THE PUDDING CLUB

KAREN WOODS

EMPIRE PUBLICATIONS

First published in 2014

This book is copyright under the Berne Convention. All rights are reserved. Apart from any fair dealing for the purpose of private study, research, criticism or review, as permitted under the Copyright Act, 1956, no part of this publication may be reproduced, stored in a retrieval system, or transmitted, in any form or by any means, electronic, electrical, chemical, mechanical, optical, photocopying, recording or otherwise, without the prior permission of the copyright owner. Enquiries should be sent to the publishers at the undermentioned address:

EMPIRE PUBLICATIONS
1 Newton Street, Manchester M1 1HW
© Karen Woods 2014

ISBN: 978-1-909360-29-7

Printed and bound by CPI Group
(UK) Ltd, Croydon, CR0 4YY

ACKNOWLEDGEMENTS

I would like to thank my readers for following me and reading all my books. Without you all I would never have had the inspiration to carry on writing. Life has taken me on such a journey and I'm loving every minute of my new found talent.

A big thank you to Front Line fit, for all their help and support and their banter whilst I've been writing this book, especially. James Largey, Nik Dodd, Mark Elsdon, Louise and Annette Swan, Lisa Cary and all the other members at strength camp, it's been a pleasure working with you all.

Thanks to my children Ashley, Blake, Declan, Darcy, for all their support. Also thank you to James - you all stand by me and support me no matter what I am doing.

Thanks to my mother Margaret for all her hard work helping me get the books ready and thanks to my father Alan for the endless storylines he gives me. Thanks to Ashley Shaw and John Ireland for their continual support throughout my writing career and always believing in me. A big thanks to Carol Godby too, a friend always.

My next novel 'Team Handed' should be out soon folks so hopefully not long to wait. Thanks to all my Facebook followers, twitter, etc I love you guys. My last thanks is to my son in heaven Dale, you're never far from my thoughts, goodnight God Bless, love you always.

Karen Woods
www.karenwoods.net

ONE

I DON'T EVEN KNOW where it came from to be honest; it just crept up on me without any warning, like a preying lioness digging its claws deep into my body. I've heard people speak about it in the past, but I never thought it would happen to me. If I turn sideways in the mirror and suck my stomach in, it looks better. Well, a bit better, but, come on. I can't walk around all day holding my breath can I? I'd explode. What the hell am I going to do?

My friend Gemma gave me some special spandex knickers and told me they could help with my problem, but I need a shoehorn just to get them over my thunder thighs. It's no laughing matter. I'm at my wits end. My arms too, bingo wings they call them. Well, they're not really wings I know that. Derr... I'm not that thick; if they were real wings I would have flown away and starved myself until near death. My cheeks too, what the hell is going on there? I look like a squirrel storing nuts for the winter. Hamster cheeks my other half used to call them, the cheeky fucker. I hope one day he has a weight problem. He'll know how it feels to be fat. My breasts too, empty lifeless skin dangling on my stomach. They used to be so perky, they just look like they have given up on life now, just like me, I suppose. Floppy spaniel's ears they are. As I look closer at them they have a sprinkle of dark hair on them. Oh my God, I'm turning into a man.

Today is the day it all stops, it's official. I've made my mind up. I'm going to be a carrot cruncher, lettuce and fruit from now on. No chips or cakes will ever cross my

The Pudding Club

lips ever again. So, yes correct, let me get this straight in my own head. No more kebabs for me, or even those little balls of dark creamy chocolate I love to eat after my bath each night. Well, perhaps I could have one? It's not going to kill me is it? And, may I add, the doctors said chocolate releases serotonin into your body, you know, that happy drug? So, I'm all for making myself feel happy again. God knows I need it right now. I'm at breaking point and could kill somebody stone-dead.

Well, my knickers are finally on, it was a tight squeeze I can tell you. My face looks blue and I'm sure my lips are turning purple. This was a bad idea, thanks a bleeding bunch Gemma. I need to get them off. I'm suffocating in a pool of thick blubber. Phew, my breathing's returned to normal - that was close. I could have been stuck in these for days if I hadn't cut them off myself. Why is my mind shouting to me in loud tempting sweet voices? I bleeding know there is a raspberry trifle in the fridge, for crying out loud you don't need to tell me. I'm on a diet, please let me rest, go away, and leave me be. I have self control now. I'm no longer a slave to your demands. The voice is getting louder, much louder and I'm covering my ears with my palms humming a tune trying to take my mind off it. Oh, it's no good this always happens. I'm in the kitchen now and through no fault of my own; my hands grip the trifle bowl for dear life. Come to mammy my fruity friend, this diet is over. Sweet fruit juices dripping from my mouth as the trifle is ploughed inside my hungry lips. The diet can start tomorrow.

It's always been the same with me, I have no self-discipline. One little bit of trauma in my life and I always find my comfort in food. Lots of it, once I start I can't stop. In fact I eat mountains of it. I can't get enough of it when I'm upset. We're not just talking about one piece of chocolate to ease the pain in my heart either. Oh no, we're talking bars of it, soft creamy calorie filled chunks of it.

So, let me introduce me myself. I'm Rebecca Rooks. I'm recently divorced and have nothing in my life to keep me company but my old blue budgie Joey. He's on his way out too, his usual immaculate plumage is bald and tatty, and even he's given up on life too. I think I'm actually talking him to death. He's the only friend who never judges me. Joey used to turn his head away from me when I went to his cage for a chat. I knew he hated the woman I'd become. I hated me too. A wing curling around his small pin sized eyes was a sign he hated my sorrowful voice. Even he's had enough of my doom and gloom stories. I can't blame him really. There he was in his twilight years and all he had each day was my droning voice of self-pity. I remember the times when Joey would sing his head off as he chirped into his little green mirror looking at himself. He doesn't do that anymore, he's like me I suppose, washed up and miserable. I wasn't always like this you know. Oh no, the life and the soul of the party I was back in my day. Everybody wanted to be in my company. I could make anyone laugh, well, except myself. Life can be so cruel sometimes and I think I just lost my way. You know the story; wrong time, wrong place. So, how did I end up a fat slob with whiskers growing on my chin? Yes, you heard me right. I have several hairs like wire wool growing under my double chin. And let me tell you, no matter how many times I plucked them; they always grow back thicker and bring another hair back with them, the bastards. I am turning into my father. I swear to you, hairs are appearing all over my body that no woman would be proud of. My nipples even have a few of them now, too; totally unreal they are. In fact, a bleeding disgrace. I've seen the adverts for hair removal on TV, but laser therapy, I'm not ready for that yet, but, maybe in time if this continues. I feel like a Russian shot-putter to be honest with you. I'm a man trapped inside a woman's body for sure. Anyway, let's get back to my story and I'll tell you where all this misfortune began. Just let me grab a fag first though, I'm going to need it.

Josh bleeding Thompson, just the mention of his name still makes my legs buckle from underneath me. His name on my plump lips still makes me want to vomit. I can actually feel my stomach churning as his ugly image hits my mind. Whenever I look back on my life, anything that he touched was ruined, and you know what? That includes me too. He fucked my head up big time. I'm a nutter now because of him. I'm starting to get upset, hold on, I need a chocolate bar to get me through this. And, if I'm going to be telling my whole story I better go and get a Tena Lady on too. My bladders not what it used to be and one bit of laughter could result in a waterfall of warm liquid all over my legs. Yes, let me go and sort that out first before I begin.

Right, "Tena" lady pad is positioned in my knickers and chocolate cookies to hand. Well, just in case I need them. I'm not saying I will eat them all but, just as a security measure I'll keep them close by as an emergency.

I was thirteen years old when I first set eyes on Josh Thompson. He was every girl's dream. He was popular at school and everyone loved him. I suppose I was in love with him from an early age and I never knew it, but, he was never in my range if I'm truthful to myself. I was more, let's say, in the geek circle. The ginger kids and glasses group you know the one, the undateables. Yeah, that describes my kind of friends, overweight and unhealthy cake munchers. We were all afraid of any male

The Pudding Club

attention and we all shivered if we were ever approached by one of the good-looking squad. They were gods in their own right and us calorie addicted girls were nothing but mere mortals compared to them. No, we kept to our own sort. We never crossed the line. There were five of us in the circle, each afraid of life. I knew I was punching above my weight, thinking Josh would ever look at me. He was every girl's dream. Many a night I would dream of him; hot, sweaty, passionate dreams. I was always slim in my mind though and he was lifting me up and kissing me with those hot, red sexy perfect lips of his. In reality though, if he was ever to try and lift me up he would have needed a hoist to get me up from the floor. And, if he ever found my lips hid away under the mounds of lard he would have been hailed as Christopher Columbus, the discoverer of a new continents. My lips were yet to be discovered by any man. It would have been an insult to my body to ever try and place anything like lipstick on the thin lines of my mouth. I did try some chocolate flavoured lip gloss once though but it just tasted so good, and before I knew it, the tube was empty and I was one hundred and twenty two calories heavier. I ate the full bleeding tube of it. My lips are barren now; dry, cracked, and barely visible. Rebecca Rook is still a podgy woman with greasy hair and more spots on her face than a Dalmatian dog. It's true, I'm a mess. I'm a greasy hormonal ticking time-bomb that needs locking up behind closed doors before she hurts someone.

All the girls in school ran after Josh Thompson and tried to get his attention. Not me though, I was so unfit. I would have had a heart attack if I would have run for a few minutes so there was no way I was chasing after him. I was no Usain Bolt like some of the girls in my school. I was an egg on legs; pale, round, and hard on the outside.

The Pudding Club

I blame my mother for that though. I was taught from an early age that tears meant you were soft and weak. I stopped crying in front of my mother. I cried alone in my bedroom with nothing but a few iced doughnuts to keep me company. I think my mother knew I was a lonely child and the only way she ever showed me her love was with food. No hugs, no cuddles, just food. I can recall a time when I was upset and down in the dumps. She went straight down to the bakery in a hurry buying me the biggest cream cake she could get into her shopping bag. It was her way of showing she cared, I think. Calorie filled love I called it back then, overdosing on carbs and saturated fats. I was addicted from an early age. I still am. "A fat, podgy, waste of space", my brother used to call me, and he was right. I was a calorie consuming beached whale that needed harpooning.

Tonight though, it is all going to change. This is going to be the first day of the new me. The new slimmer, confident me who loves her life and is scared of nothing. The cupboards have been cleared of anything that looks remotely nice and I've already replaced everything with healthy food like rice cakes and green tea. Well, nearly everything. I have to keep a few treats, don't I? My friends call the place I'm going to "The Pudding Club" but I know they are only having a laugh and I'm used to all the banter we have about my weight. I just take it on the chin these days. Well, I take it on my double chins. My friend Gemma is coming tonight too. After Christmas she piled on a few pounds and she's desperate to get rid of the extra weight she's gained before she goes on holiday in the summer. Holidays, what on earth are they? I go to Blackpool if I'm lucky and neither man nor beast will ever see what lies beneath my tent dress, unless I was raped and pillaged. Well, even that would be a blessing these days,

The Pudding Club

because any male attention for me is zero at the moment. My legs are sealed and I don't even think Moses could part them. It's not as if Gemma has a lot of weight to lose either. It's just a fart, well, compared with what I have to lose. Around ten stones I need to shed to be accepted back into modern society. And even then I won't be in the stick insect collection of clothing. I will still be in that section described as 'the fuller figure' in women's clothing stores. They should just label the clothes 'give up on life department' because tent dresses and knee length skirts, come on, that's just giving up on how you look isn't it?

Gemma Morley has been my friend since junior school, we fight like cat and dog, but still we're friends. She's changed so much since back then; she seems to have forgotten where we both come from. We were both bullied you know, and even years later it still plays on our emotions, scarred for life we were, I was anyway. Gemma won't talk about the dark days anymore. She's blocked them away in the back of her mind. That's what she calls them now, "the dark days". Every time we stepped foot inside the school gates our misery would begin. 'Professional pie eaters', the kids called us, not Josh Thompson though; he never joined in the banter. He was much too cool for that. I remember one day he did tell Catherine Bennett to ease off us, so he must have cared about me even then. Gemma and I spoke about our knight in shining armour for months after that. The day Josh sexy Thompson spoke up for us both and saved us from the hands of the school bully. My diary was filled with real gossip that day, not the usual "I wish I could stop eating cakes" comments that I usually wrote down. No, that day I had real news. Gemma's here now, so it's time to go to my first meeting at the pudding club. Wristwatch off, earrings out and I'm only wearing lightweight clothing. They all add up you know? I've even taken my hammock bra off, "letting the girls swing free" I call it. Tonight is the start of the new confident me. Bye bye fat, ugly, social reject Rebecca Rooks, and hello to the new confident woman who is fearless and scared of nothing. Hold on; let me grab a piece of chocolate before I go. I need it to calm down. My heart's racing, sweat is pouring from my armpits. Breathe, breathe, I'm starting to relax, come on Rebecca, breathe girl. Chocolate is now in my blood system, everything is calm again. Sweet tasting, silky chocolate always calms me down. Oh, how I've missed you my creamy friend.

TWO

LOTS OF WOMEN are stood about in a small room, nattering. You would have thought the venue organiser would have known that such a large gathering of heifers were heading her way, the room is way too small for us porkers. The noise is deafening. I can hear a slimmer stood in the corner talking about the new cabbage soup diet and how she's shed eight pounds in one week with it. A miracle diet she calls it. Do I really need to hear this? Every diet under the sun I've tried, and the cabbage soup diet is just one of them. The only thing I really lost from that diet was friends, yes friends. It's mad isn't it how one diet can make you lead such a solitary life. I mean, the excess gas or methane was like a gale force wind surging through my large bloomers every time I dared to move. I was forever sat on the toilet and I knew I was dicing with death if I even tried bending down too quickly. No, the cabbage soup diet is not for me.

Gemma is parading her slim-line figure to all the fatties knowing how intimidated she makes them feel. She was an overweight woman once, but no more. I've seen more fat on a chip. As soon as she started losing her puppy fat, as she calls it, she always made me feel like a quitter. Yes a drop-out. I'd done everything she did but didn't shed an ounce of weight. I cut my portion sizes down, cut all the cakes out, but still my body never changed. I gave up after three weeks of complete starvation. And it was starvation I can tell you. I was weak, and I couldn't focus. The hunger pains kept me up all night long and because of the lack of sleep I was constantly moody. I did have a

The Pudding Club

few cheats though; come on everybody cheats when they are dieting don't they? I never told Gemma though. Oh no, she would have gone ballistic if she knew I'd cheated. I kept my little secret eating habits to myself. I worked alone, a lone ranger I called myself. Six chocolate éclairs I shoved into my body each night after Gemma left me to go home. I was hungry and sad, what did she expect? She knew how hard it was for me, but still, she stood on guard by the fridge like a soldier guarding the crown jewels. Gemma made sure no forbidden foods touched my hungry desperate lips when she was with me. I was cunning though, this was child's play to me. I'd been a secret eater for years. The cakes I'd bought were stashed away in my bedroom, hid away, deep under my bed where nobody could see them. I knew each night when she left, my rewards would be waiting for me. I even faked illness sometimes so she would leave early. I was desperate, what else could I do? Even to this day, Gemma doesn't know that I cheated on that diet, and that's how it's got to stay. She hates quitters, and she'd hate me too for deceiving her.

Gemma is still talking to some ladies huddled together in the corner of the room. She's wearing her extra tight skinny jeans tonight. I'd love to wear jeans like that, but for now, elastic waists is all that fits me. I wouldn't get my arm in them skinny jeans anyway, never mind my bleeding legs. And me, where am I stood? Yes, correct. I'm stood in the corner of the room hid away like I've always been, I'm a loner. My hands are stuck deep inside my grey quilted jacket pockets. They used to fit perfectly inside these pockets months ago, but now my sausage like fingers are like bananas; big, fat, podgy fingers. My wedding ring is still lodged on my finger too. I've tried cutting it off but nearly ended up sawing my finger off.

The Pudding Club

So, until I lose the blubber, it's staying put for now. I hate looking at the gold wedding band too; it's just a reminder of the bastard I foolishly married.

Rebecca, breathe girl, you're starting to hyperventilate. Hands wafting with speed in front of my face. I can clearly see the image of my husband's face. It's going, it's going and it's gone. Breathing returned to normal. Gemma is approaching, she's working the floor and you can see all the other women whispering to each other. Gemma walks to my side and whispers in the side of my ear. "So, are you going to take that coat off or what?" My head is dipped low, why does she always make me feel so small and vulnerable?

Everyone's looking at me now and they are waiting for me to unveil what's hidden underneath my jacket. Face blushing, mouth dry, fidgeting. I nudged her in the waist. "Will you stop bringing attention to me? I said I was coming here to lose weight, not lose bloody friends. Stop trying to boss me around. You know what it's like to be fat, so just turn it in."

Oh, she's on her high horse now, yeah, she hated being reminded that she was ever fat. Her face has gone beetroot and her fists curl up into tight little balls at the side of her legs. You could have heard a pin drop in the room and she knew all eyes were on her waiting for her to reply. It didn't take long before she exploded. "I was fat over twenty odd years ago Rebecca. Why you feel the need to keep bringing it up is beyond me?" There it was, the sympathy vote she always got, all eyes were on me again and I was the baddy in the camp. The other people in the club all looked at me now with disgust. How dare I mention that this woman right here in front of me had ever had a weight problem? This should have stayed in the circle of trust. This was the unwritten rule of any slimmer, or so I've heard. Pulling her by her arm, I knew I had to try and make amends and fast, but she was milking it now trying to get the sympathy of other slimmers. Here it was; the tears, the low shaking voice, she was going for gold. Gemma was putting on a show any actress would have been proud of; she deserved an Oscar for this performance. She has a habit of falling to the ground and playing dead too, she's brilliant at it and many a time she's fooled me with her death act. She could even stop her breathing for a short time, it was unbelievable. Stamping her feet she made sure she had everyone's full attention.

"Rebecca! I was fat because I was unhappy. Go on; shoot me for finding comfort in the odd cream cake. I've worked my arse off for this body and yet over twenty years later you still feel the need to remind me of the days I was overweight. What a low blow Rebecca, you should be ashamed of yourself." Women were shaking their heads in the room, as looks of disgust shot over at me. I was hated by everyone in the room. I had to try and pull this back.

"Gemma, you know I don't mean anything by it. I just don't like you telling me to take my coat off. You know it's my comfort blanket. Please, don't start all this drama, not now, just forget about it. I'm sorry, what more do you want from me?"

Gemma turned her head slowly to the other women in the room and rubbed her knuckles into her eyes. she snivelled a few times and reached for me with wide open arms still looking at the women in the room from the corner of her eyes. "I'll forgive you this time, Rebecca. I'm not one to hold grudges. I'm bigger than that. It's all in the past now as far as I'm concerned. Let's move on."

Now Gemma was working the crowd alright, and poor me, I was the bad one yet again. I never replied. I just kept my lips sealed and wanted to melt away quietly into the ground where no one could see me. The door opened and in walked the team leader, she looked familiar. "Good evening girls and welcome to 'Slim With Confidence'. Please take a seat before we all start with weighing ourselves." Gemma rapidly moved to the front of the room, she was a right brown-noser; she always had to be the centre of attention. Smiling at me Gemma patted the chair next to her. This was torture and no doubt now I would be the main focus of the evening. I was double the size of some of these ladies in the room and probably the one who needed the most help.

My seat was reserved as I waddled to the front of the room. "How small are these chairs?" I whispered under my breath. My single bum cheek doesn't even fit on it. I wobbled, trying to regain my balance. Could this evening get any worse? The team leader introduced herself in a friendly voice. "Hello class, and thanks for coming tonight. I know it's quite scary the first time we step on the scales, but we're all in this together, we're a team. We're all here for the same reason, to lose weight." If I was being honest with myself I was at this class for more than just weight loss, I wanted a life. I wanted a new circle of friends who were just like me and knew every day what I went through challenging my addiction with food. This class was my last hope of ever being normal. I never felt normal you know? I always felt different from everyone else. I'd thought about having my jaw wired in the past, you know? Thick metal wire stuck into my mouth so I could never eat a crumb of food again. That thought didn't last long though, let's face it; the reality is that I'm just meant to be fat. I would have probably pulled the wires from my teeth anyway, or squashed pieces of chocolate through any tiny gap I could find. I'm cunning like that I am. I'd always find a way to eat.

"Right ladies, the moment of truth, let's make a nice line to get weighed," the team leader said. Gemma sprung to her feet, and guess what? Yes, she was first in the line... There was no way I was going so near to the front. These scales needed testing first; they could be broke and not giving out correct readings. No, I'll let the other slimmers go before me. I'll hang back and check it all out first. Everyone's walking slowly. It's like the walk of death to us all, well, everyone except Gemma. She's stretching and getting ready to jump on the scales, she's like a champion boxer getting ready to defend his title, bobbing and weaving, never standing still. The rest of us are all cautious. We know this is no laughing matter. We're all the same; dipped heads, sweating brows, and dry mouths, it's not looking good. There's cheering from the front of the room. Gemma has got her hands in the air clapping rapidly. "I only have one more pound to lose and I'm in nine stone valley again, superb result. Ay Becks, just one pound more to lose and I'm at my goal weight. It's not as bad as I first thought." The other women look at each other and shook their heads. The last time I saw the number nine on anything digital was on my alarm clock. I knew I would never see it again, especially not on any weighing scales. My nine stone days were long gone... a distant memory.

There is movement in front of me, the line is moving forward. My hands dig deeper in my coat pockets, sweaty, hot palms. I'm sure I can feel an old boiled sweet hiding in the corner of my pocket. Rummaging deeper, head tilted to the side, concentrating. I was right, I've found a lemon boiled sweet. I'm not really keen on lemon flavoured sweets that's why I must have left this one behind. Nobody is looking; the ball of calories is in my cupped hand slowly being raised to my mouth. My jaw opens slightly and as I cough I drop the bomb of flavour into my mouth. I'm sucking hard now, there are two more ladies in front of me and there is no way I want to get caught with this forbidden contraband on my first meeting. Sucking, crunching, swallowing, it's nearly gone. Mary Baker is next on the scales. I've just heard the team-leader call her name out. She's big this woman, and she's probably as heavy as me. She's holding some timber around her butt too, lots of it. Mary's swollen legs look sore and she has fat pouring over the side of her shoes. Yes, literally hanging over the black leather like a curtain of lard. Some people have no shame do they? I would never walk around like that. My black ankle boots hide any sign of my blubber, and my tent dress covers my boots, so no one ever sees an ounce of my flesh, ever.

Mary is closing her eyes; I can see her knuckles turning white as she clenches her fists together at the side of her legs. It's not looking good; the team-leader is shaking her head before she speaks. "It's not all doom and gloom Mary, seventeen stone is not that bad. We can work hard and start losing weight now we know what we are working with."

Mary was helped down from the scales by two of her friends. Tears were streaming down the side of her podgy cheeks and she was distraught. "I don't know how this has happened. I really thought I'd cut down on my food, this is a disaster." I was smiling now; the corners of my mouth were rising at speed. I know I shouldn't have been happy, but the pressure was off me now. I knew I was around fifteen stone so there's no way I was going to be the heaviest in the class. Mary Baker held the title of the fridge raider this time and not me. This day was getting better by the minute. Peeling my coat off I looked at Mary

The Pudding Club

Baker, she knew I was confident now and growled at me. "Rebecca Rooks, can you step on the scales please," the team- leader asked.

Gemma sprinted from the other side of the room and made sure she had a bird's eye view of the digits she could see on the scales. Smiling at me she urged me to take the next step. "Come on Becks, let's see what you weigh. You've cut down on loads of food so you should have good results!" Eyes still staring at Mary Baker I took the leap of faith. I was on the scales, shoulders back, standing proud. My eyes looked down at the numbers on the scales dancing to and fro. Nothing was on the display screen yet. My heart was beating faster than normal. Gemma lifted her head up slowly and covered her mouth with her hand. She bit down on her lips and shot a look to the other slimmers in the room. Mary Baker was now on her feet and she was in a rush to see the scales too. A circle of women were forming in front of me. My stomach is stopping me from seeing my new weight; I can't even see my feet. I'm smiling waiting for the round of applause from the class. Surely they are impressed with my results. Mary is giggling and smiling at me. She's taking being the fattest in the group well now, and good on her too, you shouldn't dwell on the past. It's good that she has moved on.

The team- leader coughs loudly and looks me straight in the eyes. You could have heard a pin drop in the room. Come on woman, just congratulate me and let me get off these bleeding scales. My legs are hurting now I thought to myself. The team leader began to speak. "Rebecca, your weight is…" I closed my eyes and dipped my head. I hated being the centre of attention. All these ladies were going to be hugging and kissing me any moment now and asking me what my secret was for losing so much

The Pudding Club

weight. I'm already preparing my speech in my head.

"...twenty stone five pounds," the leader said.

Not a word was a spoken, silence. Eyes from all directions burned into me, whispering and sniggering filled the room. This must be wrong; I've not heard her right. I challenge her to repeat herself. "Can you tell me my weight again? I'm not sure if I heard you right?"

Gemma was more than willing to help the team leader to repeat her answer. Stepping forward she announced my weight again to everyone standing there. "You are twenty stone and five pounds. The heaviest in the group I think."

Oh, Mary Baker was loving every second of this now, she was nearly pissing her knickers with excitement as she too voiced her opinion, the smarmy bitch. Mary sucked her stomach in and pushed her breasts out in front of her before she spoke. "Yeah, Rebecca is the heaviest in the class. I was only seventeen stone. Is anyone else here heavier than Rebecca?" They all shook their heads. My face was turning beetroot, blood rushed around my body, boiling hot blood surging into my round fat cheeks, my eyes were bulging. This is not happening to me. I'm going to explode, this can't be true. It's a cruel joke, surely? Breathing rapidly I smiled at Gemma with my flat palm resting on my chest. Oh, I get it now, she must have played a joke on me for revealing that she was once fat. Good joke Gemma, I thought. Now come on, tell the class it was all a big mistake and I am still fifteen stone. This joke has gone far enough. I stand with my hands on my waist waiting for her to uncover her prank to the class. Nobody is talking, there's just silence.

I step off the scales, it's no joke, the scales are correct. It's official. I'm a super sumo. I'm a walking disgrace. I watch the other people around the room. I can see Mary Baker has perked up now; she's laughing and giggling with her friends. Where have all her tears gone now, ay? The attention grabbing bitch. I know she's discussing my results and I can see she's happy now that the fattest woman in the group is now me.

Gemma puts her hand on my shoulder. "How has this happened Rebecca? You told me you've been eating rabbit food for weeks?"

I'm actually stuck for words. I don't know the answer to her question. Right, thinking on my feet. I'm usually good at this. I need to find an excuse and fast, but first, where is my bleeding coat? I need it now more than ever. I'm dying without it. I feel vulnerable. "It must be my thyroid glands playing up again Gemma," I lied. "I'll be going straight back to my doctors first thing in the morning. I mean, I've cut out a lot of stuff from my diet; cheese, biscuits, chips the lot, so I should have been more or less fifteen stone still." Gemma agreed with me, she had the answer to give to the team leader now who is hovering around me waiting for some kind of statement.

The team leader is slim but the baggy skin wafting about under her arms suggest she has also struggled with her weight in the past. She now introduces herself as Catherine Bennett. My mind's racing, where do I know that name from? It sounds very familiar? All of a sudden Gemma pokes her bony fingers into my non-existent waist and whispers in a low voice. "Oh my God, it's Catherine Bennett from school. Do you remember her, you know, the bully?"

My eyes squeeze tightly together. I try and focus, my vision is poor without my glasses. "Well, fuck a duck, so it is, Gemma. What the hell is she doing here?" my voice was low and just the sound of this woman's name on my lips made me tremble to the bottom of my stomach. This woman was dangerous and even though years had passed

I was still aware she could break me in two at the drop of a hat. She was such a bitch when we were all back in school. And I can honestly say she made my life a misery.

Gemma is wasting no time putting the record straight; she's right in Catherine's face. The time had finally come for her to get her own back. "Don't tell me you're the Catherine Bennett from St Patrick's junior school? Did you go to St Margaret Clitheroes in Collyhurst too?"

Catherine was speechless; she was on the spot and it was her turn to crumble. "Yes, I did go to those schools. I don't remember you though, what's your name again?" Gemma made sure she spelt out every letter in her name and she turned quickly to me. "This is Rebecca Rooks, surely you remember her too? Do you remember her, you used to call us the Go Lightly Sisters?"

Catherine remembered us now, her face was bright red. I'm sure she was going to pass out, she wobbled. There was no way Gemma was backing down now; she was loving every minute of Catherine's pain. "So, I see you banged a bit of timber on when we all left college then? You was as thin as a rake the last time we saw you," Gemma flicked her long blonde hair over her shoulders and looked directly at me for back up. "Wasn't she Becks, if Catherine turned sideways she would have been reported missing, she was that thin. Isn't that true Becks?"

My lips seemed glued together. I was on the spot, and even though years had passed I still felt fear in my body from this woman. After all, she was Catherine Bennett. The body beautiful, the girl everyone wanted to be back in the day. I couldn't speak. Gemma giggled and made sure Catherine knew she was no longer the fat ginger haired kid she could taunt anymore. At last, years later, Gemma Morley was holding her own and she was the one calling the shots now. 'Go on Gemma, bring her down', I thought in my head. This was a day to put in my diary for sure. The downfall of Catherine Bennett had finally come. I'd often dreamt of doing this woman in, yeah honest, I wanted to wipe her off the face of the earth, a painful slow death I'd planned for her when we were back at school. In the end Gemma smirked at me and walked away from the group leader with a smile fixed firmly on her face. She'd humiliated her and put her back in her place. Gemma was no longer a victim; she was a strong fearless (thin!) woman.

Catherine growled at me, she knew I was the weaker one; she clenched her white teeth together tightly and spoke to me directly. "So, twenty stone five pounds Rebecca? What are we going to do about that then?" There it was, the sword of revenge stabbed straight into my heart. Gemma was gone now and I was like a gazelle grazing on the Serengeti. I was alone and I had no protection. Catherine was ready to go in for the kill and rip my jugular out. "You've always had a weight problem haven't you Rebecca? Even back in a school you was always one of the..." she paused and smirked checking no one else was listening, "...let's say, one of the bigger girls."

There was no way I was standing for this. I wasn't a kid anymore; she was getting a piece of my mind. I swallowed hard. "I was big in school you're right, but I did slim down to under eleven stone. It's only these last few years that I've put the weight back on. It happens to us all doesn't it? I mean, how did you cope when you put your weight on?"

Catherine was like a cat playing with a mouse, she was ready to end my attempt at fighting back. "Oh, I only put weight on after my third child, but I lost it all almost straight away. Do you have any children Rebecca, or did you get married?" There it was the killer blow. I couldn't

The Pudding Club

fight back anymore. There was no way I was discussing my private life with this woman. I changed the subject quickly and turned away from her.

"It's lovely seeing you again Catherine. I have to go, Gemma is waiting for me." Gemma was now calling my name from the other side of the room. What a relief! The class was almost over and after Catherine had given us the tip of the week regarding counting calories we were all free to go home. I smiled as I waddled from Catherine's side and hurried to sit down with Gemma. She was my protector now and she was no longer a 'Go Lightly', she was a thin, confident woman. A fully pledged member of the good looking squad.

There was no way Catherine Bennett could bully us anymore.

THREE

GEMMA WATCHED ME from her car as I entered my front door. Waving back to her she left the cul-de-sac. She had seemed edgy tonight and not her usual self. Something is going on with her at the moment but I just can't put my finger on it, she's so shady and keeps a lot to herself.

The heat hit me as I stepped inside my home. Lovely soothing heat waves tickling my skin. I hate being cold. I've always been a frozen arse when it comes to keeping warm. I can hear Joey singing from his cage as I walk further into the house. He often sings when I'm not in the front room with him, he's got such a pretty voice. My feet are swelling and my coat is soaking wet. I need to get them off as soon as possible before I catch a cold. The weather is so bad outside, it's pissing down. Winter is such a depressing season. I've always hated it since being a small child. I think everyone hates it; dark nights and freezing temperatures. Right, let's see what's on the TV tonight. I've already missed Coronation Street so I know I won't be watching television for much longer it's a load of shite. Just repeats on every bleeding night, and they have the cheek to charge you over one hundred pounds for a TV licence. I'm going to write a letter of complaint to the BBC, it's a joke. I suppose I could read a book. Erm... No, on second thoughts, my mind's too busy to concentrate on any storyline. Reading a book is not a good idea tonight.

I know. I'll talk to Joey for a bit, he's had no company all night. He'll be glad of the attention. I think he's been lonely. Head pushed up against the thin metal bars I can see Joey jumping about at the bottom of his cage, he's burying his head. He's funny to watch sometimes. His life is so interesting to me. I could watch him for hours. How on earth does he cope on his own every day? I did think about getting him a companion a while back, another blue female budgie perhaps, but what would happen to me then? He wouldn't have the time for our chats anymore would he? I'd be tossed to the kerb without a second thought. No, we're both better off alone. We have each other. We don't need anybody else.

Joey looks at me with sadness in his eyes. I would let him fly about the room and be free but the last time I did that, he was out of his cage for over a week the little bleeder. Joey wouldn't go back in his cage for love nor money. I had to get Jerry to come in from next door to capture him and put him back. No, Joey is staying in his cage for now. Well, unless I fancy a bit of company, then that's a different story. Sometimes I let Joey out of his cage on purpose so I can get Jerry the neighbour to come in again. Jerry Jones is an attractive man and right up my street. I'm sure he fancied me before I got bigger. I suppose I'll never know now will I? Joey is staring at his little green mirror swinging about in his cage. When it was new, he was constantly singing into it and he was very rarely away from it. Not now though, he's lost all interest in it. He's given up on looking good, just like me I suppose. So, how did I end up like this? Joey loves this story and he's heard it over a million times before, but he still enjoys it. I know he does. Right, let me get my cigarettes and a cup of tea before I start to tell him again. Perhaps I'll get a couple chocolate chip cookies too? I'll need them to get through this story, I always do. "Be back in a minute Joey, just going in the kitchen for

The Pudding Club

some provisions, don't go anywhere, I'll be right back".

Right, eyes closed tightly. I'm going back into my miserable past. I can see myself stood in my PE kit wearing a navy pleated skirt that just about covered my arse-cheeks. I should have been arrested by the fashion police. I'm fat and hanging. A scruffy, spotty greasy teenager. My off-white t-shirt barely covered my podgy gut and I'm always trying to pull it down. It was way too small for me, I can't believe I even wore it. I hated sport with a passion and I knew for the next few hours I was going to be pushed to my limits, gagging for breath, on the verge of a heart attack. Mrs Jones, our physical education teacher, hated lazy kids and she hated me with a passion. I was afraid of any strenuous exercise. For the previous two weeks I'd forged my mother's signature on letters explaining to the teacher why I was unable to take part in any activities. I was crafty like that. I was a wise head. My game was up when Mrs Jones told me straight that she would be contacting my family to discuss this matter further. I begged her not to call my parents and admitted I wasn't really ill. I never missed PE again.

The weather was cold outside and the other pupils were jumping around trying to stay warm, jogging on the spot. There was no way I was doing that, I just stood still shivering and rubbing my arms at speed. Gemma came to join me, she'd been crying, her eyes were red raw and snot was dribbling down her big red nose. "What's wrong with you?" I asked her in a kind caring voice, because I was caring back then you know. I had a heart of gold. Not like I am now, a heartless bitch.

"Somebody has nicked my packed lunch from the changing rooms. The teacher said it's not the end of the world, and I won't starve, but it is, isn't it? She isn't even arsed about it. What am I going to do? I've got no money

The Pudding Club

to buy any more food. I'm going to starve to death."

I didn't answer her straight away, I was thinking. I'd put an extra sandwich in my box that morning but that was for the extra energy I would need after playing netball. Gemma was looking at me, she was waiting for me to say I would share my lunch, I know she was. I was fidgeting about under pressure, trying not to look her directly in the eye. Then she asked the dreaded question. "Will you share yours with me." Fuck, fuck, fuck. I was on the spot I answered her after a few seconds had passed.

"Of course I will," I answered trying to be understanding. I hated sharing my food, and now just because the school bullies had nicked her lunch I was expected to share my only comfort in life, my food. Mrs Jones made all the pupils pick teams for the netball game now. I hated this part of the lesson. Catherine Bennett was picking her squad and Maria Smith was picking the other. All the fatties were always the last to get picked, it was always the same with anything in school life. Nobody wanted a hindrance on their team and that meant me. Stood with my arms folded across my chest I covered the two enormous boulders that were now my breasts. They just seemed to have come from nowhere. One minute I was as flat a pancake, then, boom, two heavy sore pink breasts appeared on my chest. My mother said I was going through puberty, whatever that meant. I was only twelve years old and my body was being taken over by pubic hairs and lumps and bumps. Gemma was going through puberty too, but I think hers was going at a slower rate than mine. I hated puberty and the changes it was making to my life. My neat little vagina was now covered in monkey fluff and it looked like a ball of wire wool. I also started my periods. This was all too much to take in for my body. My hormones were raging and my appetite had doubled since junior school. "A twelve stone slob" my brother Spencer called me. "A disgrace to the human race" he often said. My brother was a right tosser, he was so full of himself. Thin as a rake he was and he loved all the things I hated. He was sports mad, a carrot cruncher who worshipped his own body. Gemma had the hots for him and she often sat drooling over him if she ever came to my house for tea. Spencer was horrible to her really, he called her names and always commented on her weight, but she just took it on the chin and seemed to want him even more than before.

I was used to the names my brother called me; it was water off a duck's back. I never let him get to me. Well, I hid my pain well and nobody knew how much it really hurt me inside. I was trying to lose weight, you know? Don't ever think I was blinded to the fact that I was obese. Even back then I always wanted to change. I wasn't just sat there every day getting bigger and bigger as people might think. I did lose five pounds once, and guess what? Not one person noticed my new flatter stomach. I was even tempted to buy some Lycra shorts but the time I'd saved up the money to buy them, I'd banged the weight back on, so I just bought more chocolates instead.

The school bully Catherine Jenkins screwed her face up as she growled at me and Gemma. You could see she was disgusted by our big round sweaty bodies. "Miss, why do we have to pick one of these two fat cows? They can't run or even play the game. They both just moan, can't they just sit on the side and watch instead?"

Mrs Jones wasn't happy; she marched straight up to us and dragged us by the arms towards Catherine Bennett. "This girl will be on your team and she will play the full game, netball is about team work. Now, shut up moaning and let's get this game started. Gemma, you're on Maria's team." Catherine was snarling at me, her teeth were showing and she was ready to explode. She came to the side of me and her hot breath was in my face. "Right, Bessie Bog-Trotter, you can be the Goal Keeper. You don't have to move about much in that position, so get your arse down to the other end of the court." That was music to my ears. I waddled to my position and stood with my hand resting on the post.

As I looked over to the playing field behind me I could see a group of lads playing rugby. Something was stirring in my groins and from the first moment I saw him, my heart skipped a beat. There he was, the fittest boy in our school. The boy every girl dreamt about. Josh 'sexy' Thompson. My mouth was wide open and I was dribbling. He could see me watching him and he actually smiled over at me. This was love. I was sure of it. He wanted me and I wanted him. This love match could change my life forever. Every girl in the school wanted to be with Josh and yet he'd smiled at me, oh happy days. From nowhere a ball came crashing into my head sending me flying across the floor. I slid across the gravel and my navy PE skirt lifted revealing my ridiculously oversized skanky knickers. Laughter filled the air. Gemma was a true friend and she ran straight over to me pulling my skirt back down covering my bloomers. It was too late though, everyone had seen them. The snide remarks had already started. "She's wearing circus knickers", "Oh my god, look at the size of her arse."

The teacher ran over to me and grabbed me up from the floor. She shot her eyes to my legs and looked concerned. "Gemma please take Rebecca to the nurse that looks like a nasty wound, it needs cleaning up. Come on, quick, quick, before she bleeds to death." Staggering to my feet, I dipped my head low and headed from the playing area. The other pupils were still giggling at me. I could hear them all shouting insults at me. I felt a rage in the pit of my stomach and I wanted to run back and kick ten tons of shit out of loud- mouthed Catherine Bennett. I would have destroyed her too, you know? Once I snapped, I snapped, there was no going back for me. My mother said my temper would get me in trouble one day and she was probably right. I just saw red and lost control when my temper broke; I was like a wild woman.

Gemma helped me calm down; she made me count to ten slowly. Just before we left I looked over my shoulder and I could still see Josh watching me. It was official. I was in love with Josh Thompson. Gemma was beetroot; she was more embarrassed than me, I think, as we trudged away from the lesson doing the walk of shame. We were the school geeks for sure. No one was ever going to change that fact. After the nurse had cleaned my knee she told me to sit outside and wait for her. It was only then that I revealed my secret to Gemma. "I'm in love. He was watching me I know he was."

"Who," Gemma asked in a concerned voice.

"Josh Thompson, I think he likes me, he was smiling at me."

Gemma chuckled and tilted her head to the side. "I think you've got it wrong Becks. Josh Thompson could have the pick of any girl in the school and yet, you think he's picking you," she smirked. "I'm not being funny or anything but you're not in his league." Her words stabbed deep into my heart, she was jealous. She was always the same. The thought of me having a boyfriend before her terrified her to the bone and I knew she secretly fancied the arse off Josh too. She thinks I don't know, but I've seen the way she looks at him, she's smitten.

I answered her in a confident voice. "Well, let's see

The Pudding Club

then. I'm going to make a move on him and see if he feels the same."

Gemma's eyes were wide open and she was covering her mouth with her hands. "Get a grip Becks, don't do it to yourself. He might have smiled at you just being friendly that's all. I think you've read it all wrong." This was now more than a mission of proving I was right, this was a life or death situation for me. For once in my life I wanted to prove Gemma Morley wrong. Just for once, I was going to be right and watch her eat her words. We both sat outside the school nurse's office waiting for her to come back. I could have bled to death the time I'd spent sat there but still no one was tending to my needs. They thought I was a mard arse really and just sat me there to keep me from crying. Gemma nudged me in the waist. "Here's Josh now, go on ask him out then." My heart was in my mouth, my eyes couldn't focus. It was true he was heading up the corridor to where we were sat. Josh had been injured; blood was trickling down the side of his mouth, thick red claret pouring down the side of his face. I wanted to jump up from my seat and tend to his needs. He was in pain I could see it in his eyes.

"Is the nurse about," he asked as he reached our sides. My mouth was glued together and even though I was trying to answer him, my words were glued to my tongue.

Gemma took advantage of the situation and answered for me. "You have to wait here; she said she'll be back out in a minute."

Josh plonked down on the chair at the side of me. I could smell his body scent, he smelt so good. I could have eaten every inch of him there and then. Gemma prodded me with a firm finger. "Go on then shit-bag. Let's see if you're right, "she whispered.

Inhaling deeply I prepared to speak to Josh. My heart

was beating in my ears and I knew it was now or never. "Have you been injured Josh?"

Gemma was amazed that I'd even spoken, I was usually so shy. She sat back with her arms folded in front of her in a strop. Here it was, the moment he would ask me out. The moment I would be no longer Rebecca Rooks the fat bird from year one. I would be now known as Rebecca Rooks the girlfriend of the one and only Josh Thompson the fittest lad in year one. Josh held his hand out and looked at the blood on his hand. "Yeah, I got head butted in the scrum." He'd spoken to me; Josh had actually had a conversation with me. I was over the moon. Gemma sat forward and she was biting hard on her fingernails.

"Do you want me to clean you up; I've done a bit of first aid before. I can stop the bleeding if you want?" I asked him. I stood up and walked closer to his side. Pulling the blood filled t-shirt from his head. I could see a small gash. It was only small, but still the blood was pumping from it. "Gemma, get me some clean water from the toilets, let's get him cleaned up."

Gemma was gobsmacked and she left to obey my orders. Josh's hair was dark and thick. As I applied pressure on the top of his head to stop the bleeding he howled out in pain. I was so heavy-handed. "Sorry," I chuckled. Looking down onto my hand, there it was a single dark hair from Josh's head. I quickly closed my hand and placed it in the centre of my sweaty palm. I was going to keep it forever and treasure it. Gemma was back now and she'd wet some tissue paper. Before I had chance to apply it to my true love's head the nurse came outside and asked who was waiting to see her. I smiled and stood tall. I sucked my stomach in and replied. "Josh, you can go first, you're in more pain than me."

Josh was gone and Gemma was stood gawping at me.

The Pudding Club

"Well, did you get a date or anything, surely he asked you out?" I was in a trance, and for the first time in my life I wasn't hungry. I felt sick, deep to the pit of my stomach. I was actually lovesick. I was sweating and small beads of sweat were forming on my forehead. I was in love for sure. Sitting down slowly my knees were trembling. I was shaking from head to toe. I was in shock, I think. Gemma nudged me in the waist and brought me back to reality. "So, what happened then? Are you two an item now or what?"

Opening my hand fully I revealed the single hair from Josh's head. Gemma screwed her eyes tightly and looked down at it. "What is it?"

Holding the lock of hair to my breast I closed my eyes and took a deep breath. "It's one of his hairs. It fell onto my hand when I was nursing him."

Gemma chuckled and made sure nobody was listening. "Becks, it's one hair from his head. It's not a wedding ring or anything."

I retaliated there was no way she was ruining my special moment. "Oh, be quiet jealous arse, it's better than nothing." To me it may as well have been a diamond ring, this was my first taste of Josh Thompson and I just knew in my heart it wouldn't be the last. Sat in a daze we could hear a gang of girls approaching from the other end of the corridor. At a closer look we could see it was Catherine Bennett and her mob. I sat back and prepared myself for the usual torment she gave me. I felt strange now and I didn't feel fear in my bones like I normally did, I felt stronger. The hair from Josh's head was magical and it had given me strength. If this bitch thinks she can just disrespect me as normal then she had another thing coming. Bring it on Catherine Bennett, I'm ready for you.

The Pudding Club

I was more than ready for her too. My head dipped low, I could see her feet near my chair, she was giggling with her friends. "Orr what's up fatty, did you burst when you fell over or what?" Gemma moved closer to my side, this was what she always did when trouble was lurking. We never fought back; we were always too scared, shit bags we were. "Ay fatty, do you know you lost us the game, you waste of space?" Catherine hissed.

From nowhere I stood to my feet and a red mist appeared in front of my eyes. Catherine Bennett had pushed me too far this time. "Catherine, just fuck off will you. You don't scare me anymore, so just piss off." The words just came out of my mouth on their own, and there was no going back now. I'd dropped a bollock for sure. Catherine grabbed my long ginger hair in a tight grip and dragged it down towards the ground. I could see her fist clenching and ready to strike.

"Just back off Bennett," a voice shouted from behind us. I lifted my head up and there he was again. My knight in shining armour, he'd come to save me. Josh pulled Catherine Bennett from me and pushed her to the other side of the corridor. "Listen bitch, stop picking on people who are weaker than you. Everyone hates a bully you know?"

Catherine was hysterical, she started bouncing about wafting her hands about at the side of her. "Orr do you fancy the ginger fat bitch? Is that what's wrong with you Josh?" she turned to face her friends. "Ay girls, Josh likes ginger minges." The other girls were laughing and Josh just brushed them off. The words he said next melted me inside. Even to this day I'll remember every word he spoke.

"Rebecca is a nice girl, not like you shag-bags. I'd rather have one Rebecca Rooks than ten Catherine

The Pudding Club

Bennett's. You're bad news you are, you always will be." My heart skipped a beat. I could have kissed him there and then. I wanted his babies. I wanted to marry this boy. Catherine left and Josh turned his head back to me. I puckered up and prepared myself for my true loves first kiss. My eyes closed for what seemed like a lifetime, lips getting dry, must moisten, I licked my lips slowly. Arms stretched out in front of me waiting for our lips to touch. "Come on Josh just kiss me," I whispered under my breath. One eye opened first then my other one. Josh was stood watching me, with a look of disbelief in his eyes.

"I think you have some serious mental issues Rebecca. Do yourself a favour and go on a diet or something, or get some help. Don't give people a reason to call you names. Being fat is the last thing you need at the start of high school, it's hard enough without it. Get on a diet or something." Josh walked away from me and Gemma was at my side. My life was over; I would never love another again. Well, not the way I loved Josh. Heat took over my body and my brain was boiling hot. I fell to the ground like a sack of spuds and lay staring into space. My short lived relationship with Josh Thompson was now over.

FOUR

Joey's eyes were closing, he'd had enough for one night. Flicking my eyes to the clock on the wall I realised I'd been talking to my budgie for over an hour and a half now. The biscuit wrappers at the side told me I'd eaten every single one in the packet. I was a greedy cow, no wonder I was the heaviest woman at The Pudding Club. Stretching my arms over my head I could feel the fat flapping about under my arms, I touched it and pulled it vigorously. I needed to change my life and fast.

The morning light shone in through my bedroom window. It's a nice day outside, a bit windy but all the same, the sun was shining. I like it when the weather is bad these days because I can leave my coat on and nobody can see my figure underneath it. My sleep was poor last night. I was wriggling and fidgeting about all night long. I think I'm going through the menopause. Dripping in sweat I was all night long, a big sweaty fat porker. The alarm clock is buzzing now so that's means it's time to get up. I need to be in work by nine o'clock so I better get a move on and move my arse. Perhaps not, what if I fake an illness, and just spend the day in bed watching some chick flicks, or better still watching the Jeremy Kyle show. I love talk shows, it just makes me realise that it's not just me with problems in this world, other's have issues too. No, second thoughts I better get up. I could lose my job and I don't need that at the moment do I? I can hear Joey singing downstairs - sweet sounds. I hate leaving him alone when I go to work. I did consider taking him to work in my handbag once, a kind of support for me when I was finding it hard to cope, but he would have hated it in my handbag all day wouldn't he? And plus, my manager is no animal lover; she's a heartless bitch who never understands me and what I've been through. Joey would have pecked her eyes out; he can sense a wrong-un a mile off.

When I first told my line manager Helen of my separation from my husband she just smiled and patted me on the arm. "Men are like dresses my dear, they're alright for the season and after that then it's time to update your collection." That was the end of her sympathetic ear to my problems. Helen has been married three times and she's a man-eater. Her latest husband is a weird one though. I think he's a crank. There's just something about him that sends shivers up my back. The women in our office say Helen is like a bitch on heat; she's always gagging for a blast of testosterone, from any man who'll have her. She likes swingers parties, or so the rumours goes. She's bi-sexual I've heard, so I think she likes ladies too as well as men, that's just pure greed, if you ask me. I've always wished I was a bit more adventurous in the bedroom, but it's just not in me. I did wear suspenders once for my husband, and I even shaved my lady garden just to spruce things up. I'll never do it again though; you should have seen the state of me. Between my legs was a mess, a big red fiery rash I had for weeks. No sack that idea; I like to keep the grass on the pitch these days, no more shaving for me.

I haul my legs from under the covers and with a quick roll I'm out of bed. Sometimes, I just sit here for hours looking out of the window, at the world going by. I can also see in my neighbour's bathroom too from where I'm sat. He's a sexy sod, but much too young for me, he's only about twenty-six. He's got a body to die for, and he's got six large muscles across his stomach area, a six pack they call it. I know that for a fact. I've counted them when I was perving on him. I did buy binoculars once, you know, I thought I would do a bit of bird spotting in my free time, because let's face it I have a lot of free time on my hands these days. It just kind of happened; I didn't plan to do it. I was at my window looking through my binoculars, it was the season for the blue tit and I was more than willing to stay looking for one all day long if needed. Turning my head from side to side with the binoculars glued to my eyes, I suddenly spotted my neighbour for the first time at his bathroom window. I know what I should have done before you tell me, I should have turned away and carried on looking for the species of bird I was trying to find, but I just couldn't do it. The passion inside me was burning high. I was a woman with needs, big needs for some male attention. It was like he had a magnet and he was drawing me closer with it. His body was wet, and the droplets of water seemed to be dribbling from his body in a sexual manner, hot, steamy droplets of testosterone. I wanted to lick him all over. I'd never seen a man like this before and something deep between my legs started to happen; a tingling, a warm sensation, flowing through my body, it felt like heaven. My Greek god had been found. That was my first taste of Jungle John from across the road. That's the nickname I've given him. In my dreams I play his wife Jane. He holds me in both his arms, biceps bulging, swinging freely through the jungle like two passionate primates. Eventually we land in his tree house and he rips his loincloth off and makes mad passionate jungle sex to me ravishing every inch of my body. The whole jungle hears my moans but I don't care, I scream louder. I'm alive and I feel like a real woman in the arms of my true love.

The Pudding Club

It's been a few months since I've looked at Jungle John from across the road. I've just not been in the mood. I've been depressed lately haven't I? The last time I looked at him anyway he'd piled a few pounds on and he seemed to have found his own jungle Jane, a slim, pretty, sexy new Jane. He was no longer of any interest to me. I still look out the window for a blue tit to pop up though, but up until now, I've still not seen one.

My back's aching today, I'm sure I've got a trapped nerve or something, or even some trapped wind. I hear that can give you pain in your lower back. That could well be the culprit of the pain I'm feeling. I feel bloated too. My stomach is twice the size it normally is, so perhaps a good old fart may shift it. I'll try touching my toes to help release it. That sometimes helps. The doctor has told me the pain I'm feeling is because of my weight, but what does he know? He blames all my ailments on my weight, the bloody know it all. I swear to you, I had pain in my fingers about three months ago and once I'd told him my symptoms he looked at me with the same expression he always holds when he speaks to me. "It's your weight Rebecca," I switched off after hearing that; he was talking through his arse. I very rarely go and see him anymore; he can no longer help me. I go and see a new lady doctor at the surgery now, she's a bit more sympathetic, and she seems to understand what I'm going through. She actually listens and tries to help me on the road to recovery.

This house is so cold in the morning, I'm sure I've just seen a polar bear running into the bathroom. As soon as I go downstairs I'm flicking the central heating on. I do this every morning. Since my husband's been gone, this is now my job, well, amongst all the others. Putting the bins out each week is the worst job and I'd get into a relationship just to save me the job, it's the

The Pudding Club

pits. I hate living alone; quiet nights, no conversation. No loving arms to hold me. There used to be a nice cup of tea waiting for me each morning when I got out of bed, not any more. I make my own. The kitchen is freezing and my teeth chatter together, it's like the bleeding Antarctic in this house it takes ages for it to get warm. I could do a few star jumps to get the blood flowing around my body I suppose. No, on second thoughts I'll just put an extra jumper on, I can't be arsed with any exercise so early in the morning.

The time's ticking away and I'm still not ready. I'm just sat looking at the half empty cup on the pine kitchen table. This table has seen so many tears over the last few years. It's a wonder it's not rotted away. "You need to keep positive" Gemma says, but it's easy for her to say when she has everything she wants in life. I know I'm feeling sorry for myself again but if I don't, who will? Breakfast was terrible this morning, half a grapefruit and a small piece of wholemeal toast. I can feel it reaching my stomach as we speak. There is no way that's going to keep me going until my mid-morning snack of nuts. I'll put an emergency bar of chocolate in my handbag just in case I collapse.

Right, it's time to get washed and apply some make-up to try and look normal. I don't know what's happened to my hair lately, it's like a balloon has been rubbed on the top of it, it's just thin and lifeless. It's never been my crowning glory, but at least it used to be thicker. Just my lipstick to apply now and it's time to go to work. I hate my job and hate that I can't find the courage to leave. I've threatened to search for another job lots of times but I suppose its better the devil you know isn't it? I work in a doctor's surgery as a receptionist. It's so depressing listening to other people speak about their illness every day. One old lady always tells me about her haemorrhoids. A full description I get every time I speak to her. "Oh, it's like sitting on glass," she moans to me. I try to be understanding, but there is only so much you can listen to isn't there? Gladys is a lovely old soul but she's in the surgery nearly every day with another minor ailment she's found on her body. When I'm bored I read through patient's notes. That's quite interesting, it keeps me entertained for hours. Nobody knows I do this, I would lose my job if I was ever discovered. I keep it to myself.

Helen, my line manager, loves the control she has over me and the other girls, she's like Hitler. I'm sure she's been screwing our new locum doctor. She's always in his office for some reason or another, she spends hours in there. Right, I've just got to say goodbye to Joey and I must leave to catch the bus. I used to drive, but since my legs started to swell, it's just too painful. Joey looks lonely today. I think he's going to die soon. This would be the straw that broke the camel's back if that happened now. I'm not ready to face any more misery. I've had Joey since he was a chick. He was a present from my ex-husband. It was either a budgie or a dog and my husband said there was no way he was walking a dog every night, so a budgie was my only option. "I'm off to work Joey, so have a good day and I'll be home soon. I've left the radio on, so you can have a little sing-a-long. See you later, mummy loves you." Joey closes his eyes and I'm sure he's gone back to sleep. Anyway, off to work I go.

Helen was checking her wristwatch as I walked into the surgery. Do I need this stress so early in the morning? I growl at her and she knows I'm in no mood for her lecture. "Good morning Rebecca, do you know you're fifteen minutes late? I hate to remind you that you start work at nine o'clock on the dot, not at quarter past." My fists are curling at the side of my legs and I can feel a hot flush taking over my body. The tips of my ears are burning and I'm ready to explode. Turning her back to me Helen walks off and speaks over her shoulder. "I'll come and speak to you later in the day when I have a bit more time, surgery is open now and the patients are waiting to see the doctor. Please, get straight to work."

Sharon sniggers over to me and rams two fingers up behind Helen's back, she moves closer to my side. "Who the hell does this woman think she is? She's so much up her own arse it's untrue. Just ignore her. Her barks worst than her bite. Anyway how did your first slimming meeting go?" Taking my coat off I smile at Sharon, she was a good friend and she never failed to put a smile on my face each morning. She was a joker and always up for a laugh. Sharon had had her own share of heartbreak too, but she never let it show when she was at work. "I leave my personal life at the door," she always told me. "My smiles, my make-up I wear for work. I can always cry and be miserable when I get back home," she always told me. It was a great outlook, but I could never seem to grasp it.

When I first split up with my husband, she took me straight into see the doctor and told him I needed help. In fact, she demanded he gave me some anti-depressants, and some sleeping pills, she wasn't taking no for an answer. The tablets the doctor prescribed made me feel sick. I was acting strange on them and weak. I threw them all out after two weeks of taking them. They messed about with my head too much. I don't take tablets anymore. I self-help usually and that means eating pallets of cakes. It works for me somehow, cakes should be available on prescription, they heal the heart and calm the soul.

"Rebecca, have you typed up that report for Doctor Wilson yet? He should have had it last night before you

The Pudding Club

left. Don't tell me it's not done?"

Face blushing, hands sweating I have to use my poker face. I keep calm and look her directly in the eyes. "Of course I've finished it, just give me a few minutes and I'll take it into him."

Helen nearly collapsed; she never expected it to be ready. "No, just hand it to me. I'll give it to him. I have to go and see him anyway," she said.

Sharon raised her eyebrows at me from the other side of the room and started smirking. "I'll print it off now Helen and put it on your desk. Just give me a few more minutes."

Helen walked away and she was at the reception window dealing with a patient. Sharon ran to my side and she kept her voice low. "Oh, I bet she's having sex with Doctor Wilson you know. I swear to you, let me find out and I'm going to land on her like a ton of bricks. Office rules are office rules and dropping your knickers for your boss is a no-go area. Mind you, if Doctor Wilson ever came onto me. I wouldn't say no. What would you say Rebecca?"

Just the thought of sex with a man made me feel uncomfortable. Sex was just a distant memory for me now and I was in the mindset that anything that went anywhere near my feminine region would require batteries and Duracell plus, ones at that. "Oh Sharon, stop it, I'm going to piss my knickers if you make me laugh anymore."

Sharon wasn't giving up that easily, she wanted an answer. "Just answer the question, would you have sex with him yes or no?" I hated being put on the spot, her eyes were dancing with excitement and she was rubbing her hands together.

"I think I would, well, if I lost my weight, and I felt

right about myself," I answered. Who was I kidding? If any man offered me sex at the moment I would have been such a grateful woman. The men say overweight women make the best sex partners as they work harder for it. And do you know what? They are probably right. Just the chance of having a man in my bed would make my body move like never before. I would be a gymnast and swing from the light fittings given half the chance. My heart is pounding at just the thought of sex.

Licking my dry lips I turn to Sharon who's now on a roll. "He could bend me over his office table and spank me like a naughty child. I think he would be quite good at sex don't you?" I'd never really thought about Doctor Wilson like that before, but as I closed my eyes I could see the scene that Sharon had just set in my mind. It's official; I'm a menopausal pervert who's gagging for sex from anywhere I can get it. As I print the documents off I can see Helen at her desk, she has it all you know. Her figure is slim and she's full of confidence. Sneaking past her I decide to give the Doctor his letters myself, there's no need for Helen to take them, I'm not disabled. What's come over me today, I feel confident, naughty even. Calm down, calm down I whisper to myself. Knocking on the door quietly I hear his masculine voice telling me to come inside the room. Pulling my black top down slightly I reveal the top of my breasts. Deep breaths and I enter the room. This man is drop dead gorgeous and my mind is working overtime again. He's ripping my knickers off and carrying me to his examination table. I'm groaning with sexual pleasure and he's riding me like the wind. I'm in heaven, I'm...

"Hello doctor, here's the letters you wanted. Sorry I didn't get them to you last night. I totally forgot about them." Hi Rebecca, don't you worry about them. They are not important. Have you lost some weight? You look different somehow, slimmer even?" Patting my skirt down, sucking my stomach in, I turn to the side. Could this be true? Could I actually be shedding some timber in such a small space of time? Bleeding hell, it's only been a day since I joined the slimming club, it's a miracle.

"Thanks doctor," I reply in a timid voice. "I am on a diet. I've got a long way to go yet but hopefully in a few months or years even I will be at my goal weight again."

"You look lovely as you are Rebecca. Such a pretty face," he replied. Now I was burning up, a compliment from this good looking man was sending my head into a whirl. Was he coming onto me or what? I wasn't sure. I hoped not, I'm wearing the biggest knickers known to man, and I'm sure they have a hole in the front of them. Trust me to wear passion killers on a day like this. I'm devastated.

"Do you need me for anything else doctor?" I asked in my now sexy voice.

"No Rebecca, you've been more than helpful. Enjoy the rest of your day, and don't be a stranger, call in and see me again. I never get to chat with you." This was amazing; I was officially on the doctor's list of women he wanted to sleep with. He must like the fuller figured woman. Sharon was never going to believe this in a million years. Me, fat, greasy Rebecca Rooks, had finally got an admirer. This was going to be a good day.

FIVE

So, let's go back to days gone by. I'm sixteen now and ready to start my first day of college. A beautician I wanted to be. I need any help possible to try and turn my life around. I feel like Frenchy from the film Grease, except I'm a lot heavier, and maybe not as pretty. Who am I kidding? I look nothing like her really, but I can dream, can't I? My weight is heavier than ever and somehow I think that's the reason I've never had a boyfriend. I've never been kissed or even fondled, never been touched by a man's hands. Gemma has had a few encounters though, the dirty mare. She got fingered last week at some party we went to. She's a right slapper these days. I know a few girls now who've done it too and its trending in our circle of friends. I never really go to parties but, if that's what's on offer at these all night raves, I'm seriously thinking of attending more of them in the future. Well, once my monkey fluff has been sorted out. I don't think even Bear Grylls would get through my pubic mound at the moment; it's like the Amazon forest. Gemma never stops talking about her sexual experiences; she's told me every detail of how this sordid encounter happened. I'm jealous, I want to get fingered too, or even touched anywhere on my body, a flick of a nipple, anything. I've told my mother that I no longer want to eat carbs. They are the devil in my eyes and the root of all evil. A protein diet is the way forward for me from now on. I watched a diet programme about it and it just all makes so much sense, cut out the bread, and all the stodgy foods and I will have the body beautiful. This is day one of the new me.

I felt nervous as we met the new pupils in our class. Gemma is sat next to me and she's chewing on her fingernails. I would munch on mine if I had any left, but all that's left is blunt sore red stumps, I've always been a nail biter. My mother got me some medical liquid to put on them to stop the biting, but after a few tries of it, I loved the taste, nothing works anymore. Catherine Bennett is in our class. I hate this girl with a passion. She's still up her own arse and thinks everybody loves her. She did speak to me last week though; she actually told me that she would talk to me this term. Catherine said, even though I was in the geek circle in high school, she was now willing to let me and Gemma talk to her just as long as we were alone. The cheek of her! I was about to tell her to take a run and jump but Gemma craved any kind of friendship and agreed to her terms and conditions. Catherine is dressed to impress today, her hair is swept back from her face revealing her high cheek bones. I wish I had cheek bones. I know somewhere under all this blubber on my face they do exist somewhere. I did see them once on an old photograph my mother had of me. I was about seven when the snap was taken. I actually had cheek bones. I often look at the photograph when I'm feeling down just to remind me that cheek bones do really exist. Gemma has pledged that she also will be dieting to lose some weight. Catherine told us if we started to look after ourselves we could actually sit with her at lunch time and perhaps share a cigarette with her. Oh, yes, I forgot to tell you about that. I'm a smoker now and so is Gemma. We've replaced food with tobacco. I think I'm smoking nearly fifteen a day now. I mean, my appetite is bigger than Gemma's and I need to curb it somehow.

I watch myself sometimes in the mirror when I'm

The Pudding Club

smoking. I feel sexy, naughty even. I practice the scene in Grease where Olivia Newton-John meets John Travolta at the fairground for the last scene. I just love the way she stubs her cigarette out with her foot on the floor. "Tell me about it stud," she says in her sexy voice. I've tried that scene so many times but my feet are like an elephant's and I don't own any high heel shoes as of yet, so I do it in my sandals, it doesn't seem to have the same effect. I'm going to buy some though, as soon as I start earning any money. Black high-heeled shoes, and black Lycra pants are going to be part of my wardrobe. I may as well dream big if I'm going for the whole Olivia Newton-John look hadn't I?

I often watch the film "Grease" it just makes me feel alive. I sing the songs from it too. I'm a good singer really and I hope one day someone might hear my voice and give me a recording deal. My mother said I sound like a strangled cat, but what does she know about talented singers? "Hopelessly Devoted" is my favourite song. I tingle as the thought of ever loving someone that much sails through my mind. Will I ever be loved? I hope so, because I have so much to give in a relationship. I can cook and even bake cakes, well, that's if the cake ever reached the bleeding table. I usually eat it all as soon as it comes out of the oven. "Becky Bogtrotter," my brother calls me. I just can't help it when I'm about any food. It's like it calls me and takes over my whole body willing me to eat everything in sight. I don't bake anymore. No, I'm sticking to this diet.

Today is the first day of learning how to apply a colour to hair. I've volunteered to have my hair coloured and cut by the teacher. I'm the class guinea pig for today. Mrs Lavay is hopeful she can get rid of my ginger locks too, so fingers crossed it all goes to plan. Gemma is watching me keenly as the first drops of colour hit my head. I can

The Pudding Club

feel it itching and burning, is this normal? I've had the skin test done and it was fine, what the hell is going on? It's burning my scalp. I want to scream out, everyone's watching me. I'm beetroot; breathe, breathe. My scalps cooling down; breathe, breathe. The teacher said the bleach can sometimes do that to your scalp. Bloody hell, I thought I was a goner for a minute there. I can see the headline in the newspapers now. "Fat bird, fried to death by hair colorant." Oh the shame of it!

Catherine Bennett is hovering over my head, she's checking the colour every few minutes, she's a right busybody. Gemma is glued to her side trying to get a conversation going with her, she's a right arse licker, she's changed she has. Gemma's just so desperate to make friends with anyone who will have her. I call her a beggar buddy. She hates it, but she knows it's true. I much preferred it when it was just us two but Gemma is more confident these days and I feel like she's leaving me behind. Being fingered has definitely changed her. She thinks she's a woman now. I suppose she is in a way, in a dirty easy, trollop kind of way.

"Right girls let's get this colour washed off. We will need lots of hair treatment rubbed into the scalp because it's been through a stressful time." I felt like the queen of Sheba. All the students were running about after me. I was being pampered by them all and I loved it. Cotton wool was dabbed across my brow and I was passed a cup of milky coffee. I ordered that myself from a student. And guess who made it? Yes, Catherine 'up her own arse' Bennett. I bet the bitch spat in it, she's evil like that. I could get used to this kind of treatment. I wish I was rich. My head is dipped into the sink. I can feel the warm water sliding down the back of my neck. Hands massaging my scalp, smells of lemon tickling my nostrils. Oh what a

The Pudding Club

vision of the beauty I've become. I love being me.

Mrs Lavay combs through my hair. I haven't even seen the new me yet. My hair needs cutting and styling before I can see it. It's the surprise element that excites me most. This could be the change I've been waiting for, the change of the whole new me as a person. Gemma is sat alone in the corner of the room; she's just staring at me as if she's in a deep trance. She's a right smacked-arse, I'm sick of it all being about her all the time. Bleeding hell, I'm just getting my hair done; it's not the end of the world. Hot pockets of air across my face, eyes down on the floor I can see my new hair colour for the first time It looks blonde, really blonde. Mrs Lavay seems to have cut a fair bit of my hair off, she said it was full of split ends and needed a good trim. I suppose she's right. The last time I had my hair cut was about three years ago. My mother used the wallpapering scissors to cut it. One quick snap of the steel scissors and I was done. She did try to cut my fringe too but let me tell you, it was a disaster. My hair was wet when she cut my fringe and once it had dried it rose about two inches above my eyebrows. I looked like a mental case. My mam knew she'd messed it up but offered no apologies. Well, a Victoria sponge she gave me with extra cream in it did seem to ease my pain. My mother gave up the DIY hairstyles after that and she never once said I needed to go to the hairdressers. When I think about it, mother never went to the hairdressers either. I think she cuts her own hair even to this day. What a tight arse she is.

It was time to reveal my new look. Catherine was running about the room looking for her handbag. "Hold on, let's put some make-up on you first. You'll look amazing, trust me. Just hold on while I get my make-up," she shouted in excitement.

The Pudding Club

Gemma rejoined the class and came to my side. "You look gorgeous," she whispered under her breath. Everyone's eyes were on me and whatever they were about to reveal was something I would be happy with. Catherine was applying some make-up to my face, her own make-up may I add. The same brush that had touched her sacred skin was now touching mine. This was a magical moment to remember forever. Her hot sweet breath was in my face. I could see down the front of her blouse too. Two perky breasts were staring at me. I'm not a lesbian or anything like that but they did look great. They were absolutely nothing like what I had swinging about in my hammock bra. These were the real McCoy; firm, sexy and enclosed in a black lacy bra. I had to stop looking. I dipped my eyes. If any of the girls would have clocked me spying on them they would have branded me a rug-muncher. Yes, a full time lettuce-licker. That's all I need in my life isn't it, to be stamped as an overweight lesbian who'd been turned on by her own classmates breasts. No, I averted my eyes. I would no longer be looking at other females breasts, ever.

Here it was, the moment I had been waiting for, the unveiling of the new sexy me. There was a strange silence in the room and I would hear whispering behind me. It was time to look in the mirror. Gemma was by my side for support, she was squeezing my hand tightly. "Come on Rebecca, take a look and see what you think?" The mirror was just in front of me and I needed my spectacles to see the blurred image. Clipping them behind my ears I could see a blonde-headed young woman facing me. She looked like an overweight Olivia Newton-John, or so I thought. I loved it, and by the look on everyone else's face they loved it too. Catherine Bennett was my biggest fan.

"You look so much better Rebecca. In fact, there is a

party this weekend and you can come along if you want?"

Gemma jumped into the conversation, "And, what about me, can I come too? I mean we're joined at the waist us two, there is no show without punch, so to speak."

Catherine brushed her off and didn't really care what she had to say. I was the new kid on the block now and Catherine Bennett had finally accepted me as one of the good looking squad. Gemma was disheartened and I knew she hated the attention I was getting.

As the crowd from around me scattered she sat down and rummaged deep into her bag. She pulled out a great big sandwich and devoured it like a hungry animal. "What are you doing Gemma? That's not in the protein diet, don't spoil it for us. Just throw it away, it's full of carbs."

Gemma was munching hard, she was nearly biting her fingers off. My arm draped over her shoulder, she was upset. I could see it in her eyes. "Catherine has said you can come to the party too, so what are you upset for?" I asked.

Gemma licked the mayonnaise from the side of her mouth; she was speaking with her mouth full. "It's only because you're going that I've even been asked. What's up with these girls? One minute you're the flavour of the month and the next no one wants to know you. When I got fingered everyone wanted to hear my story, but now, it's like I never existed." Oh, this girl could put on a great show, the crocodile tears were flowing down the side of her cheek and she was blubbering like a small child, what an embarrassment! As she cried next to me I looked at my new hairstyle in the reflection I could see in the window. After all, this was my special moment and there was no way Gemma's tears were spoiling it for me. The old Rebecca Rooks was disappearing slowly and the new

The Pudding Club

girl I've always wanted to be was about to be uncovered.

That Saturday, I stood in my new outfit staring in the mirror, I was waiting for Gemma to come to my house, she was late. Timekeeping was never her good point. She'd be late for her own funeral I'm sure of it. Tonight, it was the party night. My first ever invitation to be with the good looking squad, I still couldn't believe it. I smiled at myself in the mirror puckering my lips together trying to look sexy. I've got sexy underwear on tonight just in case it's the night I get fingered. It could happen anytime now, just look at what happened to Gemma! She said she never expected it either, but it just happened to her. So, I need to be prepared. I'm so ready for it. I have even sprayed my lady garden with vanilla musk fragrance from the body shop. There is no way I want any name calling after I have done the deed. Michelle Bailey got her name through the same kind of thing. Tuna flaps, the lads nicknamed her. There's no way I ever want to be labelled with a name like that. Gemma was downstairs, I could hear her talking to my mother. She's loud and full of confidence tonight. I bet she's been swigging some brandy before she came around here. She likes a drink does our Gemma, she's a right piss-head. A last look in the mirror and it's time to face my mother and father. My dad never really says much, he's a man of few words, but my mother, she's a different story. She can't keep her big trap shut for one minute, anyway, here goes. Time to face her.

"What the hell are you wearing Rebecca Rooks? That skirt doesn't even cover your arse cheeks. Alfred, just look at the state of what your daughter is wearing. She could be raped and pillaged looking like that." I stand alone twisting my body slowly, playing with the cuff of my blouse, unsure of my next move.

My father never replied, he looks old these days and

The Pudding Club

his skin has turned yellow. I'm sure he's not well. "Mam, this is all the rage, everyone's wearing these kinds of skirts, its fashion, derrrrr. Tell her Gemma, isn't this what everyone's wearing?" Gemma, who was wearing a similar skirt to me might I add, never said a word. She dropped her eyes to the floor and smirked. What a coward she was. I always had her back, and the only time I ask her for a bit of support she leaves me like a lamb to the slaughter.

"I don't care what the bloody fashion is Rebecca, get back up the stairs and get something decent on. Alfred," she screamed at the top of her voice, "will you tell this child of yours that if she bends over you can see her dirty washing? Alfred," she yelled again, "will you have a word with her?"

My dad just shot his eyes over at me and smiled. At last, I had some support. "Mary, leave the kid alone. She's a young girl, and if that's the fashion let her wear it. If I remember rightly you wore mini-skirts when you were younger, and may I add, yours were a lot shorter."

Mary ran to his side and poked her stumpy fat finger into the side of his head. "I'm not talking about me Alfred. Are you going to tell her or what? And, for your information, when I wore skirts like that, I was eighteen years old not bleeding sixteen. And, plus I was a lot slimmer than Rebecca." She covered her mouth with her hand after she realised what she'd just said. You could see Gemma giggling at the side of me. This was it; it was time to stand up for myself. My mother was always putting me down and now it was time to put an end to it all.

Face boiling, heart pounding inside my chest I stepped forward and went nose to nose with my mother. It was now or never. I could feel my fists curling at the side of my legs I wanted to punch her lights out. I was losing control. "I'm not always going to be fat, mother. I've

The Pudding Club

started a diet already and I've lost a few pounds for your information. What, just because I'm not like a stick insect I can't wear nice clothes? I bet Gemma's mother doesn't always call her weight like you do to me. What kind of mother are you anyway, speaking to me like that?" My dad turned his head slowly and he was actually listening to the disturbance. I'm sure he was smirking. My mother just stood gobsmacked and she swallowed hard as she watched me get my coat from the side of the chair. "I'm going out. I will be in about eleven, and..." I paused. "I may just be a little intoxicated too, so don't wait up for me." There was no reply. "Are you ready Gemma or what? Let's go to the party." Gemma moved slowly passed my mother, she avoided any eye contact with her. Today was the day that I stood up to my mother, my feeder. I was not being controlled by her anymore.

The party was buzzing. Lots of people I knew were there. When I say knew, I mean, I'd seen them around. I'd never really spoken to any of them. Gemma was behind me as we headed inside the house to the party, she was quiet tonight. People were dancing on the tables and couples were kissing on the stairs. Catherine welcomed me from inside the kitchen. "Rebecca, I didn't think you would come, what drink do you want?" Blushing, unsure of the answer I nudged Gemma in the waist for some help; she whispered back to me. "Can we have some cider please, if not lager." Josh Thompson was in the kitchen too and he was looking straight at me, there were goose-bumps all over my body. If he would have said to me "let's have sex", I would have dropped my knickers for him there and then. I had no shame. Catherine passed us our drinks and she told us to mingle.

Gemma headed into the front room. This was going to be the best night of my life. I'd never been to a party

The Pudding Club

like this before. There were no cakes, no jellies, no Swiss rolls; it was just alcohol and drugs. Downing my first glass of cider I felt it hit the bottom of an empty stomach. It tasted sweet and refreshing. I wanted more. Gemma looked like she'd seen a ghost; she was trembling and hiding her face with her hands. "Just stand in front of me please," she begged, "don't let him see me for crying out loud!"

My head spun about the room. "Who? Don't let who see you?"

Gemma was nearly hid behind the sofa. She mouthed the name Peter Jarvis. Hunching my shoulders she knew she would have to explain further. She crept up at the side of me and cupped her hands around her mouth as she repeated his name. "He was the one who fingered me," she said with an anxious tone. My eyes shot straight over to Peter, he was a good looking lad and as far as I knew he had a girlfriend. How on earth had she ever got any attention from him? "He's gorgeous Gemma, why are you hiding away from him?" She stood to her feet and looked faint, licking her lips slowly she confided in me. "Well, when I said he just fingered me, that wasn't the complete story," she paused and blew a laboured breath before she continued. "There was more."

No words were spoken between us whilst I digested what she'd just told me, I was confused. "More to it like what?" I asked in a curious voice.

Gemma held her hand around the top of her neck and her words stuttered, she was going bright red. "I gave him a blow-job too."

This was hot gossip. I'd never known anyone who'd ever performed this kind of act. I thought it was just sluts who did oral sex or prostitutes. Oh my God, this was so unreal. Gemma was a slut. A dirty cock swallowing slut.

The Pudding Club

I couldn't help but look at her mouth now. The thought of a man's genitals sliding in and out of her mouth was too much for me to handle. I felt sick inside. Why had she never told me this before now? I was her best friend. A friend who'd supported her no matter what she was going through. I was in a mood, and I was well within my rights to be. She'd been sucking willies and she never thought to tell me. Gemma wasn't the girl I thought she was anymore and I made that quite clear to her that I was upset. "Gemma, why didn't you tell me about this? I mean, that's something you share with your best friends isn't it?" She never replied she just sank her head low and slid her finger around the top of her glass.

Josh Thompson was in the room and he was heading my way. With my heart in my mouth, I flicked my new hair style back from my face. I was wearing my new contact lenses tonight and although they were itching my eyeballs I loved not having the big black frames hanging from my nose. "Your hair is nice Rebecca. It suits you much better than being a redhead. Ay, I hear blondes have more fun, let's hope it's true."

He walked away and stood with a gang of lads opposite me. He was playing with me for sure; he would never look at me in a million years, he was out of my league. Plodding into the kitchen I grabbed myself another drink. This was a party and I was going to enjoy myself no matter what. Gemma stayed where she stood sipping the rest of her drink. UB40's "Red, Red Wine" played loudly in the house and before I knew it my hips were swinging to the beat of the music. I was alive, confident, and a party animal. The drinks were going down my neck at speed and I was doing things I would never have done if I was sober. I was actually talking to people I never knew. Peter Jarvis was now by my side and his arms were around my

The Pudding Club

waist. "You look sexy tonight Rebecca, do you want to come outside for a bit of fresh air. It's boiling in here?" I agreed, he was right, it was hot and I was dripping with sweat. Gemma was nowhere to be seen and I was alone with Peter. "Do you smoke?" he asked.

"Yeah, I've just put one out though. Why do you want one of mine?"

My head was inside my black handbag and I was searching for my fags. "Nar, I mean do you smoke weed?" I didn't have a clue what he was talking about really but he never waited for an answer. I watched as he made a reefer and smiled at him. Once the joint was lit he inhaled hard on it and passed it to me. I had a few drags on it too. Almost immediately my body started to melt, my eyes were closing, and I felt so relaxed, like everything was going in slow motion. I remember him pushing me up against the garden wall and his hot wet lips touching mine, he was kissing me. At last, my lips were no longer a virgin. Cold hands on my thighs, a slight breeze inside my knickers, he was touching me in my private area. My mouth was moving but no words were coming out. Something strange wriggling about inside me, it feels different, it feels nice. I was being fingered. Peter Jarvis sucked his finger after he pulled it out of me and brought it up to my mouth. "Lick it you dirty bitch," he chuckled. I pushed him away with all my might and stood against the wall shaking like a scared animal. His eyes looked menacing as he came nose to nose with me. There was just me and him there in the garden, no one else was about. His eyes were dancing with madness as he spoke. "Now you can suck me off. It's my turn."

A hand appeared at that moment and dragged him away from me. It was Josh Thompson, he'd come to rescue me. He was my knight in shining armour again.

The Pudding Club

"Jarvis, fuck off and leave her alone. Can't you see she doesn't want you here, just do one will you?" They both locked eyes and none of them were budging. My eyes were shutting slowly and I was finding it hard to breath, I passed out.

Eyes twitching slowly I could see a figure at the end of the bed. It looked like a man. I closed my eyes tightly and bit down on my lips with force. I must have died and been resuscitated and the man sitting on the end of my hospital bed was my father. The shame of it all, now everyone would know – I was a dirty pot smoking bitch. The doctors surely would have done tests on my body, and now the whole world and his wife would know I was no longer a virgin. I'd been violated and the only defence I had for myself was that I was steaming drunk. It was time to face the music. I opened my eyes slowly. This was no hospital room, and there was no doctor sitting on the edge of my bed, it was Josh Thompson. Reaching over for my hand he stroked it slowly, he was still drunk. "Bloody hell I thought you would never wake up. I was going to give it another ten minutes and then I was going to phone you an ambulance. I thought you were on your way out." I quickly looked down at my clothes; they were still in one piece. I'd not been raped and pillaged as my mother had predicted. Sitting up slowly my head was pounding. Josh moved closer to me on the bed. "Move over then, I can relax now you're awake."

I wriggled slowly and made room for him next to me. "Where's Gemma is she still downstairs?" I asked.

Josh chuckled and held the bottom of his stomach. "She's with Peter Jarvis; just before I brought you up here I saw her heading to the garden with him."

My jaw dropped and I tried to move my body. "I must go and help her, that lad is a raging pervert."

The Pudding Club

Josh smirked and held me back. "He's been seeing Gemma for months; don't tell me you didn't know?"

My head was spinning and this was too much to take in, surely he'd got it wrong. "Gemma's not seeing Peter, who's told you that?"

Josh held my chin with one hand and he came closer to me. "You're so innocent aren't you? I suppose that's what attracts me to you." Now I was tripping for sure, whatever Peter Jarvis had given me was making me hallucinate. I pinched myself slowly. I was not tripping, this was all real. Josh moved closer and his lips landed on mine. This was my second kiss of the night, what a party this was! Gemma was never going to believe this in a million years. There it was, the kiss from my true love; slow, sweet lips, pressing softly against mine. Something stirred deep in my groin and as if my legs had a mind of their own they opened slowly. Josh jumped up from the bed and ran to the bedroom door; he slid the bolt across the top of it. Watching him at the end of the bed I could see he was stripping off. His bare naked body was now stood in full view. I wanted to laugh. I wanted to giggle, even when I saw a penis in a book or on the TV it always made me want to laugh. I covered my mouth with the corner of the duvet and I tried to act grown up. Josh undressed me slowly, it was a good job I had my nice sexy underwear on otherwise I would have shit bricks. I was now naked too as he pulled the duvet over us. His warm flesh touched mine and it felt special. Lips connected as he entered me. It was painful at first but slowly it was getting easier. This was heaven; it was better than any double chocolate fudge cake I'd ever tasted. This was sweet hot passionate sex and if it was like this every time, it was my new addiction. Josh's face was changing, he looked angry and his thrusts were getting faster and harder. He was moaning and digging his fingers deep into my blubber. Josh fell at the side of me and he's gasping for breath. I think I've just lost my virginity. I've just had sex. Silence.

Josh gripped my double chin in his hand and smiled. "This is our secret. You know Catherine Bennett is my girlfriend don't you? She'd scratch your eyeballs out if she ever found out about this, so keep your trap shut ay, and perhaps we can do it again." Did he just say we could do it again? I was stuck for words but after a few seconds it just came out without me having no control over it.

"Tell me about it stud," I said in a low sexy voice.

Josh frowned and chuckled loudly. "What the hell does that mean?"

I sat up and tucked the duvet over my bare breasts. I was on the spot, face burning and mouth drying by the second. I had to think quickly. "I meant to say, it's our secret," I giggled. Josh pulled me back onto the bed and tickled me. A male was actually touching my body; he was licking me and suckling onto my breasts. "Oh, I just love a big bird. Catherine is all skin and bones. I like something to get my teeth into," he chuckled. At that moment I wanted to push his sexy body from me and demand that he apologised but I just let his hurtful words slide over my head. The old saying was right. Big girls were thankful of any sex they got. I relished any time I had left with him and now became a cock sucking slut just like Gemma. Oh the shame of it.

Josh Thompson got ready and sneaked from the bedroom. Just before he left he turned his head back to me. He held one finger up to his lips and spoke. "Remember, our secret." I nodded slowly and watched the door close behind him. Jumping up from the bed I found my clothes and got ready in a rush. There was no

The Pudding Club

way I wanted to be found in a naked state. Tonight was a night I would remember for the rest of my life. Two kisses from different boys and I got fingered for the first time and I had sex. Gemma was not going to believe this. I'm not going to tell her about Peter Jarvis though, no, I'll keep that to myself.

The music was still pumping as I ventured down the stairs. My head was still banging but I was still intoxicated. Looking around the room I could see Catherine Bennett stood with Josh, he was all over her like a rash. The cheek of him. Walking into the garden I could see Gemma and I ran to her side. "Where have you been? I've been looking for you for ages," she moaned.

"I was upstairs being sick," I lied.

Peter Jarvis walked to her side and pecked the side of her cheek. His cunning eyes looked at me before he spoke. "See you in a bit Gemma, and next time you can swallow it," he chuckled as he left.

Gemma was anxious and waited for him to leave before she spoke. She knew I knew something was going on and she led me to the corner of the room. "Peter is my boyfriend now Rebecca. He said he loves me."

The corners of my mouth start to rise but I tried not to laugh. I act like I don't know what has just happened. "What does he mean by you can swallow next time?"

Gemma is licking her lips with speed; she's agitated and looks around the room. "I've sucked him off again, and swallowing is what real women do. I suppose when you get a boyfriend you'll know what I'm talking about, but, until then, it's kind of hard to explain." I was about to tell my best friend all about my first sexual experience but stopped at the last minute. She's not to be trusted. Gemma is a self-centred bitch who only cares about her own world. No, this is my secret and it will never leave my lips.

The walk home that night seemed to take forever. My legs were sore and a burning between my legs was developing. Gemma asked if I was alright but I just blamed my ailments on the few sits ups I'd done before we came out. She never questioned me anymore. Gemma left my side and walked down her garden path, we only lived two doors away from each other. As I watched her I was in two minds as to shout her back and tell her my secret, but I lost my bottle. This secret was mine and it was never going to tell, ever. Lay in my bed I snuggled deep into it. I was alive inside and every time I closed my eyes I can see Josh Thompson over me, making love. Did he make love to me or not? I'm not sure what the difference really is, but to me it was hot, sticky, steamy, lovemaking.

Rebecca Rooks was no longer a virgin.

SIX

TONIGHT IS WEIGH-IN NIGHT at the slimming club. I feel a bit lighter if I'm being honest with you but you never really know do you until you step onto the scales. Gemma should be here soon, so I just have time to have a quick glass of red wine before she comes. I have had no tea yet, I'm starving. I feel like my throat has been cut. I'm going to wait until I get home from slimmer's club though before I have anything to eat. I'm thinking if I have a good result I can celebrate with a cheat meal. Everyone has cheat meals don't they? So it's not really cheating. It's a reward for all my good work. The chippy will be open when I'm on my way back home and I've smelt its aromas for days now and need a fix of the greasy grub. Steak pudding, chips and gravy is my treat tonight. In my dark days, as I call them now, I could eat that meal three times a day, plus all the other crap I could ram into my body. Cakes, sweets and Chinese food - I loved it. Just having it for one night is not going to kill me is it?

Gemma is talking about taking me to a singles bar. She said it's time for me to start meeting people again. She's right I suppose, but my confidence is still low and I don't feel I'm ready for that yet. I don't know why she is so concerned about finding me a new man, she's constantly on my case to be in a relationship again. I have looked online though, I have to admit. I looked at some dating sites and they look interesting. I'm a bit cautious though, knowing my luck I would probably end up with an axe murderer or something like that. It's a chance you have to take though isn't it? There were dogging sites too, what the hell is that all about. Who would go and watch other people having sex? Not me for sure. Anyway, I think on your first date you have to meet them in a public place, just so you're safe I think. Then you can go to other venues once you know them a bit better.

I would struggle with the conversation on my first date though. How can you just meet someone and start talking? What can you chat about, you don't even know them. I think I could talk about my weight problem, because they would want to know how I've ended up with such a round body wouldn't they? I could also talk about my budgie Joey too. I could talk for hours about him and his antics. I think that may be a bit boring though wouldn't it? I suppose they would want me to talk about my previous relationships too. They would want to know all about that wouldn't they? Questions, questions and more bleeding questions. No, I'm not ready to discuss my private life with a complete stranger. It's my business and it's staying that way. It's hard enough opening up to my counsellor. I just couldn't open up to a random individual. That reminds me, I'm with Teresa on Tuesday for my weekly counselling session. I think I'm a lost cause if I'm being truthful. Every time I think I'm making progress I just seem to fall back into being the same old sad me. Teresa says positive thinking is the way forward. She said every problem has a solution and by thinking about the problem all the time I'm just feeding it. What does she know about real life anyway? She just sits on her arse in a warm office all day listening to other people's problems? She doesn't know the answers I'm looking for, she says she's just guiding me, like a dog leading his blind master but I think it's a load of bullshit and don't think she can ever repair me.

Gemma's knocking at the door now, no doubt she's

The Pudding Club

dressed in Lycra again! She's obsessed with the fabric. I bet her knickers are even made from Lycra too. That's what I'm going to do when I've shed a few more pounds. I'm going straight to the town centre to invest in my own Lycra collection, everything I buy will be figure hugging and display my new slim waistline. Imagine Gemma's face seeing me dressed in tight, figure-hugging clothes, she would shit a brick, the jealous cow. I can see her now telling me that I'm abusing the Lycra selection of clothing. In her eyes this material should only be worn by people who are at their goal weight. What does she know about how people want to look, she was fat once or is she forgetting that? When we were younger we used to sneak into the clothing department to try on the training Lycra wear. I remember one time I tried a pair of cycling shorts on. I needed a shoehorn to get them over my knees. Gemma helped yank them over my stomach and for one second I felt slimmer, well, until they split open and burst. We had to hide them at the back of the shop. That was the end of my Lycra trying on sessions.

"Are you ready," Gemma yells as she checks her thin figure in the hallway mirror.

"Yes, just let me finish my glass of wine. We have ages yet, just relax."

Gemma is wearing pink Lycra today, it's so tight on her body and you can see her camel's toe at the front of her pants. I stare at it for a bit longer than I should have, and she follows my eyes and chuckles. "Don't tell me about it - I already know. I think I need a bigger size. I must store all my weight on my fanny flaps."

I can't help but laugh at Gemma she sure does have a way with words. She's always been the same and never thinks before she speaks. Gemma continued to speak. "The trainers at First step Gym are always gawping at my camel toe too, it must be a man thing. They think I don't know they perv on me, but all the girls are onto them, they are sex starved monsters. There's this one trainer called Arnie he's the worst. Bingo eyes we all call him, you know eyes down, look in," she giggled as she finished her story. "Do you know he used to be called Bernard but changed his name by deed poll to Arnie. He's a bleeding head case. He done it just because his hero is Arnold Schwarzenegger. He's a bit strange if you ask me. He's so serious all the time. The other girls steer clear of him but I have a good laugh with him. I think he's just misunderstood. We have good banter you know? He's there to train me he's says not to make friends. But I just know it's all a front, he's soft as shit really."

Gemma's never mentioned this gym to me before now. The crafty cow has been burning calories on her own. No wonder she's shedding the weight at lightening speed. "Can anyone join this gym Gemma? I wouldn't mind doing a bit more exercise?"

Gemma walks to the mirror and checks her body over. "It's a strength camp Rebecca, it's not for the faint-hearted, this camp is hard-core."

Who does Gemma think she is? Why does she think I'm not capable of anything other than eating food? I know I'm going to regret this but I can't stand her getting the better of me yet again. I throw myself in without thinking any further.

"I'm up for the challenge, it might do me good. Who do I get in touch with to join?"

Oh Gemma's face has dropped now; she's hesitant and trying to change the subject. No, she's not ignoring me. I want to join this camp and I'm going to sign up. I ask her again and this time she answers in a sarcastic voice.

"It's a guy called Tarzan," she chuckled as she flicks

The Pudding Club

her hair across her shoulders. "He's got shoulder-length hair and all he's missing is his loin cloth, that's how he got his name. I believe he had a weight problem too in the past and hates quitters." Gemma edges closer to me and speaks in a low sweet voice. "Do you really think you're up for this kind of training? You have to have a Bio signature done and they measure all your body fat before you start the camp you know? I don't think it's for you if I'm being honest."

Gemma was staring at me now, she was willing me to give up even before I'd started. I smiled and revealed my teeth as I replied to her. "Well, Tarzan can meet his jungle Jane. Give me his number I'm going to sign up straight away."

Gemma flicked some invisible dust from her jacket and tilted her head to the side. "Yeah, if you're serious I'll give you the number after slimming club. Trust me, it's not easy and these guys will make you work. It's not a holiday camp you know? Arnie and Tarzan are quite funny who they let join the gym. Mind you," she smirked and raised her eyes to the ceiling. "You're every trainer's dream. Imagine it, if they could get you into shape. What a promotion that would be for the camp."

Gemma was really pissing me off now and I just needed to remind her of how she got her weight down in the first place. It's about time she got a reality check. She hates it that I remind her about the help she's had to shed the blubber. "Do the guys at camp know you had a gastric band fitted to lose your weight?" I ask in a cocky tone, she knew where I was going with this and growled at me.

Gemma ran to my side almost hysterical. "No Rebecca they don't know a thing and I don't want you to be telling them. Nobody knows about the band except you, so keep it that way. Why are you always pissing on

The Pudding Club

my parade?"

I was having fun with her now and as I swigged the last bit of vino from my glass, I had to have the last word and put her in her place. "Well, that's how you lost your weight isn't it? I mean, people like me can't afford the operation you had. We have to do it the hard way, don't we?"

Gemma knew what I was saying was right and her cocky attitude disappeared in an instant. She was being helpful now. "If you're really serious about joining the strength camp I will take you there tomorrow night after work. I'll ring Tarzan and inform him I'm bringing you. Is that alright?"

Glass emptied, I placed it on the side of the table and smirked at her. "That's great, Gemma. What a true friend you are. Come on, let's go and get weighed before it's too late."

Gemma was trailing behind me tonight. My last comment had knocked the wind out of her sails. Even when we got in the car she was quiet, there was no singing tonight, just a weird silence. Her mobile phone was ringing constantly, but she never answered it once, she glanced at the screen and saw who the caller was. She was being secretive, and ignored it, something was going on with her that I couldn't quite put my finger on.

The pudding club was full tonight. There were women in the distance stretching their arms over their heads waiting to get weighed. Catherine Bennett was here too. I hate her so much and I think she knows that I will never forgive her for what she did to me when we were younger. Gemma seems to have forgotten the past though, but I never will. I hate that Catherine thinks it's all over too. The cheek of her thinking I would just forgive her for the way she treated me. It will never be over in my eyes until she takes her last breath and leaves this world forever. She deserves to burn in hell for what she put me through. I hate her guts.

Some of the ladies actually look slimmer tonight. The double chins they had weeks before look different, thinner in some way. I hope the other ladies are thinking the same about me. Hold on while I suck my cheeks in and turn to the side. Is anyone looking at me? No, no one seems to care if I've lost a bit of weight. I've been taking a few laxatives too this week. Just to help me with the stubborn lard that won't shift, you know, that blubber they call love handles. I would never take the laxatives like I used to do when I was younger. No, I will never end up like that again. I nearly died. I enjoyed the bars of chocolate laxatives I've taken today though. Sweet, rich, creamy bars. The dosage is one to two pieces three times a day but I've taken more. In fact, six pieces every dose. It's been like Russian roulette all bleeding day though, I dare not fart, I can't chance it. It just comes on me all of a sudden and when I've got to go, I've got to go. I've had a few accidents too. I'm ashamed to say. When I first started taking the chocolates I got caught short a few times. I felt the hot sweat rising through my body and my stomach started bubbling, then bad pains in my lower gut. I only managed to reach the living room door and what at first I thought was a fart turned out to be the first time I'd ever shit my pants. I just felt my knickers filling up, a bad stench rising up to my nostrils. I nearly passed out if the truth was known. I only take the odd piece of chocolate laxative every now and then now, they're like dynamite in the wrong hands. They need to be used in a controlled manner by a responsible adult.

Catherine is on her way over to me and Gemma. My body is turned away hoping she doesn't come over and

The Pudding Club

talk to me. I hate being two-faced and I can't hide the fact that this woman makes my blood boil. She's at my side now and its time to turn and face her. The cheeky cow reaches over and pats my stomach area and giggles. "Oh, I hope you have stuck to this diet Rebecca? A moment on the lips is a life time on the hips you know."

Teeth clenched tightly together I hold the words back and try not to be hostile towards her. It's hard and I'm trying not to break. No, I can't hold back, she's getting a piece of my mind. I reach over and pat her bum-cheeks. "Yes, we all know little pickers wear big knickers don't we Catherine. What was your weight when you realised it was time to stop eating?"

Her face went bright red, her nostrils flared. Gemma is stood at my side with her hand held over her mouth waiting for her answer. Catherine coughed to clear her throat and a few other people nearby were interested to hear her response. She snarled at me and I could see her thin fist curling tightly together at the side of her legs. Strike one to Rebecca Rooks, she was no longer the underdog, she was fearless. Catherine swallowed hard before she spoke. "I don't like to talk about the past Rebecca. I look to the future these days. When you eventually start losing the pounds, you will understand how important it is to stay focused and never look back," she had everyone on side now and my plan of embarrassing her had backfired.

She continued talking to the class. "Slimming with confidence is all about the future and the changes we're all about to make to lead a thinner, healthier life. I never discuss my weight with anyone." The other slimmers are looking at me now as if I've overstepped the mark. They're shaking their heads and whispering to each other, miserable cows they are. Catherine walks away and shouts in a loud voice over her shoulder. "Can all the slimmers -

The Pudding Club

make a nice neat line to get weighed please?"

She shot a look at me and gritted her teeth. I've definitely upset the apple cart this time I can see it in her eyes. I glance over to Gemma who's taking her trainers off and her jacket at the side of me. She mustn't be that confident this week, she must have been secretly munching. Watching her step onto the scales I can see her biting her fingernails, she's very nervous. Catherine looks up from her seat to check the scales a second time. "Gemma, you've put three pounds on this week. Have you been bingeing?"

Gemma bolted off the scales and quickly placed her tracksuit top on, zipping it up with speed. She couldn't look at anyone; she was fuming as she answered her. "No, I haven't been eating Catherine, for your information. I'm just premenstrual that's all, so that could be the reason I'm feeling bloated. It's probably just all water I'm carrying. I'll be back to myself in a few days, just you watch."

This was bad news for Gemma and the other slimmers stepped towards the scales with apprehension, myself included. There were some good results before it was my turn to take the scales. Cheers of celebration filled the room. It was now my turn and as I stepped up Catherine came and stood behind me breathing down my neck. All the other slimmers were at the other side of the room not taking any notice of my results. I slipped my shoes off and stood on the scales, sucking my breath in I held it for as long as I could. The scales flickered and I'm sure it read nineteen stone. I was just about to look up when the numbers started to go up again making me twenty stone eight pounds. Before I could get my words out to speak Catherine pulled me by the arm back off the scales. "That's not good Rebecca. You've put three pounds on," she yelled out so the rest of the class could hear. This wasn't true, I knew what I saw.

The bitch must have stepped on the scales at the back of me. I made my protest with a blood red complexion. "I want to get weighed again. I think something is wrong with the scales. My first reading was nineteen stone. I want to do it again."

Catherine picked the scales up from the floor and placed them in a cardboard box at the side of her table. "No, Rebecca the reading is right. I know how upset you may feel, but just try harder next week. I mean, Gemma put weight on too, so you're not alone in your weight gain."

Gemma was at my side now and she too thought some foul play had taken place. Catherine Bennett was an evil woman and you wouldn't put anything past her. Gemma stood with her hands on her hips and challenged the team leader. "Catherine, can she not just have another go? Just to ease her mind?"

Catherine ignored the question and gathered the women around to finish the meeting, every now and then you could see her smiling at Rebecca with a cunning look on her face. The meeting finished and me and Gemma headed home in low spirits. Passing the chippy I stopped and looked at Gemma. "I'm having a treat meal. I know what those scales read and I know I deserve a cheat meal, Catherine has set me up. When we get home I'm going to find my old scales in the attic just to prove a point. Catherine stitched us up tonight and I'm going to uncover that bitch for the lying cheating cow that she really is." Gemma was on side, after all she'd gained some timber too and wanted some answers. We both walked into the chippy and ordered our food like starving animals.

Watching the greasy chips slide onto the white tray was heaven. I bent forward over the counter and nicked a chip whilst the assistant was putting some salt and vinegar on them. The chip was hot but it never stopped me shoving it in my mouth. Once our order was ready we both headed home in a rush. As soon as I walked down the garden path I opened the front door and rushed upstairs. "You go and put the food on plates Gemma whilst I find them bleeding scales. I know I've got some somewhere."

Gemma went into the kitchen and opened the bag. The aroma of it filled the air. Feet pounding up the stairs, I went searching for the evidence that would prove Catherine did set us both up. Right there they are, I knew I had some somewhere. A quick wipe of dust and they're like brand new. I headed back down stairs in a hurry and stood at the kitchen door gasping for breath. "Don't eat anything yet, get on these scales and just let's see what that Catherine is really up to."

Both of us were hesitant, nobody was stepping forward. "Who's going first?" Gemma asked. This was it, the moment of truth. I slipped my shoes off and closed my eyes as I stood on the scales. Gemma was on her knees and she was watching the scales closely as the numbers flicked about. Once it was still she grabbed my legs with a firm grip.

"Well, fuck a duck. You were right, that bitch has stitched us up. You're nineteen stone."

Gemma dragged me from the scales and tossed her jacket to the side. "Well, if your weight is wrong, she must have fixed mine too." Gemma stood on the scales and her head was dipped as her eyes squeezed together tightly. "What does it read; I can't see it that well?" I bent over and looked at the digits displayed on the screen. This confirmed Gemma's worst fears. Her reading was right; she'd actually gained three pounds.

Gemma jumped off the scales and went to the kitchen

drawer. Cutlery clashing, she pulled out two silver forks. "Oh well. I can afford to gain a few pounds, but what she's done to you is below the belt. Don't worry we'll fix her just like we did years ago. Remember those who laugh last, laugh longest. Let's destroy her, she's a conniving bitch and she deserves to be uncovered"

I nodded my head. "Oh, don't you worry about her Gemma. I might be fat but I can still handle the likes of Catherine Bennett. It's about time I wiped that cocky smile right from her face. She might have won the battle but she's not won the war. Let's have her Gemma, let's bring her back down to earth with a bang." We were laughing together as we tucked into our food. Munching, chomping sounds – we were starving.

Gemma patted the bottom of her stomach once she'd finished. She let out a loud belch. "I just love food. Why can some people eat anything they want and yet me, I only have to look at a chip and I pile the weight on."

I knew exactly what she was talking about and stretched my arms over my head. "Me too, but fancy me losing over a stone though. I think this time I'm going to stick to the diet and really try to reach my goal. It's just sometimes when I'm alone, I start to think of him, and you know what happens then. I just eat till I nearly pop."

Gemma slipped her shoes back on her feet, she was anxious. She grabbed her coat from the chair and stood looking at me. She'd heard this story millions of times before and I knew she couldn't stand to hear it again. "I better be going home now Rebecca. Anyway, well done you for losing weight, it's bloody amazing. Don't you worry about Catherine either; we'll sort her out good and proper when the time is right."

I just nodded my head. "We sure will, ay before you go give me the number of that strength camp. I'm going

The Pudding Club

to go tomorrow and see what it's all about. Do you fancy coming with me?"

Gemma smirked before she answered. "Yep, I'll come with you, but be warned, this camp is hard, and it's not for beginners."

I stood up and hugged Gemma and walked her to the front door. "I've got to start somewhere Gemma, a bit of support would be nice every now and then you know? I am trying." I watched Gemma walk down the garden path; she waved over her shoulder as she got into the car. She was speaking to someone on her mobile phone and the call seemed important she didn't even look back at me to wave. I closed the front door and headed back into my warm living room, it was time to start relaxing before bedtime.

Joey knew it was that time of the night again. He jumped onto his perch and sunk his head low into his chest. I felt like jumping about the living room tonight and celebrating my weight loss, but on second thoughts I need to save all my strength for the fitness camp. Then I thought – should I wear Lycra for my first session? Gemma would have kittens wouldn't she? I might just buy some bright pink leggings and a vest top to match just to see her face drop. My brother Spencer is all about body shape, all he goes on about is his lean physique. Seven percent body fat he is and he's still training everyday to try and get it lower. I think my body fat in my finger is seven percent never mind anywhere else. I wonder what I will do when I'm thin again. I might become a raging slut. I can call it my mid-life crisis and then it will be okay. Other women do it and get away with it, so why not me?

My husband will want me back then for sure. I've already got my speech ready for him when I see him. I've practised it enough times. I'm going to stand tall, look

The Pudding Club

him straight in the eyes and speak to him as if he's a piece of shit dangling from my shoe. "I wouldn't piss on you if you were on fire, pal. Move out of my way before I have you arrested". And, just before I leave his side, I'm going to flick my hair over my shoulder, because it should have grown by then and shout behind me so that everyone can hear. "You thought the grass was greener on the other side, you should have tried mowing your own lawn, you wanker." I can see his face creasing now and everyone looking at him. All he will see then is my long slim legs walking away from him as he sinks to his knees on the floor begging for me to give him one last chance. That day will come, I'm sure of it. I want to tell you all about my husband, but I'm not strong enough yet, maybe in a few days when I can get my head around it all. I've been through such a lot lately and I don't think it's the time or the place to speak about the evil bastard that nearly wrecked my life. I'm on the verge of a mental breakdown if I'm being honest and talking about him would just push me over the edge. My mother told me he was a wrong 'un right from the minute I met him, but, would I listen, no. I was young and thought I knew it all. I knew nothing really. Joey is sleeping, his little beady eyes are firmly shut, he might be pretending though, the crafty little bugger. A quick rattle of the cage usually wakes him up. No, he's fast asleep. Right it's been a long day and my body is exhausted. Just the thought of climbing those stairs makes me feel tired; perhaps a few chocolates will help give me the energy? Yes, I think I deserve a treat after the day I've had.

Lying alone in my bed; I look at the space next to me. My husband used to lie there and we would talk all night long. Well, in the beginning we did. I should have realised things were changing between us when he moved into the spare room. He said I was too fat to sleep with anymore. He was probably right too, but it still hurts to think he left me alone and upset most nights. I bet he's in bed with her now, cuddled up like we used to be, warm, and snuggled. I wonder if he misses me. I miss him sometimes but only for the company I think, apart from that, he was quite a boring man. He liked to watch the TV a lot and play on his computer games. He was always on that Facebook chat. That's where he met her I think. Facebook has a lot to answer for. I call it slut book.

Right, one last spoonful of my Ben and Jerry's ice-cream and I'm going to go asleep. Oh, fuck it, I may as well eat the lot of it, no point in leaving it half empty is there? Head stretched up to the window I can see my neighbour in his bathroom. He no longer excites me anymore; he's lost his fit body. I'd much rather find a blue tit flying about than lust after him. I think my standards have gone higher now anyway. If I'm ever going to be labelled a lady pervert, then I'm only going to be looking at bodies of men that are ripped up, bulging muscles dripped in oil. That's the right saying isn't it? Ripped Up? Well, that's what our Spencer calls it anyway. I wish I was a bit more streetwise and understood all the slang that people use nowadays. I'm so out of date with my street talk. I need to start mixing with people again. Oh, pains in my lower stomach, griping crushing pains. I can't breathe. Is it the start of a heart attack? My hands reach out for the phone to call an ambulance. Whoops, sorry false alarm. It was just wind again, bleeding hell that smells like the drains. I need to open the window. I'm gagging. Oh, Rebecca you filthy mare that's putrid. Fresh night air sails through my bedroom window as I close my eyes. I'm restless at first but after a few extra pillows under my legs I seem to be comfortable. Well, goodnight world, see you in the morning.

SEVEN

Today is the day I go to sign up for my first strength camp. It's a twelve week course and it's very intense. I've paid my deposit and now I'm just waiting to have my body fat taken. I wonder if they will just harpoon me and stick me on the wall. I met one of the trainers just a minute ago. Tarzan is his nickname but his proper name is Johnny. Gemma said he's quite mild compared to the other trainers but watching him from the corner of my eye, I'm not so sure. I decided to dress in some baggy clothes today; the Lycra can wait until I've shed some blubber. I would have died a thousand deaths if I would have turned up looking like a thread worm anyway. Other men and women are here to sign up too. None of whom are half the size of me, might I add. Why do I always feel so different? Once my body fat is taken we are doing something called a bio-signature. I believe that will help me with all my vitamin supplements. Tarzan is swinging on some bars just outside the window I can see him swinging like an orang-utan from the bars. He's fit and doesn't mind showing off his skills to the other trainers. They are all actually stood round him, cheering him on. I thought this camp was about us, not about these bleeding lot.

Gemma puts her hand around her mouth and she seems stressed. She's whispering, and nudging me in the waist. "There he is, the one I was telling you about. That's Arnie. I think he'll be your trainer. I'm not going to lie to you Becks, the guy is brutal. He takes no prisoners."

My mouth has all of a sudden gone dry as Arnie

walks into the room and stands at the side of me. His chest is expanding and his muscles look like they are going to burst out from his t-shirt. I feel scared now, and I'm actually thinking about leaving, this is just a bad idea. Arnie's bobble-hat is pulled over his head, just above his eyes. He looks at me and stares. He's not blinking either, he's not human surely? He looks so aggressive. "Who's Rebecca Rooks?" he growls.

His voice was stern and I was quaking in my boots as I stood up. My legs buckled and I held onto the wall to steady myself. I was crapping my knickers. "That's me," I said in a timid voice. His eyes scanned my body up and down and I could see by his expression on his face that he thought I was a disgrace. Looking down at the white sheet of paper in his hand he told me to follow him into another room. My palms were sweating, and I was so nervous. My mind was doing overtime. What was he going to do with me when he got me into this room? Was he going to shove a steel pole up my arse and through my mouth and spit roast me for sure? He looked pure evil and I wasn't sure of my next move.

My feet seemed glued to the floor and Gemma had to get up from her seat and give me a gentle push. "Go on, move it," she giggled. She was smirking, the bitch, and she must have known what was lying in wait for me. Arnie stood tall with his two hands pressed firmly on his hips. His white t-shirt was crisp and perfectly ironed. He reminded me of a soldier. You could see his six- pack bulging through his top, ripped bulging muscles. "Please take your clothes off and I will measure your body fat," he said. My face went bright red, this wasn't right. Gemma had never mentioned that I would be stripping off. For crying out loud I was wearing my ex-husband's boxer shorts and a bra that was three sizes too small for me. I tried to see if I could come back another time to have this test done. Surely he would understand? "Excuse me," I said in a low sweet voice. "I would like to rearrange this appointment so I can prepare for this test, can I come back tomorrow about this time?"

Arnie jumped down from the small step he was stood on and came to stand next to me. His hot breath was in my face bubbling with testosterone, he wasn't happy. "Are you taking the piss or what? No, today is the day I am measuring body fat. It's not a doctor's surgery where you can rearrange the appointment to suit yourself. Just get your kit off and I'll be back in a minute to start the test."

Stood quivering I knew I had no other option. Peeling the clothes from my round body I could feel my head getting hotter and hotter. I looked like a pig in a fit if the truth was known. I was going to burst. Stood in a grey pair of men's boxer shorts and a discoloured bra I cringed as I waited for the trainer to return. Loud coughing from behind me made me jump out of my skin. Arnie was back and Tarzan was with him. Oh my God could this day get any worse? Arnie plonked himself down at his desk and turned to face his computer screen as monkey boy started to pull and tug at my blubber. As his cold hands touched my pink wobbly flesh I giggled. I was ever so ticklish, ask anyone who knows me I always laugh when someone touches my body. I think it's a nervous kind of thing I have going on. Anyway, I laughed that much that I farted. I was relaxed, what did they expect? Aware of what had just happened I covered my mouth and tried to apologise to the trainers, this was a nightmare.

Arnie shot a look at me and shook his head in disgust. His words were slow and he made sure I was listening to every word he said. "Dropping bombs on your spotting partners is not acceptable at this camp. Please remember

The Pudding Club

that for future classes."

I snarled at him. Bloody hell, I only farted it wasn't the end of the world was it? Johnny was now between my legs yanking at my fat with some silver clamping instrument in his hand. He was shouting numbers out to Arnie who was typing it all into the spread sheet on the screen. The two men had me sat down, then stood up, then bent over, then lying on the floor with my legs sticking up. Twelve places they took readings from. I was knackered by the end of it, completely exhausted. Once my test were complete Arnie just shot a look over at me and spoke in a deep voice. "You can get ready now." I've never been so quick to get dressed in my life.

Just when I thought it was over they shouted me back and asked me to step onto a line on the floor and have my photograph taken. "Pull your top up over your waist then," Arnie stressed. "Bloody hell, do you not listen to anything anyone ever tells you," he mumbled. I was just about to give this tosser a piece of my mind when the door opened. Because once I snap, I snap and I would have put him in the cheeks of my arse and squeezed the life out of him the moaning prick. Another trainer called Mike now walked in. He was big, huge in fact and seemed calmer than the rest of the trainers and he smiled at me softly. I liked Mike. My photograph was taken and my tests were completed. I pulled my training top down over my gut, surely the worst was over now.

The rest of the new recruits all had their body fat measurements taken too. There was an Asian man who seemed as nervous as me, he was fidgeting and twiddling his thumbs. I offered him a friendly smile. "It's not as bad as you think, its pain free," I said to him with a giggle in my voice. The man offered his hand out to me and introduced himself as Rimmer. Watching him from the corner of my eye I could see him sneaking sweets into his mouth as he waited to get measured. He was my kind of training partner, sly and crafty and knew how to hide his secret eating habit.

All the body fat measurements were completed and we were stood about waiting for our next instructions. I could see the trainers setting up a bar with weights on it in one of the rooms. Gemma was now by my side. "This is the max rep test, it's quite easy and it will determine which group you will go into." This talk was going over my head. The only thing I had ever lifted was food to my mouth, and you could consider that weightlifting because a chip butty does hold some weight. Especially the way I fill it up. Arnie is stood in front of us now, legs slightly apart and hands held behind his back. I must pay attention and listen to what he has to say. He looks a right tough nut and his eyes scare me. Gemma gives me a friendly hug and leaves my side. I'm alone now and scared and not really sure if this camp is for me, I feel vulnerable. The other trainer, Tarzan as he's known, starts to demonstrate the lift. This looks like child's play, I mean, one bend, one lift and that's it. Bring it on I'm so ready for this.

Rimmer is now called to the stand to take his lift. I can't watch him, he looks so nervous. Just before he makes the lift I can see him shoving another sweet into his mouth. I could eat a sweet now, my mouth is dry and I feel weak. Rimmer bends his body down, eyes looking straight at me; back arched, he's ready to lift. My mates have told me when you look at a man's face who is weightlifting the face he is pulling is his orgasm face. His mouth is slipping from side to side, his nostrils are flaring, and his nose looks like a squashed tomato, it's not a pretty sight. He lifts the bar up and his legs shake, he's wobbling at first, but finally gets the lift under control. Rimmer screams out like a gladiator, and drops the bar to the floor. The trainers are impressed; they give him a small pat on his back as he walks passed them.

Arnie looks at the list and lifts his head slowly. I can just see his beady eyes peering from under his woollen hat. "Rebecca Rooks, come forward please." This was it, the moment of truth. The weights were lowered and I was now stood in front of six other members from the camp. The lift was explained and now it was time to lift. Breathing heavily I gripped the cold silver bar in the middle, my knees bent and my back lowered. I can see Gemma now, she's come to support me. One, two and lift. The bar is in my hands and my grip is strong. I'm actually lifting it, my backs feeling weak, legs starting to buckle, swaying from side to side, the trainers are at my side spotting me. I can't hold this much longer! Wet liquid dribbles down the back of my black leggings. For crying out loud, I'm pissing myself! The bar hits the floor with an almighty crash. Gemma turns her head away from me and everyone is looking at the small puddle between my legs. I've always had a weak bladder and this is not my fault. I have no control over it. Head dipped low, I can feel everyone's eyes on me. Gemma shakes her head and hunches her shoulders at me as she watches the trainers mop up the mess on the floor. I'm trying to make a joke out of it but I'm rushed away by Arnie to the side of the room, he's not happy.

"Rebecca, do you have any medical conditions that you have not told me about? I mean, you seem to have no control over anything that's going on between your legs?"

Who did this man think he was talking to me like this? So what, I suffer with the odd burst of gas and the odd wet patch, surely it wasn't an hanging offence, accidents happen? He's waiting on my reply and lets out

The Pudding Club

a laboured breath. Licking my lips slowly I have to think quickly. Coughing, I clear my throat. "I've had a water infection, that must be the reason why I've dribbled. I'll make sure it doesn't happen again."

He's looking at me for something more, he knows I'm lying. Tapping his pen on his front teeth he asked me to sit down. His voice is low now and I feel calmer. I think he's taking a shine to me. "Do you really think this kind of training is for you? It's hardcore, and even the strongest of people struggle with it," he smiled gently at me. "What about a milder course for you, something easy, not as intense?"

I gritted my teeth together tightly. It was just like being back in school again in the PE lessons. I was always the kid nobody wanted to be on their team and here he was Mr bleeding Motivator, doing exactly the same thing to me all over again. I'd had enough, no. I was not giving up again, not this time. I was going to commit and finish the course if it was the last thing I did. I swallowed hard and spoke. "I want to continue with the camp." My eyes filled up and I was on the verge of breaking down. "I know you think that I won't make it to the end, but I will, just give me the chance. I just hope you can support someone like me and help and guide me through?"

Arnie was stuck for words. I think he was actually touched by my determination. Holding his head to the side, he nodded slowly. "I like a challenge and if you're saying you are going to be committed then I will let you continue. But," he paused, "you need to sort out whatever it is going on down there," he shot his eyes to my private regions.

My cheeks were bright red, and I didn't know where to look. I just nodded my head and that was enough for him to leave my side. Gemma popped her head inside the

The Pudding Club

room. She was hysterical, laughing her head off. "Oh my God, pissy knickers, what the hell happened? I've never been so embarrassed in all my life. You were like a donkey; it was gushing out of you."

Gemma was so over the top, it wasn't a gush at all, it was a bleeding dribble of water if that. "I just lost control of my bladder that's all. I'm going to get some of them Tena ladies for next time. It won't happen again don't you worry."

Gemma looked at the long mirror hanging on the wall and turned sideways in it, sucking her stomach in. "This could be your last chance Rebecca, I mean, you have high cholesterol and I'm sure you are verging on diabetes. This camp could be the answer to all your prayers if you put the work in."

There she was again, Miss fucking know-it-all. She was starting to piss me off big time. I had to say something. "Gemma, take your head from up your arse. I know what I've got to do and I'm doing it aren't I? When we were fat together I was the one who always got us exercising are you forgetting that?"

I stood watching her crumble now. Oh, I thought she'd be quiet, where's all her smiles gone now? Tucking her vest top in her skin- tight leggings she stretched her arms over her head, she was smirking. " Rebecca, we used to do a few sit-ups together that's all. You were no Rosemary Conley. And, as I remember after doing them you rewarded us both with a cream cake, so the exercising was pointless."

She was an out and out bitch. She was doing her best to break my temper. This was the time to pull my ace card out from up my sleeve and shut her up once and for all. "If I had a man who paid for a gastric band, I would be the same as you now, but we all haven't got a rich husband

The Pudding Club

have we?"

Gemma snarled and her eyes widened. "What do you mean by that ay? I married Alex because I loved him, no other reason, so wind your neck in and get your facts right."

Gemma was livid, she knew as well as I did that Alex was her sugar daddy and the only reason she married him was because he was loaded. She'd forgotten that I was there when she met him and her first words were that he was loaded. Gemma met Alex on a dating site when she was twenty-six. She was an overweight slob then, with no chance of ever finding love, desperate she was. Alex was a business man and he had several properties in and around Manchester. He was always flashing his cash about from the first moment we met him. I was Gemma's escort on her first date and Alex took a shine to me too. After that Gemma went on all her dates by herself, she was jealous of me if I was being truthful. She was always jealous of anything I had. Alex was always looking at my breasts and Gemma knew I could have taken him from her at anytime I wanted, but he wasn't my type. I did however allow him to eat chocolate sauce from my breasts one drunken night though. Gemma was drunk and asleep when it happened and to this day she doesn't know about her sleazy husband's little secret. I feel quite bad about betraying Gemma, but come on, it was only licking some chocolate sauce from my breasts, it wasn't having sex with him was it?

I'm waiting outside now for all the other people to finish their tests. It's like a bleeding military camp here – there's shouting and screaming in the distance. Once that's done we're getting our body fat results. I've never had this kind of test done before. Gemma has already told me her body fat is eighteen percent. I think mine will be double that or maybe even treble that, I'm gutted already. Rimmer is still munching his sweets on the sly I can see him concealing them. I'm starving so I'm going over to talk to him. Stood at his side I make him aware that I have seen his secret stash of sweets. He's nervous, and smiles at me. He knows I know. I can see him sucking and crunching his sweet quietly. "What sweets are you eating?" I asked in a quiet voice. Rimmer nearly choked, he dug straight in his pocket and passed me a red ball of candy. It was a Rose's apple, they were one of my favourites sweets when I was a kid. Bursts of apple flavours dancing around on my tongue, heaven, pure heaven. Where on earth had this man got them from? Nobody was selling these anymore, was there a black market for them or what, I needed to know. "These toffees are extinct, where did you get them from?"

Rimmer chuckled and stood proud. He was like a treasure hunter who had found the Holy Grail. "They're from a market stall in Bury town centre. They have all the old sweets like Floral gums, cherry lips, cop-cops and cola-cubes. I'll grab you some the next time I'm shopping up there if you want?" Rimmer was my new best friend. I wanted them now; I could taste all the old flavours in my mouth. I was craving them. Perhaps he would give me a few more sweets to last until he brought me my own supply? Would it be cheeky to ask for more? I smiled at him and slid the candy ball in my mouth slowly. Rimmer was watching me with eager eyes as it appeared on the end of my tongue. We were partners in crime now, our bond was sealed.

Gemma stood next to me and inhaled deeply. She was like a Springer spaniel on the scent of banned contraband. "Who's got Rosy apples, oh my God, I know that smell anywhere. Rebecca what are you eating?"

The Pudding Club

Rimmer turned his head and snarled at me, it was obvious he didn't want to give another sweet away. This was the circle of trust and there was no way I breaking the code of silence. Quickly swallowing my toffee I turned to face her. "I can't smell anything, what is it you said you could smell?"

Gemma was pacing up and down and she stood frozen next to Rimmer. Her eyes shot a look to him but she never spoke. Arnie saved the day for us both when he asked us all to gather round him for our body fat results. Everyone was nervous and I was chewing on my fingernails. The two trainers now started to announce the results. Closing my eyes tightly I played nervously with my fingers. My name was shouted out and Arnie looked at me with disapproving eyes yet again. "Your results are one of the highest Rebecca. You and Rimmer are both forty eight percent body fat."

You could have heard a pin drop and everyone's eyes were firmly fixed on me. Rimmer patted my shoulder and whispered in a low voice. "We can work together; it's not the end of the world is it?"

Gemma was stood with Arnie and looking at the results. Why she was doing that was beyond me, the result wasn't going to change, was it? I stood up and confronted my fear, from nowhere I found this inner strength and I was now talking to the group. "I know some of you may think I should leave now, but I'm here to make changes. Please guys, be patient with me and let me try and fit in. I'm a skinny person trapped inside a fat woman's body. I do want to change and be slim again, it's just going to take some time."

Rimmer clapped his hands together slowly and before I knew it the class joined in. Life wasn't that bad after all. The team accepted me at last. Arnie stood tall

The Pudding Club

with his wingman Tarzan stood at the side of him. They looked like marines, who were ready for combat. They discussed the next session and what was expected of each of us. I was so ready for this now, positive thinking, and life changing menus, and the whole new me just waiting to be found.

EIGHT

TODAY IS MY APPOINTMENT with my counsellor. Teresa is a lovely woman but she does talk out of her arse sometimes. She's around fifty years of age and looks so timid. I swear to you if a strong gust of wind came along she would snap in half. I like her voice though, so soft, and calming. I've been with her now for over eight months and although I'm not completely fixed, I am making some kind of progress, well, that's what she's paid to say isn't it? When my sessions first started all I used to do was cry. A full hour blubbering. I very rarely spoke. I'm sure Teresa used to read her magazine whilst I was in with her, but can you blame her? I was a walking wreck with a story of doom and gloom.

I'm ten minutes early so I will wait in the reception area and eat my snack before I go in to see her. I'm eating houmous and celery sticks today. Yep, no cakes or crisps today. It tastes alright too, a bit mushy, but still it fills a gap in my stomach. For breakfast I had a poached egg and two rashers of bacon and two mushrooms. I'm eating really well now and making big changes to my eating patterns. Breakfast in the old days was five chocolate biscuits and two pieces of jam and toast. I miss dunking my biscuits in my cup of coffee though; I miss all my old foods. This is week four now of my diet and I have lost one and half stone in total. My knickers are slipping from my arse-cheeks and even though I know I should buy new ones I keep wearing them just to remind me of how much weight I've lost.

I can nearly see my lady garden too, well if I hold my

The Pudding Club

stomach blubber up high enough. I know. I can't believe it either! It's been such a long time since I've seen my vagina, I thought it was extinct if I'm being honest with you. It's not a nice sight really, it's like an over grown bush. A chicken's napper in fact. Gemma keeps telling me to get it waxed, something called a Hollywood wax she has had done. I think that means no pubic hair at all but I'm not sure. No, I like a bit of hair on my private bits. A welcome mat I call it. My arms are thinner too; the bingo wings are slowly disappearing. I do need to tone my body now though; all this weight loss is just leaving me with lose hanging skin. I can pick an apron of fat up from around my waist and just pull it everywhere; it's hanging, rotten in fact. I feel better in myself, thinner, and more confident.

My snack lasted about five seconds, there's not a scrap left. I'm sure I should be allowed more food than this but Arnie has told me if I don't stick to the diet he's going to personally wire my jaw up. I think he would too; he takes his job to heart. He's a right dick-head sometimes but he does make me smile with some of his comments, dry, quick- witted humour. In fact, he's quite nice to me these days. His humour is not everyone's cup of tea and it takes a bit of time to get used to but I'm actually enjoying my training with him. I've not felt my legs and arms for weeks if I'm being honest. Everyday my muscles ache, Arnie said that's normal, but surely it's not, I'm constantly aching.

I had a bit of a trauma yesterday too. I'm so embarrassed about it. After a hard day of training at the camp I decided enough was enough, I needed something to ease the pain in my joints. "Deep Heat" they call the product. Nobody told me how to use it properly and I just slapped it all over my body like moisturiser. The lady in the chemist told me to just rub it over the sore areas, so I did get some professional advice. I was aching everywhere when it was time to rub the cream on. So, I rubbed the ointment all over my legs and arms, and anywhere else I could reach. I even rubbed it on my groins. The only way I can describe what happened next is by saying I was like an erupting volcano. Every second that passed I was getting hotter and hotter. I rubbed my fingers in my eyes as they started to itch also. I never knew you had to wash your hands after applications. I was a burning fat bomb. I dragged my nightie from my body and ran around the house trying to cool down. It's amazing how many places you touch when you're applying cream to your body. I'd had an itch up my bottom too, and you know you have to chase an itch don't you? It spread to my lady garden. Lying in my living room with not a stitch of clothing on I wafted my hands all over my body. My legs were stuck up in the air and my ring-piece was on fire. In fact, my body was a blazing furnace. I really thought my number was up, and prepared myself for death, ten bleeding Hail Mary's I said. My two cheeks were on fire and my eyes were closed tight, I couldn't see. I did consider ringing the emergency services but I was blinded and couldn't find the bleeding phone. I'll never use "Deep Heat" again. Well, not unless I'm supervised. I can be a right idiot sometimes, and yesterday was just one of them days. It took me hours to cool down.

Teresa is out in the reception area now saying goodbye to her last client. I wonder what her problem was? The woman who's leaving only looks young, how could she possibly have any issues at her age? Teresa waves her goodbye and spots me. "I won't be a minute Rebecca, I'm just nipping to the toilet," she whispered with a giggle. Why do people feel the need to tell you things like that? My mind just holds the vision of her squatting on the toilet now. Teresa usually has a bowl of sweets on her table in the office for her clients. I will have to tell her not to offer me any. Last time I was in my session, I ate the bleeding full bowl. I was upset, and you know what happens when I'm crying. I'm a right greedy cow.

Right, here goes, let's see if today I can have a great session with her and help Rebecca Rooks get her life back on track. It's a hard day today because we're going to talk about him, yes him, my ex-husband, the bastard. Standing to my feet I follow Teresa into her office. "It's a lovely day outside, isn't it Rebecca?"

I never really noticed to tell you the truth but a quick look through the window confirms that my therapist was right. "It sure is a bright day, hopefully we're in for a great summer," I reply.

Teresa looks at me closer and walks slowly to my side. "You look like you've lost quite a lot of weight Rebecca, you look so well."

At last, hallelujah, somebody has noticed my hard work. This was a good sign. Order the Lycra! I'm officially losing weight. I hesitate before I answer her. Is she just saying this to be nice to me, to make me feel better about myself? It's her job to do that isn't it?

"Thanks for noticing. I have been cutting down on my calories and I'm eating healthy foods now." I reply modestly.

Who am I kidding? I've been starving myself to death; my stomach thinks my throat has been cut. If she only knew the torture I was putting myself through every day, just to make sure I didn't binge on forbidden food she would collapse. To the thin people in the world, fat people are just greedy and deserve to look the way they do. Their understanding of a food addiction is nil. Teresa knows I'm being defensive and watches me closely as I take my coat off and drape it over the back of the chair. I hate the beginning of my sessions, it's just so boring talking about everyday life. I need to get to the nitty-gritty problems and heal myself. I'll bring up the subject first, hopefully we can get cracking and get this over with as soon as possible.

"I'm ready to talk about my husband today Teresa," I say in a soft voice trying to be positive. "I think it's time to face my demons." Teresa is excited and rubs her hands together. I can see it in her eyes, progress at last. There is a sofa nearby and I go and lie on it. I need to be comfortable if I'm going to talk about my ex-husband. He makes my blood boil and I can just about speak his name. My fists curl up tightly at the side of my legs and I'm trying my best to control my temper. Right, eyes closed deep breaths and try to relax. I can hear Teresa nearby, rustling paper, it's all gone quiet.

My therapist's voice is low and she coughs to clear her throat. "When you're ready Rebecca, start at the beginning."

My hands are hot and sweaty, and I can feel my stomach churning, I feel sick. I knew I would have to get this off my chest at some point in my life, but, I've never felt ready, well, not until now. Eyes closed tightly I can see his face. My heart is beating ten to the dozen and I open my eyes slightly just to calm myself down. Eyes closed again and I can see Josh Thompson as clear as daylight. There is a stabbing pain in my heart and I realise just how much I loved this man. Now is the time to talk about him. The bastard who broke my heart into a million pieces.

For the first time ever I felt loved, cared for even. I kept my secret relationship with Josh close to my heart and never breathed a word to anyone, not even to

Gemma. Don't get me wrong, there were times when I was going to tell her, but I just didn't trust her enough to confide in her, she was a right gob-shite at times and she couldn't be trusted. Gemma was in love with Peter Jarvis now anyway or so she said, and that was all she ever spoke about. Day in, day out, she never shut up about him. I never told her about what he'd done to me on the night of the party either, I was just so embarrassed. And, if I was being true to myself I think I was a willing participant in the fingering saga that had taken place. That's what I call it now, 'The Fingering Saga'. Nobody but Peter and I know what happened on that night and hopefully that's the way it will always stay.

Life at home was pretty bad at that time, my father was terminally ill. The doctor said he had months left to live, if not weeks. I was gutted and felt like ending my own life too. My mother was a walking wreck; her usual strong manner had died. She's lifeless nowadays and very rarely speaks. She just sat with my father around the clock, she was a broken woman. My brother never speaks about our father's illness. It's like nobody can face losing him. I lay in bed listening to his laboured breathing through the paper-thin walls every night and it killed me that I couldn't help him. Food was no longer a comfort. In fact, I didn't eat much anymore. My mother rarely cooked either; she's lost the will to live.

My appetite died the minute I was told my father didn't have long left to live. I was nearly seventeen at this time and I needed my dad more than ever. He was the only one person who ever listened to me. Who would give me away on my wedding day? Who would fight my corner when my mother verbally attacked me? I was alone and scared of the days that lay ahead. Gemma helped with my pain sometimes, but cream cakes were no longer the answer anymore. I refused them when she brought them for me. They didn't ease the pain like they used to. The sweet tasting calories just tasted like cardboard, everything I ate tasted the same, nothing tasted right anymore. The Friday evening I returned home from college I knew something was wrong. The house was in darkness and the front door was left open slightly. Walking into the hallway I could smell death; stale, sour aromas that gripped my throat and made me heave into my hands. Sinking to my knees I could hear my mother sobbing in the living room. I knew he was gone without even asking anyone. Drawing my knees up to my chest I rocked about just staring at the four walls. Emptiness, sadness, loneliness... I wanted my father back.

Spencer walked into the hallway and flicked the light switch on, eyes looking down at me he spoke in a shaky voice. "He's gone, he died this afternoon." A large ball of emotions jumped to my throat, I was choking, gagging for breath, Spencer just stood staring at me unsure of what to do. "Take deep breaths, it's just shock, it will pass," he said in a stressed voice. My brother was right, after a few minutes I could breathe again. My legs were so weak and I was fragile I didn't think they would allow me to stand up. Making my way to the front room I could see my mother sat in the corner of the room with her head held in her hands. We weren't a loving family and even though I wanted to comfort her, there seemed to be an invisible barrier between us. I just left her sat on her own. Sitting down on the sofa I sat chewing my fingernails.

At last, my mother lifted her head and smiled softly at me. "He passed without pain, Rebecca. He said before he left that he loved you so much and you should make him proud. He just drifted off to sleep, very peaceful it was." How could she be so calm? I would never see my dad

The Pudding Club

again, ever. I needed to leave, I needed to run away and never come back. My head was in bits and I just wanted to kill someone. Yeah, I would have taken someone's life I was that mad. Walking out from the house I just froze on the garden path. Where could I go? Who could I turn to in my hour of need? The only person who really cared about me was Josh. The walk to his house seemed to take forever. I was sobbing my heart out and people in the street were just staring at me. My heart was beating inside my ribcage at speed and I was sure I was going to pass out. Josh had told me straight that I should never call at his home, but this was an emergency and I needed him. My hands shaking, I tapped on the front door. Now I was here, I was in two minds if I should really have come. Too late, the door opened and Josh's sister opened the door. I wanted to speak but nothing was coming out.

Janice knew me from school and quickly led me into the house. "Rebecca, what's wrong, speak to me will you," she stressed.

"Josh, is he at home?" I blubbered.

She looked confused and stood looking at me a bit longer than she needed to. "He's upstairs, I'll give him a shout. Just wait here." Janice left the front room, and I paced the room unsure of my next move. I was going to leave. It was a big mistake ever coming here in the first place. Josh couldn't help me. I was just reaching out to anyone who would listen. I knew in my own head he was just interested in having sex with me that's all. He didn't care about me, I was just a bang. I made my way to the door ready to leave. A voice behind me made me stop dead in my tracks. It was Josh.

"What the hell are you doing here?" he growled as he grabbed me by the arm. Turning slowly to face him, he realised I was upset. "What's wrong? Don't tell me

The Pudding Club

you're fucking pregnant or something like that, because if you are there is no way you're keeping it, do you hear me?" he was pacing up and down and ragging his fingers through his hair.

"No, so relax. I'm not tubbed, my father has died. I just wanted to talk to someone."

Josh looked relieved, and led me into the dining room away from his sister. Closing the door behind him he kept his voice low. "Rebecca I know this is a hard time for you, but you need to stick to the rules. You can't just turn up here whenever you want. People will start talking." His words stabbed straight into my heart, he was an out and out prick. For the first time ever I saw him for the person he really was. A shallow, selfish prick. A rage from deep inside me surfaced and a red mist appeared in front of my eyes. I wanted to hurt him, I wanted to end his life. So what, yes I was fat, but I deserved respect. I was still a human being.

I growled at him and went nose to nose with him. "I know I shouldn't have come here Josh, I just thought, well, I don't know what I thought. A bit of support might have been nice. I may be fat Josh, but I'm not being your secret anymore. I'm worth more than that you know. If you're embarrassed about shagging a fat bird then that's fine, that's your hang-up not mine. I'm going now Josh and just to let you know I won't be sleeping with you again, find yourself another fuck buddy, I'm done with you," I opened the front door and turned my head back to him. "I'm going to find a man who is proud of me and doesn't hide me away because they're ashamed."

There it was, the speech of my life. Me, Rebecca Rooks from the geek camp had carted one of the good looking squad, Josh Thompson. This was history; no one had ever done this before. Josh went white; he looked

The Pudding Club

like he'd seen a ghost. I walked out of the front door. Josh filled up and I'm sure he was going to cry. Did this guy really care for me, or was this just all for show? "Rebecca, don't be like that. You know how things are between us. Me and you, well, it just doesn't make sense." Well, the cheeky bastard, there he was stood behind me telling me that he was too good for me. I was going to knock that smile right off his face once and for all.

"Josh, I'm worth ten of you. I don't have to pretend to be someone I'm not. What you see is what you get with me. And, if I was being perfectly honest with you, sex wasn't that great either. I've never had one of them orgasm things with you, I lied. And, any noises I made when we were having sex was just pretend." Oh, I was on a roll now and giving him a piece of my mind. "You're not all that Josh, so I'm going to leave you now with that thought. I just needed a friend at the moment and you couldn't even be that. See you around Josh, it's goodbye from me, enjoy your life." Josh was following behind me but he never said a word, he was gobsmacked. Walking down the garden path, I didn't look back. That was the end of my love affair with Josh Thompson. I was done with him forever, the wanker.

My father was buried the following week. It wasn't a big service just close friends and family. Gemma had been by my side all morning and she was more than helpful to my family with her sympathy. Around the graveside I watched my father's coffin being lowered into the ground. This was so final, so heart-wrenching. My dad had been in my life for so long and to never see him again or talk to him again was devastating. I had so many questions to ask him. There were so many things I should have said. I'd not told him how much I loved him and now he was gone. My head was going to explode. My mother was a

The Pudding Club

mess, she wasn't coping at all. Spencer was holding her up, her legs had buckled and she was sobbing her heart out. Death is such a bad thing. I never want to feel like this again.

A few weeks later it was like a weight had been lifted from my shoulders. I'd decided to tell Gemma about my love affair with Josh Thompson. I'm no longer ruled by emotions. I thought I loved Josh, but if I did truly love him from the bottom of my heart then why am I not crying and pining for him? I felt numb towards him. I think I hated him, I hated his guts. Gemma has just arrived I could hear her downstairs talking to my mother. Right, I was preparing to watch my best friend's face drop when I told her all about my little secret love affair with one of the good-looking squad. She'll never believe me in a million years. She's at my bedroom door, here goes.

"Are we going out tonight Rebecca or what? You've been in this bedroom moping for weeks now. It's time to start sorting your life out. I mean, if your dad was still alive he would be going mad at you wouldn't he?"

Tears filled my eyes, why is it when anyone spoke his name the pain in my heart is still there. I feel raw inside, will I ever get over this? I answer her in a stroppy tone. "Has my mam told you to come up here and say that, because she's been saying the same thing to me all day. She said my dad told her with his dying breath that after he was gone, I should live my life to the full. She's making it up Gemma, I just know she is. I mean, how long did it take my dad to die because according to my mother he relayed lots of things for her to tell me, it's bullshit, I know it is. Do you know what? Everything that she wants me to do now, she's saying my dad said it on his death bed. I'm not being funny or disrespectful Gemma but how long was his dying breath? She's making it up for sure."

The Pudding Club

Gemma sniggered, she knew I was right. "Yes, she told me to say that to you, but she is right, you do need to pull yourself together now, you've cried enough tears. Let's go out tonight, we can get wrecked. Let's go into town. I'll tell Peter to bring his mate for you, a blind date so to speak."

Smiling I sat down on the bed, this was going to be hard to tell her. I took a deep breath and began. Gemma knew I had something to say to her and she was edgy. I dipped my head low and began to reveal my secret. "I've been sleeping with Josh Thompson for months. I finished with him after my dad died, he's just a dick-head and I can't be arsed with him anymore."

There was silence, my heart was beating in my chest. Gemma looked at me and chuckled. "What, you've been sleeping with one of the good-looking squad? Rebecca, I don't believe you. Why are you chatting shit! How? When?"

Calming her down, I filled her in on all the details, she wasn't happy that I'd never told her and she was in a mood. I knew I had to make amends and it was time to speak about sex for the first time with my best mate. "Sex was shite with him anyway if I was being honest with you. He told me that I must never tell anyone about us having sex, he was ashamed of me. I was a nob-head. I don't know why I never told you. Will you forgive me Gemma? Come on, you never told me about getting fingered and sucking Peter's cock did you, so we're equal?"

Gemma smiled, she knew I was right. "Well, fuck a duck, fancy that. Right, we're deffo going out tonight and celebrating this. It's official, we're no longer geeks. We are sexy, and we are officially on the map." Gemma was rubbing her hands together in excitement. "You should tell Catherine Bennett all about her boyfriend's antics.

The Pudding Club

That would wipe the smile off her face for good."

I was mortified and stopped her in her tracks. "No, I don't want that. I just want to forget about Josh now and get on with my life. Anyway, what's Peter's mate like, I hope he's dishy?"

Gemma clapped her hands together. "He's a darling, Becks, on my life; if I wasn't with Peter I would have a go at him myself." That was enough for me, Gemma was right. It was time for me to move on. It was decided I was going out for a night on the tiles.

Later I stood staring at myself in the full length mirror in the hallway I looked different. I was thin. I could see my cheek bones and I had a waistline. The black dress I was wearing was figure hugging and for the first time ever I felt sexy. My mother shouted me from inside the front room. Walking to her side I wafted the thick cloud of grey smoke from around her head. She was blasting the cigarettes these days and she must have been on about forty a day. "Here, get this money and put it towards your night out. It's not a lot, but your dad said before he left us that I should always help you along." I smiled and tried to hold my laughter in. She was a funny old soul but her heart was in the right place. I kissed her cheek as I left, it was cold and thin. As I looked deep into her eyes, I could see the emptiness in her sad, cold eyes. I never wanted to end up like this. Love is such a strange emotion. It can make you so happy or break you in two. I don't think I've really been in love yet, I think Josh was just lust. I wanted to have sex and he was the first person who took an interest in me. No, I've never been in love.

My mother stood at my side flicking tiny fluff balls from my dress. "You look stunning tonight love," she said. This was a first, she usually told me I looked like a bag of rags. I smiled and thanked her. This was a moment that

The Pudding Club

I would remember forever - the first ever compliment from my mother. Gemma was in the mirror pouting her thick red lips. She was still overweight but she looked good. She was a fat, happy person, who seemed to be full of confidence. Saying goodbye to my mother I left the house with only one thing on my mind. I wanted to have fun and lots of it. Fuck Josh Thompson and his good looks, I'd rather have some ugly guy who loved me.

Walking into the pub, I was alive, my hips were swaying to the beat of the music and I was ready to party. No more sadness in my life. I was on the up. Gemma ran straight to Peter's side and she flung her arms around his neck kissing him. She was so over the top. I could see another man at Peter's side and he looked nervous. This was it, my blind date. From the distance he looked quite good looking, but my eyes weren't fully adjusted to the light and for all I knew he could have been a right minger. I got a drink and jiggled across the dance floor towards him. Gemma was smiling and in a loud voice she introduced me to Barry. He stretched over and hugged me. He smelt of fragrant spices, a welcoming aroma.

"Please to meet you Rebecca, Peter has told me so much about you." I could have died on the spot, cheeks burning, palms sweating. Had Peter told him about the fingering saga? I sipped my drink and checked Peter to see if I could read his mind. The coast was clear, Peter would never reveal our little secret, he would lose Gemma if he did. We all went to sit down, the pub was buzzing and the atmosphere was great. From the corner of my eye I spotted Josh. He was sat with Catherine, and she was all over him like a rash, the smarmy bastard. He's seen me now and you can see him crumbling. With a quick flick of my hair I ignored him and made sure he knew I'd moved on. I sat next to Barry and started to whisper

The Pudding Club

sweet nothings into his ear. I actually like Barry, he's nice. He makes me laugh. He's not as good-looking as Josh of course and his body is plump rather than toned, but who cares, he's just what I need at the moment. Up on the dance floor Barry is quite a good mover, he's thrusting his hips and swinging his arms in the air, this guy can dance. Me, I'm just stood shuffling around my handbag. Dancing was never my talent. I'm too stiff. It's like I've got a plank stuck up my arse. I can't dance. I'm just a swayer. Gemma and Peter are smooching. He kept looking at me did Peter, he had something up his sleeve I was sure of it. He was making me feel uncomfortable if the truth was known. The look he was giving me was sexual and he kept licking his lips. It might just be me being paranoid, this sometimes happen when I mix my drinks, but I'm sure I'm not seeing things. He's definitely coming onto me. After a bladder full, I needed the toilet.

Walking into the toilet Gemma followed closely behind me. "He's alright Barry isn't he?" she squawked. Looking in the mirror. I smirked and agreed with her. "Yeah at first I thought he was a bit boring, but he's not, he's good fun." In walked Catherine Bennett, full of life and as loud as always. I was just not in the mood for her abuse; I hoped she hadn't seen me. I just casually walk into the cubicle and pretended I'd hadn't seen her. I could hear laughing outside, and I listened closely. Catherine was making fun of Gemma, I could hear her, the bitch. "It's amazing what you fat girls can wear these days isn't it? I mean, I thought it was puppy fat when we were back in high school but it's not is it? You're just meant to be fat." I'm on the edge of the toilet, willing Gemma to fight back but nothing; she's not saying a word. Biting hard onto my fist I could still hear her loud, annoying voice. "Have you ever thought about getting your jaw wired

The Pudding Club

Gemma, it might help you lose weight? Who knows one day you might just be able to wear clothes like this." That was it; I was off the pot and out of the toilet as quick as could be. There was no way she was bullying Gemma, not on my watch anyway. Catherine smiled at me and licked her tongue slowly across her teeth. "Oh, and here's your partner in crime, Rebecca Rooks. The two fatties are still friends I see." By now blood was pumping in my brain and my temper was rising. Catherine had her own little crowd with her and they were all pointing their fingers at us. Gemma ran inside the toilet, she was sobbing. Catherine stared at me, and I never looked away, she knew I could handle myself. We were like two gun slingers at dawn, neither of us flinched. Catherine coughed to clear her throat and bent over the sink towards the mirror, she was applying more lipstick. "Here Rebecca, get some of this on your lips, it's candy flavoured, you'll love it, you fat slob." My fists curled into tiny balls at the side of my thighs, I knew it was now or never. Running forward I dragged her by the scruff of the neck and grabbed a thick clump of her hair. She seemed to fall to the floor like a sack of spuds, she wasn't strong. She was just a loud-mouthed bitch who couldn't back her mouth up. Now it was my time to talk.

"Listen, you bony little troll, if you ever speak to me or Gemma like that again, I'll make sure everyone knows what a coward you really are. We may be fat, yes, but do you know what Catherine," I paused. I knew exactly what I was going to say, but I had no fear of what the consequences might be. "Ask Josh about fat birds, he loves them. Go on, ask him about his kinky obsession with big tits and floppy bellies. At least he has something to grab onto when he's having sex with me." There was silence, the other girls were all just staring at me, wide-eyed.

The Pudding Club

I had to step up my game. "Go on, ask him about me, Catherine. Ask him about all the times he was having sex with me rather than you."

Catherine jumped up from the floor and sank her long talons into my face. She was trying to scratch my eyeballs out. Gemma came out of the toilet and when she saw what was going on, she ran at Catherine too, she was hysterical. "Yeah Catherine, he's been shagging Rebecca for months. Deal with that, you no hoper." Hands flying into the air, objects were being flung about the toilet, it was war. Somebody must have called for help because within seconds two bouncers ran in and separated us.

Catherine was screaming at the top of her lungs. "You're lying, Josh loves me; he'd never go near a fat scruffy tart like you. Come on, let's go and ask him, you lying slapper." Catherine was carried out of the toilets kicking and screaming by the bouncers, she was livid.

Josh stood next to his girlfriend as we came out of the toilets he was snarling at me and his teeth were clenched together tightly. "Rebecca, why are you lying to Catherine? I love her, why are you causing trouble for me?"

I stood tall and inhaled deeply; he wasn't getting the better of me, no way. "I've just told her the truth, Josh. If you can't be faithful, than that's your lookout."

He ran at me and he was in my face. His warm hot breath tickled my nose. "Stop lying, you fat cow, just tell her the truth."

Gemma was by my side now, she was watching my back. We were surrounded by a pack of wolves and there was no way out. "You like fat girls Josh, just stop lying to yourself. I'm not the one who's lying it's you, so piss off out of my face." I led Gemma by her hand to the exit. Peter and Barry were looking over at us, quite oblivious

The Pudding Club

to what was going on.

Josh was shouting from behind us and he made sure everyone heard what he had to say. "If were cleaning our closets out Rebecca, then tell Gemma all about Peter Jarvis and what happened in the garden. Go on, I saw it all, I bet you've not told her about that have you?"

Gemma turned her head slowly and looked at me. I was speechless, he'd caught me off guard. The saying is right that people who live in glass houses shouldn't throw stones and now here was my payback for opening my big trap. "He's lying Gemma, just ignore him." Footsteps from behind me. Josh was stood there with a cunning smirk on his face. "It's not so funny now is it Rebecca. I think we're equal now aren't we?" The cocky bastard just walked off and left me to defend myself. Gemma knew I was lying and it was now time for me to come clean. Peter and Barry heard all the commotion and ran to our side.

Gemma gripped Peter by the neck, he was turning blue, her grip was so strong. "What's this about you and Rebecca? Don't even think about lying to me, because I'll chop your fucking dick off and ram it up your arse." Peter let out a laboured breath and hunched his shoulders. Gemma turned to me and her hand swung back before it landed on my cheek. "You were supposed to be my friend, how could you?" Gemma ran off and Peter chased her.

Barry looked at me and shook his head. "It's not looking good for you is it? I think I should leave too." I watched Barry leave and I was alone. Music pumping, I just fell to my knees and wanted to melt into the floor. I'd lost my father and now my best friend.

Teresa coughed loudly and I opened my eyes. My session was nearly over. I was sweating and felt tired. "You've done well today Rebecca, it's good that you're

The Pudding Club

talking about it now, it's better out than in, I always say." This woman was so bleeding jolly; I bet there wasn't a bad bone in her body. Stretching my arms above my head I sat up from the sofa. I felt drained, like I'd relived every moment again. Taking a swig of the water from the glass I quenched my thirst. Sitting in the chair facing Teresa we had a quick chat before I left. Teresa liked to sum up at the end of each session and today was no different.

"How do you feel when you talk about Josh?"

I twiddled my thumbs and dug deep in my heart to find the emotion. "I feel numb, cold and angry," I replied. Teresa jotted it down as I was talking.

"Do you think you can ever forgive him for what he's done?" I was spitting feathers, my stomach was churning.

"No," I snapped. "This man broke my heart and left me on my knees when I needed him most. We took vows to love each other forever and he broke them. I'll never forgive him for as long as I live."

Teresa could see I was getting angry. I was twisting the cuff of my blouse as she continued. "So, if you ever saw him again how would you act?" Bleeding hell she was digging deep today, she wasn't backing off. I checked my wristwatch; surely it was nearly time to leave. She repeated the question I had to answer. I was backed into a corner.

"I would tell him what a life wrecking tosser he really is." She rolled the pen around in her fingers.

"Do you still love him Rebecca?" I wasn't ready for this kind of question. This was too much, how dare she ask if I still loved the man who broke my heart. She was staring at me waiting for me to answer. Lips dry, heart pounding, I wanted to run away and never be found again. There it was the answer to all my depression and all my eating problems. I still loved Josh Thompson.

The Pudding Club

My heart was low as I left the office. Teresa had scratched beneath the surface and found out the real reason I was never getting any better. I still loved my ex-husband. I was a failure, a drop out, a non-coper. How could I still love someone who had hurt me so badly? This wasn't good; I needed something to take this pain away, this gripping piercing pain deep inside my heart. There's a "Gregg's" bakery nearby. I can see the sign from where I'm stood. Feet pounding the pavement I make my way to the only thing that can make me feel better at a time like this, food. The queue isn't long, nobody will ever see me in here. I'm too fast. I'll be in and out like a Harpurhey shoplifter. Hands inside my purse, my mouth dribbled as I looked at the cake selection through the glass window. Cream, chocolate, fudge, strawberries and custard tarts, the shop has them all. Do I just buy one cake? Maybe two, because I have been upset haven't I? The assistant is now looking at me for my order. In an excited voice I tell her my heart's desires.

"Can I have two chocolate éclairs please and two strawberry tarts."

I know I've ordered quite a lot but my mind wasn't quite made up when she asked me, so I've bought a selection. God, it's only a few cakes for crying out loud. I'm not going eat them all am I?

NINE

JOEY IS ILL. He's not sung all day. I think he's days are numbered now, he's losing his feathers. His head is nearly bald, the poor bugger. It's a shame he can't wear a small hat to cover his thinning plumage. I dread the day when he leaves this world; he's been my best friend for years. My only friend really. Well, the one I completely trust. Never once has he passed judgement on me or let me down when I needed someone to talk to. We watched "Grease" together again last night, the fourth time this week. And Joey listened to me as I belted out some of the songs from the film. "Hopelessly Devoted" is my favourite. I even hit the big notes, at least I think I did. I act out the song with a piece of white paper held close to my heart feeling every emotion. Of course I don't look like Olivia Newton- John, but I can still dream can't I. Oh, the things I would have done to that Danny Zuko given the chance. I would have ripped his black leather T-birds jacket off him and smothered him in chocolate. Thick, creamy chocolate. He'd really get me so excited. I've always loved John Travolta and when he plays the part in the film where he flicks his slender hips, he just sends waves of passion surging throughout my body. I made my husband act out a fantasy once. He was John Travolta in it. Josh was no John T-Bird but it was one of the best nights of sex I ever had in my life. The sex ended in an argument though, so it was quite deflating. I only said, "Danny Zuko give it me hard and don't stop gyrating them hips," and Josh, he spat his dummy out. I was just caught up in the moment and just forgot where I was, I

The Pudding Club

think. Having a sexual fantasy acted out was then barred from our marital bed. I still fantasized about John Travolta during sex with my husband though but he never knew about it. I made sure I sank my head deep into the pillow when I felt myself saying his name. I love watching old films, they make me feel happy and giddy inside.

Joey is tired, his little green eyes are shutting slowly. I think he knows I'm going out tonight on a date. He's always like this when he knows he's going to be alone for the rest of the night. I put a bit of apple in his cage before as a peace offering, but he's not touched it. He's definitely upset. Gemma made me sign up for one of those on-line dating websites. At first I wasn't interested but nowadays I'm quite getting used to them. It's last chance saloon for me. Gary is the man I'm meeting tonight. I've been talking to him for a while and he seems really nice. I just hope he's not a nutter or something. I've spent hours on the phone talking to him and he's a similar age to me. He's also divorced. Dating is hard when you've never really done it before. It's been years since I've been on a date. I've had my hair done and a spray tan, just to give me that extra bit of confidence. That was an experience in itself. I looked like an Umpa-Lumpa when I first looked in the mirror, but now I've had a shower I look so much better. I was upset when I had my spray tan. The stick insect of a girl was going to charge me double the price because she said I used a lot of the lotion. I swear, she was going to get twisted up, the cheeky cow.

I told her straight, "Where in your price list does it say big birds are costly to tan?" She soon shut up and apologised after I told her I was going to have a word with her manager. I'm wearing black tonight, it makes me look slimmer. I did think about wearing a red dress but I think I'm still in mourning for my husband so black is

The Pudding Club

the only colour for me at the moment. I've got some new knickers and bra too, not the cheap ones either. I went to a top chain store and got measured for a new bra that fitted me properly. I've gone down in size too, two cups sizes in fact. I don't know why I'm buying new underwear. I think it's just in case I feel like ripping my knickers off and having a quick leg-over. I've not had sex for that long I've forgotten what to do. I have had a wax on my bikini line though just in case, not a Hollywood one like Gemma told me to though, I've left a landing strip. I can't be bald, it just doesn't feel right. My lady garden does feel cold though, it feels strange. Right, it's nearly time to go, quick squirt of perfume and it's showtime. Maybe a quick spray between my legs too and down the front of my dress, who knows I could get lucky.

Gary is stood outside the pub waiting for me. He looks nice and presentable. A bit overdressed but he looks like his profile picture, maybe a bit bigger than his photo and not as tall as I thought, but he looks okay. Paying the taxi fare I make my way towards him, he's smiling, that's a good sign. He must like me. "Great to meet you at last Rebecca," he chuckles. He's hugging me now. "Whoa, that's a bit tight, ease up on the pressure, big boy," I mumble under my breath.

Smiling at him I knew I was the more confident one, he was shaking like a leaf, constantly fidgeting about. "Shall we go inside or are you planning to stay here with me all night?"

Gary rolled his eyes and apologised. "Please bear with me, I'm a wreck. I've been ready since six o'clock just pacing the floor. This is the first date I've been on in months. I hope it's not put you off me. I'll be alright when I calm down."

Bless his cotton socks, he really was crapping his

The Pudding Club

pants. Taking his hand in mine I led him into the pub. We were booked to have something to eat, but I needed a drink first, I was gagging. Gary seems to have calmed down, at least his breathing has returned back to normal. The waiter leads us to our table. I'm starving but I know my weight day is tomorrow so I have to stop bingeing. Sitting down at the table I sip at my glass of wine. The menu looks so nice and my mouth is watering. There is nothing on here that looks remotely healthy.

Gary is licking his lips; he must be a food monster too. "What are you having to eat Rebecca? The steak looks lovely. You get onion rings with it and chips and salad and peppercorn sauce." He was right, the dish did look nice, but my eyes were drawn to the desert menu. Chocolate fudge cake with ice-cream with hot, thick custard. I could taste it in my mouth, sweet, creamy, smooth chocolate. Closing the menu with a snap I tried to make conversation with Gary. No, no Rebecca, weight day tomorrow, you've been so good. Just say no. The vision of the cake was still in my mind.

"Can I order the same as you Gary?"

He smiled and spoke to the waiter. Gary seemed to be ordering lots of side dishes, he must have been hungry. Taking his jacket off I could see his stomach was like a pot-bellied pig. The buttons were popping open and you could see the shirt was way too tight for him. "I love food Rebecca, I know I shouldn't eat all I do, but I just can't help myself. Since Wendy left me, it's the only comfort I get." This was all I needed, another bleeding comfort-eater like myself. This date was doomed from the off. I could see us both now in my mind, sat at home unable to move because we were fifty stones each. We are full of bedsores and unable to take care of ourselves. No, I don't want a fat boyfriend. I needed someone who could curb

The Pudding Club

my appetite not someone who was just like me, a fat pie-eating mess. My heart sank a little, because apart from his eating habits Gary was a nice man.

As the night went on Gary got better looking. I think the wine had something to do with that, my beer goggles worked miracles. Gary sat holding my hand, he held onto them as if I was his last chance of happiness, he was so needy. Looking into each other's eyes he leant forward and kissed me. This was amazing, his kiss made me tingle from my head to my toes. Was I just desperate for affection? This man might be the answer to my prayers. I knew then that my knickers would be coming off tonight. Why not? I deserved a bit of fun. It wasn't like Josh hadn't moved on. Swigging the last bit of wine in my glass I stroked the side of Gary's face, I was teasing him.

"So, do you want to come back to my place for a coffee?"

His eyes danced with excitement, he couldn't believe his luck.

Downing his pint of lager in one, he stood up and pulled me by my arm. "Of course I do, come on before you change your mind," he chuckled. This was it; I was moving on. I was going to have sex with another man. How was Joey going to take it when he saw another man in our house, surely this would finish him off. In the back of the taxi Gary slid his hand up my skirt as he kissed me slowly. I could see the taxi driver looking at me through the rear-view mirror. It was official, I was a slut.

When we got in, Joey was bobbing about the cage; squawking loudly, he wasn't happy. Gary goes to see him and sticks his fat podgy finger inside the cage. I knew it was a mistake, Joey hates newcomers. His beak bit down hard on the side of Gary's finger and he was trying to savage him. Gary was in a panic and tried to shake him

The Pudding Club

off. I couldn't help but smile, this was hilarious. Gary sat down and sucked the top of his finger. Joey had drawn blood. Kicking my shoes off I sat next to him and tried to comfort him. "Oh, I'm so sorry about that, Joey thinks he's a pit-bull, he's so protective of me. Hold on, I'll cover him up to calm him down. Pulling a towel from nearby, Joey was covered. He no longer could see Gary. He was still chirping loudly letting me know he wasn't happy. After a few minutes he calmed down though. Gary smiled at me and he was ready for a night of fun.

Tickling the side of my face he whispered in my ear. "Do you like tea-bagging?"

I was confused; I liked dipping my biscuits in my cup of tea yes, if that's what he meant. I asked him to make himself clearer. "What's tea-bagging?"

Gary smiled and gripped my hand tightly; he smirked and licked his bottom lip slowly. "Come on Rebecca, don't pretend that you don't know what it is, everyone's doing it these days."

I blushed, had I been off the sex scene for that long that even basic sex had changed. Hunching my shoulders I just looked at him with a blank expression. He spoke in a soft voice. "It's where you lie on your back and I drop my balls into your mouth, you know, like a teabag in a cup?"

Well, the dirty bastard. There was no way I was into all this kinky stuff. Maybe after knowing him for a few months I might have given it a go, but on our first date, no, this wasn't happening. Gary could tell I was upset, he hadn't thought this through. He tried to smooth things over. "I haven't done it before either Rebecca, it's just that all my mates are talking about it at work and I wanted to give it a go. You know, just so I could say I was a tea-bagger like them. That's all."

The Pudding Club

Something inside me felt sorry for him, he was sorry he'd spoke. It was only a bit of fun I suppose, was I being harsh and prudish? Giggling I agreed to his sexual request. Gary nearly dropped down dead; it was up to him now. We lay kissing passionately for a few minutes before he decided to make his move. Helping me lift my dress over my head he could see my new underwear for the first time. This was money well spent. I looked sexy, his eyes nearly popped out of his head. Caressing every inch of my body he penetrated deep into me. Eyes watering, I had to catch my breath, this was some penis, nothing like my ex-husband's, it was massive. Our hot, sweaty bodies rolled about on the sofa. We were both hungry for each other's flesh.

It was time for the tea-bagging to begin. I wanted to laugh as I watched him crouch on top of me. His testicles looked like a bag of gold dangling near my nose. All I had to do was open my mouth but I was giggling and I was struggling to keep a straight face. Two plum-like testicles now hit the side of my mouth, squashing up hard against my nose and mouth. I was struggling to breathe as they dipped up and down on the bridge of my nose. This was so funny. Gemma would never believe this in a million years. I was a sex goddess, a woman of fun in the bedroom, a modern day slut. Josh was always so basic in the sex department. Although he loved to smother his face into my large breasts, he was anything but kinky. Any time I mentioned a new position he always declined saying it wouldn't work as my body was too fat for him to get deep inside me. The cheek of the man, he had no shame. I remember the reverse cowgirl position that we tried. There I was sat on him like Calamity Jane riding him like my life depended on it and all of a sudden he stopped me saying I was squashing him. I never bothered

The Pudding Club

after that, my talents were wasted. I just lay in the same position watching him having all the fun on top of me.

By now Gary is turned on; he didn't tea-bag me for long. I think his legs were hurting him. We were now ready to explode, Gary was a hot lover. He was confident between the sheets and knew what a woman wanted. Hands gripping the side of the chair a wave of heat surged through my body, this was it, I was having an orgasm. My fingers dug deep into his back I screamed out with pleasure, God knows where it came from but I shouted it out without any control. "Fuck me Danny Zuko, harder, harder."

Gary heard my screams and joined in too. "Oh, Sandy, you dirty bitch, you're the one that I want too."

I smiled. This guy was so much fun in the bedroom and he didn't mind me fantasizing about other men whilst we were having sex together. This was music to my ears. Gary had found a place in my heart as my number one fuck-buddy. Gemma said fuck-buddies were a must have for women these days, no ties, no commitments, just pure sex. I wonder if Gemma has a fuck-buddy? I'm sure she's not faithful to Alex, I can just tell. Gary ticked all the boxes in the sex department. Anyway, fuck-buddy could help me burn more calories for sure. When Josh and I first started having sex we were like rampant rabbits. I very rarely ate anything back in those days. We didn't have time, we were always at it. The weight just dropped off me back then.

Once sex was over, Gary lit two cigarettes and passed me one. Lay in each other's arms we smoked our cigarettes in silence. It's funny that now the sex is over and I'm still lying here with nothing on. I'm completely naked. I am confident about my body and feel alive. Gary lay with me too and he didn't care that his fat gut was stuck out in front of him either. He called it his bumper cushion, he does make me smile with his one-liners.

"So, shall we do this again," Gary asked as he stubbed his cigarette out in the ashtray.

I had to be calm and not act like I was desperate. Taking a deep breath I flicked the ash from my cigarette. I'm sure I was doing some kind of French inhaling with my mouth like Frenchy from the film Grease. "I've enjoyed myself Gary; in fact, I've had a great time. I'm not really ready for any big time relationship but I'm up for a bit of fun if that's what you're talking about."

Gary played with the end of my erect nipple and sniggered. "I'm all up for having a good time. You were amazing Rebecca. A real woman you are. My Wendy was a drag in the bedroom, frigid in fact. I'm happy to be just friends if that's what you want?"

I nodded my head and that's all it took to make us fuck-buddies. "I'm starving," he whispered. "I don't suppose you have anything to put on a sandwich do you. You've zapped all my energy, look I'm wasting away."

I was hungry too, but there was no way I was snacking at this time of the night. I lied. "I've not been shopping Gary, I'm dieting and the only thing I've got is a bit of fruit, apples and oranges, do you want one of them?"

His face dropped, "No, I'll leave it. I shouldn't really be eating this late in the evening anyway." Checking his wristwatch he stretched his arms over his head. "I best get home." He shot a look at me and I was uncomfortable. Did he want to stay the night, was he hinting that he didn't want to go home. No man had been in my bed for a long time. I couldn't share a bed with a man again. Legs and arms touching me all night long, hot breath in my face, no, he had to go home. "I'll ring you a taxi if you want?" I said with a giggle in my voice, making sure he

The Pudding Club

knew there was no chance of him staying overnight. Gary agreed. As I stood up to use the phone a loud fart left my vagina. I was beetroot. I didn't know where to look. A fanny fart at a time like this! Could I have been anymore embarrassed?

Gary chuckled and he made me feel at ease. "Don't worry it happens sometimes after sex, it just goes to show we've had a good time that's all." I dared to move again. I was a big fat ball of air. Stepping forward just a few paces I grabbed the phone. My legs were weak and shaky. Once I'd ordered a taxi I sat down looking at Gary. This was an awkward time and I knew he was going to say something, he was just picking his moment. "So, you like a bit of Danny Zuko do you? I'll wear my black leather jacket next time if you want?" Oh, the shame of it all. I wasn't ready to talk about my obsession with John Travolta to anybody. I dipped my head low and hoped he would be quiet. "I love the film Grease too. I can get a copy of the DVD if you want and we can have a T-birds and pink ladies night. It could be good fun." This was amazing. I had a pink lady jacket in my wardrobe from years ago. I bought it for a fancy dress party that I never went to. My eyes filled with passion, I wanted to have sex with this man again and again. He was really turning me on. Was it too late to cancel his taxi? A car was honking its horn outside. It was too late I was going to bed alone tonight. Joey was chirping in his cage. He knew I was still awake and he wanted our late-night chat. There was no way I was uncovering him whilst I was like this. My hair was a mess and I was still half naked. Joey would have dropped down dead.

Walking Gary to the front door we both shared a final kiss before he left. As he walked along the garden path he started singing to me. "Stranded at the drive in, branded a fool, what will they say, Monday at school?" I was pissing myself laughing, this man was a nutter. He was a couple of butties short of a picnic. I liked him, he was just like me. "I'll ring you tomorrow Rebecca," he shouted before he got into the cab.

"Okay," I answered. Closing the front door my heart was leaping about in my chest. I was back in the game, no more crying about Josh. I was finally moving on. I was sexually active again and loved it that men found me attractive once more. Walking back into the living room I pulled my dressing gown from the side of the sofa. Once I was covered up I stepped up quietly to Joey's cage. The budgie could see me now, he was bobbing about full of life. Smiling at him I plonked down on the sofa. Popping a cigarette into the side of my mouth I lit it with shaking hands. "Joey, I've had the time of my life tonight. My eyes will no longer cry for that ex-husband of mine. I think I'm on the mend." Joey was listening; he dipped his head into his bowl of seeds and nibbled on them slowly. "I'm getting better aren't I?" I asked him. Joey bounced about at the bottom of his cage and walked about like a proud peacock, he rustled his feathers and started singing. I spoke to him and chuckled. "The girls aren't going to believe what's gone on tonight Joey, no way. Guess what? I've been tea-bagged." I sat chuckling to myself as another pocket of air squeezed out of my vagina. I was like a whoopee cushion. Oh, the joys of sex.

Lying in bed I snuggled under the duvet. I regretted not letting Gary sleep over. It would have been nice to have had some company for a change. Someone to talk to, or even someone cuddle up to. I'm going to text Gemma. I know it's late but I need to tell someone about my great night. I hope she doesn't go mad at me for waking her up. It's only two o'clock in the morning and plus, she's

The Pudding Club

rang me later than this when she's been stressed. Sod it, I'm texting her. "Gemma, I'm alive. Gary was so much fun. I don't know if you know about the latest sex crazes, but, wait for it... I've been tea-bagged. Speak soon, love your best friend AKA PG tips hahaha. (Oh, that's my new nickname, you know, teabags etc) good night from one happy woman Becks x

The Message is sent and she's not replied yet. She must be fast asleep. Oh well, I better get asleep too. I'm in work tomorrow and I don't want Helen on my back again. She's been a right bitch with me lately and I'm sure she's after getting rid of me from the surgery. Eyes closing, duvet tucked under my chin, drifting off to sleep. Night-night world.

TEN

HELEN IS RUNNING ABOUT THE OFFICE like a blue-arsed fly. What a stress-head, she needs to chill and relax. She wants a meeting with all the office staff today. I know it's me she's gunning for, the evil bitch. It's always been the same; every time she gets her collar felt by the management she calls a meeting and makes our lives a misery. Gemma has just rung me but I had to fake a bit of stomach ache so I could go into the toilet and speak to her. She was laughing her head off when I told her about my tea-bagging experience. Gemma's going to mention it to her husband and see if he fancies a bit of it too. She hates that I've done something before her; she's always been like that. Gemma likes to be the first to try anything. Well, not this time, Rebecca Rooks has officially been tea-bagged.

Helen sits down at the table and twists her blue biro around in her fingers. Looking down at her notes she licks her lips slowly. "Girls we need to improve our service," she begins. Her eyes seemed to be just looking at me, or did she have a glide in her left eye. No, she was most certainly staring at me and making me feel uncomfortable. "I think our look needs to be updated. I mean, new uniforms, a clean, refreshed look. Rebecca just take the way you look for instance. It's drab and depressing isn't it?"

Sharon's jaw drops as she nudges me in the waist. Helen was really pushing my buttons now and I was ready to give her a mouthful. Okay, I might have been a bit under dressed for work, but I overslept this morning and my black leggings were all that were clean and ready to go. Eyes down between my legs, I've never noticed I had a camel-toe today. Red in the face, I yank my white blouse over it. Doctor Wilson must have complained about my leggings. Yeah, that was it. I was just in his office minutes ago and he must have clocked my camel-toe. Oh my god, the shame of it, sacked from work because of my leggings being stuck in my vagina. I would never live this down. This would go down in history, my family shamed. I could never wear leggings again for work. I was a disgrace what was I thinking? One night of passion and I'd let my dress sense slip.

Helen looked in a bag at the side of her and pulled out a navy blue skirt and a jacket to match it. "This is the new uniform. I expect everyone to be wearing it on Monday morning. No excuses." She shot a look at me and smirked. Sharon picked up the skirt from the table. It was a nylon skirt with a small pleat in the front of it. There was no way I was going to fit into anything like this. I'd not worn a skirt for years. I voiced my opinion as the others listened in with anticipation. "Helen, I won't be able to wear anything like this. I will try and find a pair of trousers the same colour. I don't like showing my legs at the best of times and I'd feel much more comfortable in pants."

There was silence, the girls were flicking their eyes from one to another. Helen was going to blow for sure now that I'd challenged her. She walked slowly to the end of the table and dipped her head to my level. "Trust you Rebecca, I mean, why do you always have to be the one who puts a spanner in the works. Doctor Wilson has asked such a simple request and you can't even do that. Well, unfortunately this time you're going to have to do it. It's policy."

Helen walked away with her nose held up in the air.

The Pudding Club

The other girls waited until she was gone and voiced their opinions. Sharon was fuming and slid the skirt away from her on the table. "She can take a run and jump if she thinks I'm wearing that bag of shite. It's like a granny skirt, come on girls, look how long it is, we'll look like bleeding nuns. No, I like a knee length skirt and I'm not wearing it. Who else feels the same?"

None of the others were supporting Sharon. I held my hand up and spoke to the girls. "Listen, as I see it, we've not been given any formal warnings about these changes so she can piss off. I'm sure it's ninety days notice she has to give us before any changes can take place. I'm a member of the union so I'll check it out."

Sharon held her hand over her mouth and shot her eyes behind me. I knew without even turning around that Helen was there. I could feel my face burning up, it was on fire. Slowly I turned my head and there she was stood staring at me. Her face said it all; she held her head to the side and bent down slowly placing one hand on the side of the table. "Oh, I might have known it would be you who would start some kind of trouble. I'll tell you what Rebecca, if you lost a bit of bleeding weight you wouldn't have this issue."

That was below the belt, who did she think she was talking to me like that? I stood up; Sharon was now stood at the side of me as backup. "Helen, how dare you speak to me like that? Have you never heard of dignity at work," I smiled because I knew my shit when it came to office policies. I'd read them enough when I was bored and I knew she'd overstepped the mark. "I want to make a complaint about you, Helen. All the girls have just heard the insulting way you spoke to me, so if I were you I would walk away and say no more before you get yourself deeper in trouble."

The Pudding Club

Helen was white. At last I'd found her jugular and I was ready to rip it out. Rebecca Rooks you are a lioness who is no longer fearful of this cow Helen! The girls all stood by me now, we were like a pack of wolves closing in on her. she knew her game was up. Her voice changed and it was low and soft. "Rebecca, I do apologise for what I've just said. Surely we can work something out. I've had a crap day and my stress levels are going through the roof. Can we just sit down over a coffee and put this issue to bed?"

The mouse was running scared and I was playing with her now. I was going to milk it and make sure she never messed with me again. "I'm upset Helen, you have humiliated me in front of the girls. I don't know if I can just sweep it under the carpet and forget it ever happened."

Sharon poked her finger in my waist and whispered in a low voice. "You tell her Becks, it's about time that stuck-up cow was knocked off her high horse." Right, it was time for me to turn on the tears. This was sure to get me a day off work with full pay. Come on, she'd upset me, it was what I deserved. Tears streamed down the side of my face. I can just turn them on like a tap.

Helen knew what I was after and placed a comforting hand around my shoulders. "Why don't you have a day off, with full pay, and try and calm down. I'm sorry for speaking to you like that, it will never happen again." There it was, the day off I was looking for. I quickly picked up my coat and said goodbye to the other girls. I winked at Sharon as I left.

"Jammy bastard," she giggled at me as I passed her to leave.

The sun was shining and the sky was blue. The air was fresh and even though it was a bit chilly outside it was still a lovely day. Searching in my handbag for my mobile

The Pudding Club

phone I rang Gemma. She was off work today anyway and I thought it would be great to meet up for a quick cuppa. Once I'd rung her to confirm I made my way to the local coffee shop on the shopping fort to meet her.

Cakes, biscuits, sandwiches all grabbed my attention as I walked into Costa's. The cakes were scrumptious and I was dribbling from the mouth just looking at them through the glass window. Thick chocolate cakes with double whipped cream oozing from them. Sponges with layers of thick sticky jam in them. This was all too much for me, I was suffocated as my addiction tried to take over me. Gemma placed her hand on my shoulder and she giggled. "I hope you're not planning on getting one of them cakes?"

Captured in the act, I smiled at her and denied all allegations. "No, I'm dieting remember. I'm at camp tonight and Arnie can smell a carb eater a mile off. I wouldn't dare consume any. My body is a temple." I was lying of course and she knew I was tempted by the array of delights facing me. We both ordered a coffee each and sat down. I was having a hot flush again; the heat was rising up from my toes to the back of my neck. Damn you, menopause.

Wafting my hand in front of me Gemma smiled. "Why don't you just get some hormonal patches or something instead of going through this all the time? Look, the sweat is dripping off you." Reaching for a white tissue from my bag I patted it softly on my forehead. I was sweating like a pig now and my cheeks were going to explode. Deep, long, struggled breaths. I loosened my top button, cold air circling my breasts. Gemma was just sat staring at me sipping on her drink. I could have keeled over and died and she still wouldn't have batted an eyelid, she was so self-centred. The hot flush passed after a few minutes.

The Pudding Club

People were looking at me now and all I could do was smile at them.

"So, come on. I want to know everything about your date with Gary last night. And," she paused as she moved closer across the table. "I want to know about this tea-bagging thing you're going on about. I've spoken to Alex about it and we're going to give it a go tonight. I mean, we're quite adventurous in the bedroom and it's a wonder we don't already know about it."

Stirring the silver spoon around in my cup slowly I smirked. I knew she was jealous that I'd done it first. I made sure nobody could hear me and started to tell her every detail about my night of passion. Once I'd delivered the news Gemma sat back and she was really caught up by my experience. She started to giggle and covered her mouth with her hands and whispered. "I'm going to get some goggles on standby. I'm not having Alex's hairy testicles smashing against my eyes, no way."

I laughed loudly, I was holding the bottom of my stomach. I was laughing that much I wet my pants a little. It was a good job I had my Tena lady on otherwise I would have had a small puddle around my legs. Gemma sat back and continued talking. "So, are you seeing Gary again or what?" Gemma loved a bit of gossip and I wasn't going to disappoint her.

"Of course I am. I've not had this much fun in years. You told me to get a fuck-buddy, and that's exactly what Gary is, a fuck-buddy. I'm living for the moment from now on." We sat giggling like two schoolgirls, we were so naughty.

Gemma swallowed hard and sat forward in her seat. "Guess what the gossip is at strength camp? One of the girls told me last night, you'll never believe it in a million years. It's about Arnie." Scratching my head slowly I hunched my shoulders. I didn't have a clue what she was going on about. Arnie seemed so clean-cut, what could he have possibly done to cause any kind of gossip, he was whiter than white? Gemma was about to reveal his secret, she rubbed her hands together in excitement. Folding her arms tightly across her chest she let out a laboured breath. "He's only been sleeping with one of the girls who goes there training. Do you know Brenda, the one who looks like a tranny? The big butch lesbian one, who looks like Rose West, the murderer?" I held my head to the side thinking. I did remember the name, but the woman's face wasn't registering. My mind was a total blur as Gemma continued . "Well, anyway, he's been sleeping with her or so I believe. He's got a nickname now at camp, but you have to swear down that you won't breathe a word of it to him or anyone else. He'll go off his rocker if he gets a whiff of the rumours. Anyway, to cut a long story short, Brenda told Alice in confidence about the whole experience."

This was amazing news. I was really involved in some serious scandal. I'd been locked away for years from the real world and never really took part in other people's lives, but that was then, and this was now. I was eager to hear more. "Come on then, tell me, what's his nickname?"

Gemma was sniggering, she took a few seconds to stop laughing. She couldn't breathe as she continued. "Brenda said his willy is so small she could barely see it through his pubic mound. She's nicknamed him bell and bush because apparently that's all she could see when he took his boxer shorts off."

This couldn't be right, this was just a vicious rumour. Arnie looked so strong and masculine, how could he have such a small pecker? Surely, Brenda had got it wrong. I delved deeper. "Are you sure about this?" I asked.

The Pudding Club

Gemma sat upright, she cracked her knuckles slowly and looked me straight in the eye. "Rebecca on my life, I swear to you, Brenda said he's got the smallest penis she has ever seen."

This was hot news, the best gossip I'd heard in years. The slave driver Arnie was not all he made out to be, his body beautiful was not perfect. This information made me smile and I knew the next time I saw him I wouldn't be able to help myself from looking at his private regions. Arnie had screw dick, a small coiled snake. Gemma shot her eyes over to the counter. Twisting a piece of stray hair dangling at the corner of her cheek she gave me a cunning smirk. "Shall we have a cake each, just a small one, or we can even share one?"

This woman was the devil in disguise; she knew I couldn't say no. But, it was weight day soon and this cake could just push me over the edge with my weight loss. I'd already had a few cheats and I was in starvation mode to try and lose the weight I'd gained from overindulging. It's the smell from food that gets me, you know. The other day for instance, there I was walking past the local shops when a young lad came past me eating some chips. I could taste them; the smell of the vinegar was tickling my nostrils. I am a helpless food addict. I went straight into the chippy and ordered myself a portion. It didn't stop there either. I ordered myself a steak pudding and a portion of curry. And, to top it all a buttered muffin. I left the takeaway like a burglar leaving his latest job. Food concealed deep inside my bag I headed home as fast as I could. I hated myself after I'd demolished every scrap of food on my plate, but that was always the same after I pigged out. Nobody knows about my secret eating. Gemma thinks I'm doing really well on the diet, but if the truth was known, I'm always hungry. I've started to eat my toenails too just for an extra bit of nourishment. Well, I didn't intend to start eating them, it just sort of happened. I was lay watching the TV one night and I was cutting my hooves. They were massive and overgrown, just like me I suppose. I cut the nail off and just slid it into the side of my mouth. At first I just chewed on the end of it, but before I knew it I was chomping away on it, like a cow chewing on the cud in a field. I've tried to stop this new habit and I can honestly say it's been a while since I last did it. My toenails are so short now anyway, in fact they're painful I've cut them that short.

I answered her. "No Gemma, you can have a cake if you want but I'm trying to be good. I may just have a bite of yours though if that's alright? But I don't want a full slice." Who was I kidding? I did want a cake; my stomach was crying out for some calories. I could hear it rumbling as the last bit of coffee slid down the back of my throat. Gemma stood up to go and order her guilty pleasure whilst I sat back in my chair staring out of the window. The shopping fort was busy today and the shoppers were out in full force. It always amazed me watching people. If they didn't know you were watching them they would pick their noses, scratch their arses and lots of other disgusting habits. Lazily, my eyes wandered over the shoppers when suddenly my heart started pounding in my chest. I stopped to look – don't tell me that's him?

Sitting up in my chair I stretched across the table for a closer look. I'm choking, I want to vomit. Gemma where the hell are you? Please hurry up back before I make a show of myself. My eyes are glued to the window. I knew it was him for sure; I rubbed my eyes to take another look. What the hell is he doing back on the scene? I thought he'd moved away. Gemma is back and she knows something is wrong. I'm pale and gasping for

The Pudding Club

breath. I'm going to have a heart attack. "Bleeding hell it's only a cake Becks, I will share it with you if that's how it's making you feel. You're such a drama queen." Words stuck in my mouth, finger pointing to the window I struggled to speak.

"It's that bastard Josh Thompson. I've just seen him pass the window. Gemma, go and shoot the fucker. I can't stand it if he's back on the scene. Doesn't he think he's hurt me enough?"

Gemma ran to the window and stuck her face to it looking frantic. She paused and turned her head from side to side. Walking back to me she hunched her shoulders. "Are you sure it was him. I can't see anyone who looks anything like him?" My fingers gripped the chocolate fudge cake in front of me and I shoved it into my mouth, the full slice was in and I was eating it with speed. I was delirious, disturbed even, this couldn't be happening to me again. Gemma sat down and shook her head as the cake seeped out the side of my mouth.

"Well, you greedy cow. You can go and get me another slice of cake now. I've just queued up for that. Go on Miss Piggy, go and get me another one."

My head spinning I tried to digest the food in my mouth. I know it was him for sure. I wasn't seeing things and I wasn't going mad. The creep must have come back to Manchester. I needed to be prepared for the next time I set my eyes on him. I needed a gun and fast. Where could I get one from? My mind was working overtime as I made my way to the counter. Two pieces of cake I ordered this time. There was no way I was missing out on comfort food. I needed it and I needed it fast. Sat back at the table my mind was doing overtime. I needed to book in with my counsellor for an emergency session. This was pushing me over the edge.

Gemma sat nibbling at her cake and she seemed in deep thought. My cake was already gone in two bites. "Do you think it might have been someone who just looked like him Rebecca? Josh has left for good, he told everyone he was never coming back to Manchester again. So, I can't see it being him."

I know Gemma was only trying to help me, but she was doing my head in. I knew what I saw, and it was him. His walk hadn't changed either, he was standing tall as per usual, chest out and full of confidence. He walked like he owned the place. I never replied to Gemma. I didn't want to get into an argument. My stomach was bubbling, pains deep in my stomach. I was always the same when I had any stress in my life. I needed the toilet and fast. Grabbing my bag from the side of the chair, I clenched my arse-cheeks together tightly. I had to be quick, I was touching cloth. Running across the room I headed straight to the toilet. Once in the cubicle I yanked my knickers down as fast as I could. It was touch and go as to whether or not I shit my knickers. This wouldn't be the first time either. I'd had a few accidents in the past but it was never in a public place I was always at home. I was safe now, sitting on the toilet, face sweating. Relief, I'm breathing normal again. The pains are still bad but nothing like they were a few minutes ago. The doctor said I have stress-related IBS. Irritable Bowel Syndrome, it just creeps up on you and you're never safe when you have an attack. I hate you Josh Thompson. This is your fault. Ever since you've been gone from my life all these ailments have appeared. Dam you Josh, I'll never forgive you for this.

Gemma kissed my cheek as we parted company. We arrange to meet at the strength camp later that night. Watching her leave I scan the area carefully. I know he's out there somewhere and I start walking slowly towards the shops. My feet are barely moving, I don't think I can stay here any longer. I had planned to buy myself a new outfit, but I've changed my mind now. I need to get away from here as fast as I can before I spot him again. This was my worst nightmare come true. Yes, I'd imagined meeting Josh again, but not like this. I was always slim and dressed to the nines. Head dipped, I walked at pace to the main road. I was having such a good day and now it was ruined. Josh Thompson had pissed on my parade yet again. I was on a complete downer.

Later, dressed in my training clothes, I sat waiting for Gemma to pick me up. I've raided the fridge and I feel like a big fat blob yet again. Teresa, my counsellor, can't fit me in until tomorrow, so my head feels like it's going to explode. I've got so many questions, so many things needed to be answered. I feel so mixed up inside. I was alright until I'd seen him again, then all these old feelings came flooding back to me. I hate myself for still loving him. I hate that he still holds the key to my heart. I'm on a nil by mouth diet now, just fluids. If that bastard is back on the scene, I want to be prepared to meet him when I'm looking good. I don't want him to see me like this, ever. I'm booking in at the hairdressers for a complete makeover as soon as possible and I'm getting my nails done. This is it; I'm on a mission to wipe the smile right off that smarmy bastard's face for good. Gemma's here now, I'm not going to mention it to her, she only moans at me and says I should just get over my ex-husband, but what does she know about heartache? If Alex left her for just one day, she would keel over and die. She needs to practice what she preaches.

Looking back I remember when Peter Jarvis finished with her. Six months she lay crying for and I know she still blames me for her relationship ending. She's never really forgiven me for the fingering saga, and every now and then she brings it up just to remind me of my betrayal. After she found out about Peter and me she ignored me for months. She wouldn't answer my phone calls or even speak to me. That was one of the worst times of my life. My father had passed away, Josh had left me and my best friend was gone. I call those the dark days. I just locked myself away from the world and wallowed in my own self- pity. My father's death broke me in two. I was ten stone a month after he passed away. The weight just fell off me. It was the lightest I'd ever been. I didn't realise I'd shed any blubber it just sort of disappeared on its own. My mother was the one who noticed how bad I'd taken my father's death. She had me at the doctors and he gave me some antidepressants to help me through this bad time. Mother thought I was taking the pills but I never touched a single one. In my heart I wanted to die to be with my father, nobody would miss me, no one would even know I'd gone. My mother was the one who went to see Gemma too, she knew us falling out had a lot to do with my moods.

There I was just lying on my bed listening to my Grease soundtrack and in walked Gemma as if nothing had happened. The room was dark when she walked in. I hated the daylight when I felt like this. She just walked straight up to the window and yanked the curtains open and stood looking at me with her hands on her hips. "Right, I'm over it. You betrayed me with Peter but I'm willing to forgive you just as long as you never make a move on my man again." I wanted to tell her exactly what happened on the night me and Peter were together but she was having none of it. She hugged me and we both had a tearful moment together. I'd missed Gemma and I know she'd missed me. We were best mates and

The Pudding Club

didn't seem to function without each other. Even when she married Alex and she went on her honeymoon we still kept in touch, we were inseparable. She was always chatting to Josh and me whilst she was away. Gemma always warned me about Josh though, she knew he was a wrong 'un but I couldn't see the woods for the trees. I was in love, a fool, I suppose. Gemma's here now so let's go and see what I can do at this strength camp. It should be good tonight, my temper is boiling. I could rip someone's head off if the truth be known. I'm a ticking bomb waiting to explode. I need sectioning.

These weights are heavy tonight. I can feel my back getting ready to snap. Arnie has told me that my technique is crap and I have to work on it to avoid any injury. I'm sure he thinks I've done this kind of training before because he looks at me as if I should know the lifts. If he carries on I'm going to put him in his place, I'm so hormonal. I think he knows his secret is out because when we came into camp we could see him and Brenda arguing at the side of the room. Brenda was stood pointing her finger in his face and she was fuming. I can see them both shooting looks to each other, whatever has happened between them you can see Brenda is not happy. Right, hands full of chalk, legs bent, chest up, I'm ready to lift. My knuckles are turning white, my grip is strong, I call it my Kung-fu grip. Arnie is stood behind me, spotting me. I can feel his hot breath on the back of my neck. I need to lift this weight, I can't fail. One, two, three, and lift. What's happening, this weight won't move? Face screwed up tightly I try again. It's moving slightly, but only a touch.

Arnie is in my ear and he's not happy. "Are you taking the piss or what? Get your head into the lift and focus." He's angry and he's not backing down.

"I just can't seem to budge it. I think it's too heavy for me," I plead.

"You're arse is the only thing that's heavy Rebecca. We're here to do a job, so stop moaning and lift the weight."

My face was blood red, I was weak. Gemma now came into view and stood at the door. She could see I was struggling. "Come on Becks, you can do this, just concentrate," she said.

I channelled my energy and twisted my head to look at Arnie. He was smirking and he was willing me to fail. I could see it in his eyes, the wanker. Hands gripped around the bar I took the position and found my inner strength. I was actually lifting the weight up. Tarzan now appeared and I could see him from the corner of my eye sneering at me. Screams from deep within me filled the room and from nowhere I shouted at the top of my voice as I lifted the bar over my head. "There you go, bell and bush, have a bit of that!"

Legs shaking I lowered the bar back down to the floor. I'd completed the lift. I was a female warrior, a tower of strength. Regaining my breath I realised there was an eerie silence in the room. Tarzan covered his mouth with his hand and his shoulders were shaking as he laughed. Gemma was pale and she was gobsmacked. Slowly I lifted my head up and that's when I realised what I'd just said. Arnie was melting into the floor, his hat was pulled down further over his eyes and he bolted out of the room and headed straight towards Brenda who was outside training.

Gemma ran to the window and looked out. "Becky, where on earth did that come from? I told you this was secret, look what you've caused now."

Outside in the garden area, Arnie was in Brenda's face and they were nose to nose, all the other members were whispering to each other and laughing. "I'm sorry Gemma, it just come out, he winds me up so much and I just sort of lost my head for a minute." Arnie was marching back into the room and he was gunning for me, I was sure of it. Stood tall, he snarled at me and licked his bottom lip slowly. "I don't know what you've heard about me Rebecca, but it's not true. I'm here to train you and nothing else. I hope you keep your snide comments to yourself in future."

I was so embarrassed, cheeks pumping with thick red blood. I didn't know where to turn. Gemma had gone and left me and I was alone with this mad man. Reaching for my bottle of water I gulped a large mouthful trying hard not to look at him. "I'm sorry Arnie," I mumbled to him. "You're right; I should never have spoken to you like that. It won't happen again." The rest of my training session went well. Arnie eased up on the pressure and I kept my big gob shut. That day, I seemed to earn the respect of my trainer and he knew he could no longer break me in two with his snide remarks.

The training finished and Gemma came to meet me. She was smirking and speaking in a low voice. "God Rebecca, I can't believe what you said. Brenda is going ape trying to find out who told Arnie what was going on. I've told her I've not said a word, so keep what I told you to yourself, don't be blabbing on me motor mouth." I was smiling to myself, what a big idiot I was.

Sitting in the car I reached for my cigarettes. I always had a fag after training, it helped me relax. Gemma winds the car window down and struggles for breath. "I wish you would quit smoking, it's not good for you, you know?" Oh, here we go again, the smoke police is giving out her lecture. Gemma was a smoker once too but to hear her you would have thought she'd never smoked.

The Pudding Club

"I've cut down," I lied. "I'm only having five a day now. I was smoking nearly twenty a day, so I've done well."

Gemma wafted her hand in front of her face, and pretended to choke. "I don't care, you need to kick it in the head it's a filthy habit." Blowing a thick cloud of smoke from my mouth I opened my window. Gemma was doing my head in and I was in two minds as to get out of the car and walk the rest of the way home. Thinking about it, no, it's quite late, and my legs are starting to ache. In fact, my muscles feel like they are going to pop out of my skin. I'll sit here and listen to her moaning, I can't be arsed walking home. Gemma's singing, and to tell you the truth I think she's got a good voice. When we used to sing the duo of Olivia Newton-John and John Travolta she always sang the female part, she was good too. My voice sounds like a cat being strangled if I'm being honest with myself, but it never stopped me singing.

The song on the radio used to be one of my favourites. Celine Dion's 'Baby Think Twice'. But now it reminds me of him, the ex-husband. I wish she would turn it off. Pulling up at my house the song was just finishing, Gemma was howling the last few words. I waited until the song went off. "Right Gemma I will see you tomorrow. I'm back in work so I won't be home until the usual time."

Gemma held her head towards the rear-view mirror and played with her eyelashes. "Okay, give me a ring when you're home. I'm going home for a night of spicy sex. I'm going to let Alex teabag me, so I'll let you know what happens."

I chuckled and waved over my shoulder as I walked up my garden path. Gemma was gone as I entered my house. Just as I opened the front door I spot a white envelope lying on the floor. Bending my knees slowly I picked it

The Pudding Club

up with caution. The name on the front was handwritten. Screwing my eyes up tightly together I looked at the writing closer, the words are blurred. Heart in my mouth I head to the front room in a hurry. The letter was from Josh, I was sure of it. Throwing the envelope down on the sofa I stood shaking near the door. I wasn't ready to read it; I would never be ready to read what that tosser had to say. Running up the stairs, I ran into my bedroom and I pulled the covers back from the bed. Digging deep underneath it I hid away like a scared animal. I couldn't take anymore today, I was at breaking point. I desperately needed my counselling session, I was a nervous wreck. Head hid away under the duvet I closed my eyes for sleep. I wished I would never wake up again. At least then I would never have to cast my eyes on Josh Thompson. The man is an out and out bastard, he doesn't deserve to walk the face of the earth. He deserves to die a slow painful death.

ELEVEN

THE BIRDS ARE SINGING OUTSIDE, the sun is shining and it's nearly ten o'clock. I've already phoned in work sick and I plan on lying in my bed until it's time to go to my counselling session. I've cried this morning, sobbed my heart out. It's like I've unblocked the emotions that have been stored deep inside me for months. The letter is still downstairs and I can't bring myself to read it. I sat on the stairs for over an hour debating if I should. I'm not strong enough yet, I'll never be strong enough. I think I should just throw the letter in the bin, at least then he can't get back into my head. I'm so mixed up inside. I've been ringing Gemma all morning too but she's not answering. I hope she's alright; it's not like her not to answer her phone. It's always by her side twenty-four hours a day. I can hear Joey singing downstairs, he's probably wondering where I am. I usually have a chin wag with him before I go to work. I bet he thinks I'm dead. I suppose he could be right too. I'm numb and feel emotionally drained.

Staring at four walls I feel like I'm losing the plot, my head is all over the place. Why does Josh always make me feel like this? It's a letter he's sent me not a letter bomb, what do I have to be scared of? I'm going downstairs right now to read it. Why should I be a prisoner in my own home just because that tosser has raised his ugly head again? Deep breaths, I can do this. Housecoat on I'm tiptoeing down the stairs. As soon as I walk into the front room I run to see my feathered friend. "Good morning, sorry I'm late Joey, I've just been having a bit of trauma in my life again. I bet you're sick to death of hearing about my troubles aren't you?" Curtains open, I cast my eyes over to the white envelope lying on the chair. Popping a cigarette into the corner of my mouth I light it with shaking hands and touch the letter slowly. I can smell his aftershave on the envelope, sweet, spicy fragrances. Josh always smelt good, he always smelt fresh and clean. Fingers trembling, I slowly slide my fingernail under the top of the envelope. There are words, lots of words written on the piece of paper. I need my glasses; I can't see a bleeding thing. Eyes focused, I begin to read the letter slowly. My hands itch at my neck and a red rash starts to appear, small red blisters. Hundreds of them.

Dear Rebecca,

I know you don't want any contact with me again, but I do need to speak to you. I'm sorry for how things turned out between us but you know I never meant to hurt you. I hope we can meet up and sort things out. I'm nothing without you. I miss you every day. Please try and forgive me.

Love Josh xxx

Tears are pouring down my cheeks I dab the cuff of my pink housecoat in the corners of my eyes. This isn't good, why doesn't he just leave me alone. He can't just toss me aside like an old toy when he feels like it and then come back thinking he can just pick me up again. It's always been the same with Josh; he wants what he can't have. When we last spoke, he made it quite clear that he hated me and never wanted to see me again, what's changed since then? I've got so many questions running around in my head, I can't think straight. I need food and lots of it. That's the answer, I will eat my heartache away, food has always been the cure for any upsets I've had. Rashers of bacon sizzling in the frying pan, two eggs on the go and more mushrooms than I could ever eat. I'm having four pieces of toast today, and butter, yeah, Lurpak the best butter, I'm having that too. Sitting down at the table I tuck into the feast before my eyes. I feel alive, I feel comforted. The meal didn't last long and just as I predicted, the feeling of heartache returned after the last mouthful of food hit my stomach. It's nearly time for my therapy appointment too so I best get a move on and get ready. Gemma still hasn't rung me back, where the hell is she when I need her most?

Teresa invites me straight into her office. She can see I'm anxious. In my hand I have the letter gripped tightly. Once I was inside the room I headed straight for the sofa. I kicked the shoes from my feet and lay down flat ragging my fingers through my hair. Teresa sits down quickly and tries to reassure me that everything is going to be alright. "It's that bastard again Teresa, he's posted me this letter. Why the hell is he back in my life again, why can't he just leave me alone? I've never done anything to deserve this kind of treatment, he's just trying to play with my head again isn't he?"

"Just relax Rebecca, take deep breaths and let's talk this through. It's not life threatening that he's been in touch, it's quite positive really because at least we now know he still cares about you."

I know I shouldn't have, but when I get upset I just blurt things out of my mouth without thinking. "Like I give a flying fuck if he cares about me or not. He left me on my hands and knees begging him not to leave, if he cared about me he would never have put me through that. He's a wanker, an out and out wanker nothing else." My

The Pudding Club

chest was rising with speed and my palms were sweating. I needed a drink, I was hyperventilating. Teresa got me a drink and watched as I gulped back the cold water. Once I'd calmed down again she spoke to me in a soft voice.

"I think it's time to go back to the beginning Rebecca. Start from when you met him and how it all went wrong." This was a nightmare, I had to relive every minute of my life with Josh Thompson yet again. I'd tried my best to forget him but now I had to speak about him to move on with my life. Closing my eyes slowly I could visualise my life back then. I could see myself and I was happy for a change.

I was twenty four and my weight had been under control for a few years and at last I was a size twelve. My hair was shoulder-length and I was blonde. It was all Gemma's idea to go on holiday, you know? She said we deserved it after all we'd been through over the years. Gemma had split up from Peter Jarvis and the death of my father was still looming on my mind. We booked to go to Ibiza, the party resort. Sex drugs and rock and roll were heading our way and I for one was ready to let my hair down. I'd not had sex since my short-lived affair with Josh. I wasn't interested anymore. In my head I thought the only man I would ever love was Josh, nobody would ever come close to him and how he made me feel. I was young and vulnerable, a proper dick-head when I think back. Josh was still with Catherine Bennett at this time and the word on the street was that they were engaged. I hoped she'd drop down dead or contract some lethal, incurable disease; I hated her with a passion. My head was set to have some fun. I was washing Josh right out of my hair.

Still living at home with my mother I knew if I didn't pull myself together now I would end up a lonely old maid sat at home all day doing crosswords, baking and knitting. Stood with my suitcase in the living room my mother sat staring at me. "You look lovely, go and have some fun. It's about bleeding time you come out of that bedroom anyway."

My mother had her way with words and I smiled at her. "You're right you know mother, I'm going to have more nob-ends than weekends. I'm going to have hot steamy sex and lots of it."

She nearly choked. I'm sure she smiled but quickly straightened her face and spoke to me in a stern voice. "You don't need to get your knickers off to have some fun you know. You'll get a name for yourself if your trolleys are down all the bleeding time. Be careful and don't end up pregnant. And…" she paused as she hunched her shoulders. "Get some condoms or something for protection. The last thing you need in your life is a baby."

My mother always knew how to knock the smile from anyone's face. Here I was a free spirit ready to head into the sun for nights of hot steamy sex and all she could think about was the bad points. She was right though, I did need some condoms and there was no way I was riding bareback. I mean, I could contract some foreign vaginal disease or something like that, couldn't I? I can see it now; me stood humiliated in the clap clinic, with big warts all over my fanny. No, as soon as I get the chance I'm getting a pallet load of condoms. This holiday was one I was going to remember for the rest of my life. I was a young, free woman and nobody was going to blow the wind out of my sails, not even my mother. Gemma arrived in the taxi and my mother stood at the front gate waving us off. She looked old as I looked back at her over my shoulder and my heart sank as I waved goodbye from the car. Gemma was giddy and she was already drunk, you could smell the alcohol on her breath as soon as I got inside the taxi.

The driver was a right misery too and he kept telling her to keep the noise down, she was singing at the top of her voice. "Oh, live a little you miserable fucker," she screamed. "Were you never young you old fart?"

The driver slammed his brakes on, and turned to face Gemma in the passenger seat, he was livid. "Listen, I've been working all night and I just want a bit of peace and quiet before I clock off. If you can't button your lips for the rest of the journey then you can piss off and walk the rest of the way. I don't need this kind of shit when I'm tired."

The driver pulled off again and Gemma raised her eyes at me. "Someone's in a bad mood aren't they?" she whispered. This holiday was going to be mental. Everyone and anyone was going. It only started out as a few girls booking a holiday but now everyone in Manchester seemed to have booked on our flight. Boarding the plane I smiled as I took my coat off. I could feel the heat from inside the cabin. Loud singing from inside, gangs of men sat staring at me. Gemma pushed past me and she was flirting with the guys as she walked past. Her confidence was high, she'd lost a lot of weight since splitting up from Peter and she was easily in a size twelve now. Squeezing through the small aisles I could see Gemma putting her hand luggage in the box over the seats. She turned to face me and she was alarmed as I came to her side. Before she could speak a voice from the side of me spoke.

"Don't tell me you're still in love with me after all this time Rebecca?"

Quickly turning my head I could have dropped down and died where I stood. It was him, the bastard, the tosser, the wanker, Josh Thompson. I was speechless; he was just sat smiling at me as if nothing had ever happened.

Gemma sat down near the window and she was poking her finger into my waist. "Say something then," she whispered.

Taking a deep breath I answered him. "Why would I be still in love with a prick like you? Those days are over, pal. I was young and didn't know any better. I'm going on holiday to have fun, so just stay out of my face. Anyway, where's your girlfriend Catherine, I hear you two got engaged?"

Josh chuckled loudly as he flicked the invisible dust from his jeans. "Me and Catherine are history, Becks. I don't want to be tied down at my age. I want to have fun." He was such a liar and I knew instantly he was talking through his arse.

"Yeah, whatever Josh. Enjoy your holiday."

I sat down next to Gemma and I was shaking inside, I felt sick, my heart was pumping inside my ribcage, this wasn't good. Josh was sat in the seat next to me. This was a nightmare, how could I make the journey with him so close to me. I asked Gemma to swap seats with me but she refused. Twiddling my thumbs I sat staring in front of me. As soon as the air hostess came around with the drinks trolley I ordered a double vodka. Josh was looking at me for sure. I could feel his eyes burning into me.

Leaving my seat to go to the toilet I was aware he was following behind me. "Come on Rebecca, let's be friends. The past is the past, let's start again. I'm sorry, okay. I was just mixed up back then. Will you at least speak to me about it?"

I would have spoken to him if I could breathe, my lips were moving but not a single word was coming out. Staring deep into his blue eyes I was captured by him yet again. I had to turn away, looking into his eyes was causing

The Pudding Club

some kind of movement in my vaginal area, waves of excitement tickling inside my groin. Josh quickly looked around and pushed me into the toilet. He was giggling and held a mischievous look on his face. "Come on let's have some fun. Let's join the mile high club. Come on Becks, you used to love a quick knee-trembler. Get your knickers down whilst I slip my cock inside."

The man was pure filth, but I loved it. I loved him. He made my heart beat again. Digging my long talons deep into his back I sank my lips onto his. The toilet was only small and we were struggling to move about. I felt wetness in my lady garden. The barren land had now started to work again. Hands inside my knickers, he quickly inserted his fingers inside me. This was heaven, pure, filthy, lustful sex and I loved it. This was my time to shine, no more holding back I was going for gold. Josh Thompson would be begging me to stop by the time I'd finished with him. I was horny, a sex starved crazy woman grateful of any male attention I could get. Moans, groans, sexual noises; we were having full blown sex in the toilet cubicle. This was naughty. I was naughty, and if we got caught we could have been thrown off the plane, banished, humiliated, named and shamed in front of all the other passengers. The holiday had only just started and I was having the time of my life. Josh was whispering sweet nothings into my ear telling me how much he'd missed my body. He was gagging for it, you could see the passion in his eyes. A knocking at the door, someone was waiting to get inside. Josh was just about to reach climax and I covered his mouth with my hands. For that few moments I didn't care who knew what I was doing. I was alive and in the arms of the man I loved, Josh Thompson was back in my life.

Sliding the small lock from the door I was met by

an old man's frustrated face. He was holding between his legs and growling at me. "Bleeding hell woman, I've nearly pissed myself here, what on earth were you doing in there?" Josh now came into view behind me and the man was startled. He chuckled as he pushed past us both. "Oh, to be young again. I wish my Olive would be a bit more adventurous in the sex department. I'm lucky to get a leg over every six months. Bleeding arthritis has ruined her; she can't move her legs anymore."

I burst out laughing, and people were starting to look at me. The horny pensioner went inside the toilet and I headed back towards Gemma. She was never going to believe this in a million years. I was a sex goddess, a dirty filthy slut who didn't care where I had sex anymore. My outlook on life was certainly changing. I was taking life by the balls and enjoying every moment of it. Gemma sat upright when she saw me heading back to my seat. Cheeks blushing, my hair all over the place, she looked at me closer. "Where the hell have you been, you've been ages?" she squawked.

As I sat down I looked at Josh and he gave me a cheeky wink, my heart was in my mouth. "Sssshhh will you," I chuckled as I hid my head into her shoulder. "You're never going to believe what's just happened."

Gemma was eager to hear more, "Spill the beans then, come on, tell me."

Taking a deep breath, I prepared to tell her. I was as proud as punch and if I could have I would have shouted it from the rooftops. "I've just joined the mile high club," I whispered with one hand covering my mouth.

Gemma looked confused, I knew I would have to explain things further. "I've only just gone and had sex with Josh in the toilets."

Gemma's face dropped, she folded her arms firmly

across her chest. "Why are you doing that, are you forgetting how that plonker treated you or what? You're just so easy; no wonder he thinks he can just bang you whenever he feels like it."

Wow, she was so upset, I think it's because I'd joined the mile high club before her, she was so jealous and she couldn't hide her feelings one little bit. "Oh, get a grip Gemma. I'm on my holidays not on a bleeding religious retreat. I'm sick of being boring old Rebecca Rooks. I'm going to have fun from now on and live my life." Silent, Gemma just sat staring out of the window. She was in a strop. I could tell by the way she was tapping her fingers rapidly on her knee. Turning my head slightly I could see Josh, he was smiling at me. Why had I just let him walk straight back into my life? I always told myself I would never go near him again. I was a fool in love.

Once we reached our hotel I smiled at Josh as I left the coach. He was staying at another accommodation not far from where we were staying. Gemma was still acting strange and I knew I would have to do some serious creeping when we got to our rooms. She hated being left out. I watched the coach leave and Josh waved as he passed me, it was love, I knew it was. Gemma marched into the hotel and dragged her suitcase behind her. "I hope you're not planning on spending all your time with him, Becky. This is our holiday, just me and you remember. If you think for one minute I'm just watching you two have sex for seven days, then you can think again."

Gemma was such a drama queen and I knew had to sweeten her up. "Oh be quiet Gemma. Don't begrudge me a bit of fun. I've not had sex for as long as I can remember so just show a bit of bleeding support will you?" Gemma ran to the balcony and opened the patio doors. The heat came straight into the room and I felt

The Pudding Club

sick. I was never really good with the sunshine and my skin was that pale that I went as bright as a lobster as soon as the heat rays touched it.

Gemma was stripping off. "Come on let's get around the pool. We need a tan for tonight; we're not going out like two bottles of milk. Gemma stood naked and this is the first time I could see how much weight she'd lost. She was actually skinny. Digging deep in my suitcase I found my special body control swimming costume. It said on the label it flattens your stomach and makes you look two sizes smaller. I needed the magician Paul Daniels to make my blubber disappear. I wasn't holding my breath that any piece of material could take inches from my body. Stripping off, I sucked my stomach in and slid the black costume over my thighs. I looked like a threadworm.

Gemma was watching me out of the corner of her eye, and she was smirking. "Why didn't you just get a bigger size? It would have fit you then?"

There she was again, super bitch. Mrs Love my fucking self, strikes again. I bit hard on my lip and continued shoving my fat inside my swimwear. The costume was on, it was a tight squeeze yes, but there was no way I was admitting it to Gemma. She would have loved that she was right. Grabbing my beach bag I placed my sunglasses on and headed to the door. "Come on then, let's see what Ibiza has to offer two girls like us?"

Gemma quickly followed behind, she was giddy and back to her normal self. "Becks let's make sure we have the time of our lives. I swear to you now, what happens on tour, stays on tour. I want to be a slut, yep, you heard me right, Becks. I want to be a sperm bank," she sniggered. "Anyone can make a deposit in me." This girl was so off her head, she could be ruthless at times and vulgar, but I still loved her, she was my best friend.

The Pudding Club

The pool was packed, there were so many golden bodies lounging on the sunbeds. As we walked past a group of girls one was spewing her ring up at the side of the pool. Ibiza was a party resort and anybody who went there knew sooner or later they would crash and burn as the nightlife took over. Gemma nudged me in my waist. "We need to get some pills for tonight, ecstasy, or something. Who do you think supplies all that kind of shit around here?"

I shrugged my shoulders; I didn't have a clue to be honest. Drugs really weren't my thing. I'd taken them before in the past for a quick buzz. I suppose I just did it to fit in, really. I did enjoy the night though. I never stopped dancing. I was on the stage all night strutting my moves and off my rocker. I try and stay well clear of drugs nowadays, it's not for me. Eyes to the left of me, he's there I can smell his aftershave. I quickly looked over my shoulder and I'm met by Josh's eyes. "Come and get on these two beds here Rebecca. Ay, Gemma," he shouted, "come and meet my mates." Gemma smiled and flicked her hair over her shoulder. She was a right flirt and her eyes lit up when she set eyes on Josh's friends. They were all good looking.

"Long time no see Josh," Gemma giggled, she was flirting. "I hope you're behaving yourself and keeping out of trouble."

Gemma knew about Josh's past. He was a wheeler and dealer and he was always looking to make a quick few quid. There she was again, the two-faced bitch, arse-licking as per usual. It wasn't that long ago that she was slagging this man off, telling me he was bad news. Gemma had double standards for sure. Josh clocked my swimwear and giggled, he was blatantly staring. "Check out your camel's toe Becks, is your hairy muffin hungry or what?

The Pudding Club

It's nearly chewing the bloody crotch away from your swimming costume."

There was laughter, everyone's eyes were on me. Eyes down between my legs, he was right. I had the biggest camel toe I'd ever seen in my life. My flaps were like two car doors. I knew this costume was too tight, why did I ever listen to the sales-assistant, I should have gone with my own instincts. Quickly, I sat down and tried to release the grip my vagina had on the material. I lay down and pulled my beach towel over my private regions. Josh bent over towards me and chuckled. "I bet it's swollen from before, you know how big my cock is don't you?" This was too much, I was blushing and sweating. There was no way he was doing this to me again. I was a woman now, not a young girl anymore. I had to find my inner strength and answer him back. Josh wasn't making me feel small like he always did.

"Get over yourself Josh, your so called cock didn't even touch the sides so wind your neck in."

He was laughing his head off and as he smiled his big white teeth were revealed. "I like the new you Becks, in fact, you're someone I could fall in love with."

Oh my God, he was playing with me for sure. Josh, one of the good-looking squad has just said he could fall in love with me. Surely he was playing mind games. His words turned over in my head and my heart was beating ten to the dozen. I wanted to sing, I wanted to jump up in the air and shout it out so everyone could hear me. I wanted to serenade him with a song from the film Grease. "Hopelessly Devoted" was on the tip of my tongue and without thinking I just belted out the chorus. Everyone was watching me, I was the entertainment and I was putting on a show of a lifetime. Now it was Josh's turn to blush. Gemma joined in the song from where she was

The Pudding Club

sat. Any Grease fan will tell you how hard it is not to sing along when a track comes on from the film. Josh's mates were cheering now as I hit the final big note; I was out of tune but nobody seemed to care. A round of applause filled the air. Josh looked around and he was impressed.

Walking to my side he bent down and pecked me on the cheek. "You're just so horny. I can't believe I ever let you go."

Josh walked away and headed towards the bar. Gemma was in deep conversation with one of the lads in the group and she was in her element. Lying down flat I placed my sunglasses on. I was smiling and I couldn't stop checking my swimwear. If another camel toe appeared I was throwing the costume right in the bleeding bin. It never said that on the label when I bought it. And, if it did, I would never have got it in the first place. I sniggered to myself as I stretched my legs out fully. It was a good job I'd shaved them otherwise they would have had a field day with me. Josh is walking back towards his sunbed and he's holding two drinks in his hand. When he gets to where I'm sat he passes me one of the drinks. I'm a princess at last, somebody actually cares about me. I wanted to shout over to Gemma and tell her but her back was turned away from me. I thanked Josh and tried to remain calm. I could feel his eyes all over my body, when I looked at him, he never flinched.

"You're so sexy Rebecca. I've never really forgot about you, you know. In fact, I've missed what we had together." This was too much, so many compliments, so much love in his eyes for me. Was I imagining it, or was it the truth? Had Josh Thompson really fallen for me?

The day ended and I was bright red. Gemma was a golden brown colour, but me, I was a lobster, bright and sun burnt and blotchy. We all arranged to meet at a bar

The Pudding Club

later that night. Josh touched my hand as I left. "I can't wait until later, do you fancy coming to my room for a bit? The lads are staying by the pool, so it will be just me and you?"

Gemma snarled as she listened into the conversation, she wasn't happy and she stood twisting her hips and playing with her hair. I had to decline. "No, I'll meet you later on. If that's alright." He was gutted, his jaw dropped and you could see the disappointment in his eyes. My, how things had changed, he was the one who was doing all the chasing now. Rebecca Rooks was loved.

My hair was like a ball of fluff. Even though I'd washed it, the humidity had caused it to frizz. Looking in the mirror I looked mental. A bright red body wearing a white pair of shorts and a pink vest top. Knowing how hot it was I grabbed a headband from my suitcase and slid it into my hair, the rest I just clipped back. Gemma was rubbing some aftersun on her body. She stroked it evenly up and down her legs. "What did you think of Andy, Josh's mate? I thought he was well fit," Gemma asked.

I looked in the mirror and answered her. "Yeah, he's good-looking. Are you going to get into him or what?"

Gemma tapped her fingernail on her front teeth. She chuckled loudly as she squirted some perfume up her skirt. "Of course I am. This is our holiday. I'm here for a good time not a long time."

I grabbed my handbag from the side of the bed and looked for the last time in the mirror. "I agree, just let us be ruthless and show these guys what we're all about."

Gemma ran to my side and hugged me. "I'm glad Josh is here you know. I know he hurt you in the past, but he does seem to have changed. I just want you to take it easy; don't let him rule the roost if you know what I mean?" Gemma was right, I was the one holding all the cards now. There was no way this man was hurting me again. Once bitten, twice shy sprung to mind. Hand inside my bag I pulled out some euros. I wanted to make sure I had enough to last me the night.

My father had left me quite a lot of money when he died and until now I'd never spent a penny. It just didn't seem right me having a good time on my father's hard earned cash. I suppose I was rich, but, I never told anyone. Money meant nothing to me. I would have given every penny in my bank account back just to have my father by my side just for one more day. I still missed him a lot. Whenever I was upset I would talk to him. I know he wasn't actually there in the room with me, but I did feel his presence whenever I was upset. Its funny death isn't it? It's so final. One minute your loved one is there and the next they're gone forever. Life is so precious; you need to enjoy it while you can. You never know what's around the corner. Right, we're ready to go and paint the town red. One last mouthful of vodka and we left the room.

The heat is sickly, I feel so hot and sweaty. My neck and forehead is covered in sweat. I think I'm chaffing too. Every time I take a step forward I can feel my thighs rubbing together. Josh is shouting me, his hands in the air and he's calling us over. "Come on sexy lady, get a drink down your neck and let's party." Gemma is straight over to Andy and I can see her hands all over him, she means business. I'm glad she's off my case now and I can relax without her judging me. At least now I can spend some quality time with the man of my dreams. I can't stop looking at him you know. He's at the bar ordering me a drink. His arse is perky and his golden body is covered in oil. I so want to lick him all over. I'm undressing him with my eyes. I need to get a grip of my emotions. What the hell is happening to me?

The Pudding Club

"Shall we sneak off Rebecca and spend some time alone. Gemma looks happy enough with Andy she won't even know we've gone?" he whispers. Head turned over my shoulder, I check Gemma out. She's laughing and dancing and having the time of her life.

"Come on then, but we can't be long, she'll kick off big-time if she thinks I've deserted her."

We sneaked off into the night. Josh had a bottle of vodka under his arm and we were set for a night of fun. The beach looked so romantic tonight and the stars in the sky shone brightly. Taking my shoes off I could feel the sand beneath my feet. It was cold and felt nice. Josh sat down on the beach and patted the space next to him. The sea breeze was in my face and it was helping my body cool down. This must have been the most romantic date I'd ever been on. We were Olivia Newton-John and John Travolta. Opening the bottle and taking a large mouthful he passed it to me. I was already half cut and I knew if I drank anymore I would be totally wiped out. I had to pace myself. Taking a deep breath I reached over and touched his warm hands. I was confident and knew I had to get what was on my mind off my chest.

"Why do you want me now Josh, is this just a holiday fling or do you really want me?"

He let out a laboured breath and looked deep into my eyes. "I do fancy you like mad Beck. Back in the day when we were younger you were a fat bird," he quickly backtracked and realised what he'd just said. "I don't mean fat bird, I mean, well, you know what I mean."

The rage inside me filled my throat. I know I was a fat cow back then but he was still having sex with me. "So, you're saying just because I've lost weight you feel like you can be seen with me now. That's a piss-take Josh and I don't think you should be here with me if you feel like that. I'm a person you know with feelings and if I'm fat or thin it shouldn't matter."

He was quiet for a few seconds and he dipped his head low and played with the sand. "You're right, I was more concerned about my image back then and what everyone else said about you."

I was choking with emotion. I know I was ugly and fat back in our schooldays but he was actually admitting that he thought it too. "I think you should go Josh, I want to be alone."

There was silence, you could have cut the atmosphere with a knife. "Rebecca, from the bottom of my heart I can only apologise. I was young and foolish. I'm not like that anymore and if I was being honest with myself, you've never been far from my thoughts." I didn't know if he was telling the truth or not. I looked deeper into his eyes. I was smitten and he'd captured my heart once again. I leaned forward and kissed him. The passion was strong between us and before I knew what was going on my knickers were off and we were having sex. I didn't care where I was or who could see. At that moment I was in heaven and in the arms of the man I loved.

Sex was over pretty quick and I was gagging for breath. I was a porn queen, and I'd made sure I left my man fully satisfied. He was lying on the sand blowing his breath at rapid speed. Lighting two cigarettes up I passed one to Josh. "See, us fat birds work harder, don't we?"

Josh nearly choked on his cigarette. "You can say that again," he chuckled as he pulled his shorts up.

Every hour of every day in Ibiza I spent with Josh. We were in love and inseparable. I know Gemma would say I sold her out for Josh, but I had to take control of my life and do what was best for me. Anyway, she was with Andy and it wasn't like she was on her own. Josh wanted me

The Pudding Club

to be his girlfriend when we got back home. I'd told him about the money my father had left me and he seemed eager for me to invest it. Josh always knew how to make money and I trusted him when he spoke about investment plans. My heart was filled with so much love for this man, and it's true, I would have done anything for him.

Once we landed in Manchester it was time for us to go our separate ways. Of course we would see each other again, but for now he went home to his parent's and I went to mine. As I waved him goodbye my heart broke. Gemma told me to pull myself together and stop making a show of myself, but I was honestly heartbroken. I felt empty and like part of me was missing. Gemma pulled me closer as we walked outside to get a taxi to go home. "My fanny has never had as much fun. I swear to you now, Andy is brilliant in bed. I never knew that many positions existed before he showed me. This is going down in my book as the best holiday I've ever had." Gemma was right; this holiday would be one I would remember for the rest of my life. I think I went away as a girl and came back a woman. I was in love. Yes, hook, line, and sinker. Josh Thompson was my world, my everything.

Opening my eyes I could see Teresa sat at the side of me. I'm sure she was texting someone on her phone. Here I was pouring my heart out and really digging deep into my past and this woman wasn't one bit interested. I sat up quickly and reached for a tissue. Dabbing it in the corner of my eyes I sniffed hard to get her attention. She looked at me and pretended to jot something down on her notepad. I bet she was writing on her paper, "A waste of time, this woman is potty." But I didn't care what she'd written. I just wanted to get out of this place as fast as I could. Why did I ever think she could help me in the first place? I had to face my own fears and go and see what

The Pudding Club

Josh wanted. He was a human being after all, what could he do to me that he hadn't already done? I was immune to his charm, there was no way he was having me over again. I was too wise for that now. I was older and wiser. I said my goodbyes to Teresa, she knew I was in a mood with her and tried to make amends. "You've had a good session Rebecca. You are really turning a corner in your life. Just keep positive and keep smiling." I nodded my head as I left but never replied.

The weather was poor and the Manchester skies were dark and cloudy. Zipping my coat up tightly I waddled to the bus stop. I was an emotional wreck and I felt like I would burst into tears at any time. Digging deep into my pocket I found a sweet. Fudge was a favourite of mine and this one must have escaped my latest binge. Unwrapping it with speed I rammed it into my mouth. This was the sugar rush I needed. Sucking it slowly I closed my eyes and enjoyed the flavours circling around in my mouth. I seemed to be in a world of my own as I sat on the bus travelling home. I knew people were there with me but they just didn't seem real. Eyes looking out of the window I watched the world go by. I just wanted to be at home. I was safe there and away from the grip of Josh Thompson.

Joey is quiet, he's no longer singing. Slowly I walk to his cage and see his small blue body lay on the bottom of the cage. Opening the cage, I call his name but he's still lying there frozen. Hands gripping him I bring him out of the cage and hold him to my chest. He's died alone, without me by his side. Was he in pain? Could he have been saved? I sobbed my heart out as I collapsed onto the chair with him still in my hands. "Joey, I'm so sorry I wasn't here with you. It was that bastard again. I had to go and get some help for myself. Please wake up Joey, please

The Pudding Club

I need you. My feathered friend was gone. He'd been part of me for so long now and without him I felt like my life was over. I know he was only a budgie, but we had a special bond together. He needed me and I needed him. Hours passed and I knew I would have to bury Joey. I found a small box and filled it with tissue paper. Reaching inside the cage I hooked the small mirror down and placed it into the box with Joey. He loved that mirror and spent hours looking into it. I placed a small note into the box too, telling Joey how much he meant to me and how my life would be without him. I suppose you think that's sad, but he was my best friend, and without him my life felt like it was going to end. The heavens opened as I walked out into the garden. The small hole I'd dug was ready to place Joey in. Flicking the switch on my stereo I played a song Joey loved. He enjoyed Grease too and he always jumped about his cage singing his head off whenever Grease Lightning played. Patting the soil down with the small spade I sat down and looked up to the sky. I suppose I was hoping someone could answer my prayers and just sat crying. Nobody did answer me though. I don't know why I ever thought they would. I was beyond any help and set for a life of misery.

The house phone had been ringing for hours. It was strength camp tonight and it was probably Gemma ringing to see where I was. I wasn't going tonight. How could I go when my head was in bits. I needed to be alone, time to heal. My meals were set out in front of me. Steak chips and beans and for dessert I'd taken out of the freezer a double chocolate cake. Yes, I was pigging out. I was upset and I needed comforting. I would be back on my diet tomorrow but for now I was comforting myself the only way I knew how. Food in my mouth, I savoured every mouthful of the forbidden food. I know I should

The Pudding Club

have had only one slice of cake but I was very upset. Spoon digging into the cream like a maniac I devoured every scrap of cake on my plate. I always felt guilty after a food binge, but it never stopped me re-offending. I would have tried to be sick, but I had no energy to stick my fingers down my throat. I was broken-hearted and just sat alone thinking of the days that lay ahead.

Reading over Josh's letter again and again I picked up the phone and dialled his number. I had to see what he wanted. I couldn't hold out any longer. I was shivering with fear and needed this to end as soon as possible. Listening to the ringing tone I waited for him to answer. The sound of his voice sent shivers down my spine. Hairs stood on end at the back of my neck, I couldn't speak. Taking a deep breath I found the courage to begin.

"It's me Rebecca, tell me what you want and get the fuck out of my life."

His voice was calm. He told me he didn't want to discuss what it was over the phone, he wanted a face to face meeting with me. At first I was going to tell him to take a run and a jump but I surprised myself and agreed. The meeting was set for the next day at noon. Once I hung the phone up I ran back to fridge as quick as my stumpy legs could carry me. Head inside it I found the last of the Ben and Jerry's cookie dough ice-cream. This was only ever used in emergencies; I needed it more than ever. The house was in silence, no Joey chirping anymore, no sounds at all accept my rumbling stomach. Oh, and the odd fart that came out unexpectedly. My head was whizzing and I feel so much anger inside my body. Reaching for my cardigan I rolled up in a ball and closed my eyes. I wanted to die, never to wake up again. Everything I'd ever loved was gone, what did I have to live for anymore, nothing.

TWELVE

AFTER A LONG PHONE CALL to work explaining why I wouldn't be in today I sat slurping my cup of coffee. Gemma was on her way round and she was fuming that I'd only just answered my phone. Once I'd told her about Josh and the meeting she knew how much my head was up my arse and told me she'd be at my house as quick as she could. This was weird of her because she never went out of her way for anyone. Gemma loved a trauma and I know secretly she was enjoying every minute of my pain. She's still never really forgiven me for Peter Jarvis, even after all these years she still holds a grudge, I can just feel it. I hope she doesn't bring her son with her, I'm in no mood for him today, he's draining. The letterbox is rapping hard it must be her at the door, she always knocks like the bleeding police. I better shift the empty food containers from the kitchen side. She'll go mad if she knows I'd been bingeing again. Evidence gone, I open the door.

"Bloody hell, you look a mess Becks. Have you been crying?"

Was she right in the head this woman or what? Of course I'd been upset. What did she expect from me, gales of laughter? "Joey died last night that's why I wasn't at training with you. I just came home and he was lay at the bottom of his cage." Gemma smirked, she never knew how you could love a bird like I loved Joey. "Why are you smiling Gemma? It's not funny, you heartless bitch. I know Joey was only a budgie, but he was part of me."

Gemma tried to keep a straight face, but she was still

smirking. "I've not said a word. Don't start attacking me because you're upset. I'm here to help that's all. If you don't want me here just say so and I'll leave."

I did want her to go, but I needed a friend and she was my only option. I tried to calm down. "I'm meeting Josh this afternoon. He said he wants to meet me face to face, he's not willing to discuss it on the phone."

Gemma was white in the face, she looked uneasy, fidgeting she sat down and tapped her fingers on the dining table. "What does he want to talk about that's so important. You should have told him to fuck off. Are you forgetting what he did to you? The money he stole from you and everything else he's done. No, phone him back and tell him to speak through your solicitor."

Gemma was serious and she meant every word she said. This was so out of character for her. "No I'm going to see him. I need to close this door on my life if I ever want to move forward. He can't hurt me anymore so I'm going to see him."

Gemma stood up and walked to the sink for a drink of water. "He's a liar Becks, don't listen to anything he's telling you. You know how much of a bull-shitter he is."

I didn't need to hear this from her; she was just making things worse than they were already. "What do you think he's going to tell me that I don't already know? He left me yeah, he stole my money and he was fucking somebody else. God, Gemma, how can anything be worse than that?"

Gemma swigged a big mouthful of her drink and played with the cuff of her sleeve. "I'm just saying that's all. You need to tread carefully where that tosser is involved. He's probably out for something from you so be careful he doesn't fill your head with shit again and have you over."

The Pudding Club

Gemma thought she knew it all, who was she to give any advice about relationships? It wasn't that long ago that her and Alex were nearly getting divorced, she told me she'd met somebody else and she was all set on leaving her husband until I made her see the light. "Have you seen anything of Gary or what, he said he's been ringing you all the time but you never answer his calls." This was correct, I was ignoring any calls from Gary but that was only because I was mixed up at the moment. It wouldn't be fair on him if I pissed him about. I knew I had to sort me out first before I could move on with any other relationship. Don't get me wrong, the sex was brilliant but I needed more than just a quick knee trembler, I needed to be loved.

"I'll ring Gary later on. I've just had so much on my shoulders lately. Tell him to relax; I'll be in touch soon."

Gemma was acting strange; she was edgy and didn't seem focused. "Have you been to see your mother too? She rang me last night asking me if I'd seen you. You can't just ignore people Becks, you need to start sorting your shit out and get your life back on track. If you ask me, you should leave Josh to rot, and just get on with your own life. He doesn't deserve the time of day."

"Gemma, I'm going to see him, end of. Why are you so hyped up about him, anyone would think it was you who was married to him not me."

Gemma let out a laboured breath and grabbed her car keys from the table. "There's no helping some people, I'm going, I'll speak to you later when you've calmed down. Let me know when you've spoken to him. Perhaps you'll be in a better mood then ay?"

Gemma marched out of the room and slammed the front door behind her. "Hormonal bitch," I muttered under my breath. Heading upstairs I knew I would have

The Pudding Club

to get ready, it was nearly time to meet Josh and I wasn't even ready yet. Opening the wardrobe door I paused. Do I dress to impress, or do I dress casually? Opening the underwear drawer I grabbed my spandex body controller. Whatever I chose to wear this was going to be needed. Pulling the extra-large garment over my thighs I held my breath. If anyone would have seen the state of me they would have laughed their head off. One breast was over my shoulder and the other was hung low near my stomach. I had to literally pull my breast down and put it back in the right position. Looking closer in the mirror I realised how much I'd aged. Thick creases at the side of my eyes and my cheeks that had lost all shape, I was a hopeless case for sure. I knew I should have had some botox the last time Gemma had got some. I like the thought of looking younger, but needles scare me. Knowing my luck anyway I would have had some reaction and ended up in the hospital. Gemma has had fillers before and her lips were always being topped up, she looked good but swore me to silence. She never wanted anybody to know that she was cheating the ageing process; she wanted everyone to think she was ageing well. I will get some botox in the future though. Gemma was right I'm not dead yet, I do need to look after myself.

Right, I'm ready to go and face my demons. I wish I would have planned this meeting more at least then I could have had my hair done and my nails. I've settled with my old black dress. It's plain, I know, but it hides my round figure. Josh always loved me in black, he said it made me look kinky. We've arranged to meet for a coffee on the shopping fort near the town centre. I'm going to drive today. I feel I'm ready to get behind the wheel again. I've lost a fair bit of weight since the last time I drove, so I should be able to move my legs. Checking my make-up

The Pudding Club

in the rear-view mirror I realise I'm not stunning but I suppose it's the best I've looked for a long time. I never slept a wink last night either. I kept imagining I could hear Joey singing downstairs and I was up and down all night long, I do miss Joey.

My head feels like it's going to burst. I can feel the pressure at the front of my head pounding, pumping with pain. This stress is going to be the death of me. I wish it was just all over and I was me again. I've often wondered who 'me' really was. I don't know her anymore. Josh kidnapped her and I think he's holding her hostage somewhere. Perhaps when I meet him today if I pay the ransom he will give her back to me. There has to be a ransom, some kind of payment, he always wants something from me and I can't see today being any different.

He knows my money has gone, he knows that more than anyone, after all, the bastard spent every last penny of it. The money my father left me was gone in months after Josh put a wedding ring on my finger, twenty thousand pounds just gone and nothing to show for it. Josh told me the investment was foolproof; it was going to set us up for life. What a nob-head I was. How could I have ever believed such a lying toe-rag? I know why, because I loved him, and I was blinded by the power he had over me. I should have known earlier how cunning and sly he really was. It was only after he found out I was loaded that he asked to marry me, you know. Gemma told me too, she said "Are you sure he's not marrying you for the money?" I was young and foolish back then and thought she was jealous of me and the man that I loved. I should have listened to her but ay, it's gone now and there's nothing I can do about it.

Josh was always dressed in new clothes at the time I gave him my money. A new car was a must for him, too;

he said that meeting all these big people he needed a set of wheels to impress them all. I agreed with him, I even went to pick it with him. I loved seeing him smile. I loved making him happy. I just loved him, end of. My mother went ballistic when I told her about the money all being gone. "A fuckin idiot," she called me. "A daft, lovesick dick-head." She still goes on about the money even today. I can't blame her really, it's true, I was an idiot. I could have had a comfortable life if it wasn't for him. I had everything I needed to set up the salon I'd always dreamt of. Rebecca's Studios it was going to be called. It just goes to show you that love can take over your life and lead you to places you never knew existed. I've often asked myself if I was really happy with Josh. I was, I think. Well, maybe at first but I never felt good enough for him. I always felt like I was second-best. He must have loved me though; no one could have put on that much of a show just for the money.

Ten years we were married and I loved being called his wife, proud as punch I was. I know there were times when he wished he'd stayed with Catherine Bennett, but that was me shouting at him telling him to get his sorry arse back to her all the time. I was pregnant with his child too. The happiest time in my life to know the man I loved with all my heart had planted his seed deep inside me. I miscarried after fourteen weeks. Josh was upset and we said we would wait a while before we tried again. We never did and I was set to be without children in my life. I would have been a good mother too. I would have loved that child with all my heart. Josh bought me a budgie after the loss of our baby; he said he hoped it might ease the pain in my heart. I suppose Joey did when I think about it, he definitely filled a gap. He needed caring for and loving just like me and that's how we ended up as best friends.

Josh changed after I lost the baby. He was on his mobile phone constantly, and he was always texting or doing something on his phone or laptop. He told me it was business and I never had any reason to doubt him. Josh's job meant he was always called out whenever something came up. I just thought it was strange that a car-showroom sales manager was asked to go to the office so late in the evening but he told me this was normal. Special clients he said he was meeting, rich clients who were famous and wanted to browse at the cars when the showroom was closed. I could kick myself now when I look back at what he got away with. He must have been laughing at me all along. Josh and his knock-off must have been having the time of their lives with me out of the picture. He must have been having sex with the dirty bitch at work. I never did find out who she was either, he said I didn't need to know her name. I always imagined her to be skinny and blonde-haired and good looking. I don't know why, I just did. Josh was all set to leave me when something strange happened. There he was packing all his clothes when his phone rang. I could hear him arguing with someone on the other end of the line and he was angry. Josh never left me that day, he just put all his clothes back in the wardrobe and told me he was staying. I never asked why he'd changed his mind. I was just relieved he wasn't leaving me. I would have shared him you know. Pathetic isn't it, but he was my life. I couldn't breathe without him. To even think of him not in my life sent shivers down my spine. I would have turned a blind eye and let him have his mistress just so long as he never left me.

When you watch the TV sometimes you see women like me and wonder why they put up with what they do.

The Pudding Club

It's that thing called love again. It makes you mad and unable to think straight. Josh used to stay out until late three or four times a week. I could feel him sneaking into bed behind me smelling of her perfume. Floral, sweet aromas. I tried to buy the same kind of fragrances hoping I could win his love back but it never did, he wasn't interested in me now that the money was gone. I did try and spice up our sex life though and every now and again we did still have sex. Well, if you could call it that. It was more me just sucking him off than having sex. I was just trying to please him. I remember one night I was on my knees giving him oral sex whilst he was watching the TV and I had the urge to bite his penis right off. I could taste her on it and it knocked me sick. He was such a hard-faced bastard. I never did bite his dick off though, I was a coward but I should have when I think back, I should have chewed it up in tiny pieces and spat it back at him. He would have deserved it too. I would have rammed his cock right up his arse just as a token of the way he'd treated me. I always talk the talk I do, but when it comes to walking the walk, I'm a right shit-bag.

Just the thought of going to prison makes me feel ill inside. I do have some crazy thoughts though and with this temper of mine I know one day I'll do something that lands me up in jail for a very long time, I'm a nutter when I lose my rag. Prison does scare me though. I mean, a big bird like me would be much sort after in the nick. I would be some butch lesbian bitch for sure. I've seen it on the TV you know. The quiet ones always get attacked. I've run the thought of going to prison over in my mind a few times and even had a plan to make sure I was not sought after by the chief lettuce lickers. I would tell them I was a murderer; a psycho, a bleeding nutter who would stick a blade in them if they ever fucked with me. I liked the image I created of myself in my head. I wasn't the underdog for a change. I was strong and ruthless and feared by all inside the prison walls. It's such a shame I was never going to be that person. I would never have the guts to bite my husband's cock off or even stick a knife in anyone. I am just me - Rebecca Rooks, fat, single and desperate.

Marching across the car park on the shopping fort I froze. What on earth was I doing meeting this prick in the first place? He'd only written me a letter and there I was at his beck and call again, just like I always was, desperate. Stood thinking I kicked my foot on the floor trying to buy some time. I was arguing with myself like some kind of head the ball. Hot, sweating I decided I needed to face him. I needed answers, closure on our relationship. Did I just want that though? Or did I just want to see him again. Oh, I don't bleeding know I am in bits. My stomach is rumbling and it needed comforting. Head twisting around, my nostrils were filled with an aroma. A Kentucky Fried Chicken outlet was just steps away from me. Why hadn't I seen this earlier? I loved chicken. Head dipped, coat zipped up fully. I headed into the store. I was a bit early anyway and I had ten minutes to kill before I met Josh. And, in that time I would have devoured a family bucket of chicken on my own, so it was all good. I paced quickly to the counter and placed my order. Twelve pieces of heaven were in the bucket they passed me, twelve deadly sins in the form of chicken pieces. Finding a seat where nobody could see me eat this meal was all that mattered now.

Before long, all that was in front of me was a plate full of bones. I'd skinned the chicken completely. It was finger licking good, just like they said it would be. I love the wipes you get with your meal too. It wipes all traces of the food from your fingers. Face cleaned, I check my watch. It's D-Day. I'm feeling a little better now, not as nervous as I thought I would be. Food has calmed me down and I can think straight again. I declined the ice-cream after my meal though; it would just go through me straight away. I mean the proper shits too. I've always been like that with ice-cream, that's why I only eat it when I'm at home. It's like dicing with death if I eat it anywhere else; it's not a good idea.

I can see the coffee shop in front of me now. A few people are sat outside using their mobile phones. I can't see him yet, I hope I'm the first here. At least then when he walks in I can be sat down and not make a show of myself. Loud noises, people talking, I head inside the coffee shop. I love the smell of freshly ground coffee, it's so calming. I can't see Josh though, he mustn't be here yet. Ordering my skinny latte I find a place to sit. It's in the corner of the room and not as busy as the other spots in the shop. The cakes are in the cabinet facing me too, big thick slabs of chocolate fudge cake, devil's food I call it. Licking my lips I close my eyes and rid the thought of getting a piece. It's so hard for me and I'm struggling.

"Anything else," the assistant asked. I just shake my head and pay for my drink.

I love this coffee shop, it's always so welcoming. The decor is warm and it feels like home. Even the leather sofas are comfy. Sitting back I could easy have a quick nod off before he gets here. Food always make me feel sleepy after I've just binged on it. I think it's my body telling me I've overdone it yet again. Before I know it I'm snuggled deep into the sofa and my eyes begin to close slowly. I'm dreaming and I'm in the film Grease. I'm thin and my black Lycra pants fit me like a glove. I've got a pink lady jacket on too and I'm strolling at the funfair looking for my heart's desire. I just love this dream. I always dream of wearing black Lycra pants. I suppose it's my mind telling me that it is possible if I stop eating crap foods. There's a cloud above me now and it's raining. It's pissing down if I'm being blunt, wet droplets on my face, this can't be true. I've not even danced with Danny Zuko yet. Eyes open quickly and I see the silhouette of a man in front of me. Rubbing my eyes I become aware of my environment. My dream is over and the reality hits me right in the face.

"Some things never change do they porky? Don't tell me you've been scoffing your face again. You're always like this when you've had a good feast."

Wriggling about in my seat I snarl at Josh. Who the hell did he think he was calling me porky? He should have been trying to lick my arse not wind me up. When we were together that was his pet name for me, but now, I hated it, just like I hated him. "Keep your insults to yourself Josh. Just say what you have to say and leave me alone to get on with my life."

Josh squeezed in next to me and leant in to kiss me. There was no way in the world this was happening. Who the fuck did he think he was thinking he could just stroll in here as if nothing had ever happened? I pushed him away with my teeth gritted tightly together, he knew I meant business and backed off. "Bleeding hell, loosen up Becks. I'm here to make amends, just relax will you?"

Was he having a laugh or what? Was I imagining this or was it really happening? This man had no shame. "I've missed you Becks. I know what happened in the past was wrong but I'm sorry from the bottom of my heart."

I examined his face carefully. When he was lying his left eyebrow twitched at the top, it wasn't moving. "That's all in the past Josh. I'll never forgive you for the way you treated me and if you think you can ever be forgiven for that then you need your head testing."

Josh smirked and licked his lips slowly. "I want you back. I want us to be like we were in the beginning. I'm nothing without you by my side." This was unreal. I had to pinch myself to make sure I was hearing him right. This was my time to clean out my closet and be done with this bastard once and for all.

"You smarmy wanker. What, because you say a few nice words to me you think I'll rip my knickers off and jump into bed with you? Go and fuck yourself. You'll never get in my knickers again. I'm so over you Josh. You had your chance and messed it up. I'm nobody's doormat anymore."

He was desperate, and I'm sure he was welling up, yes, real tears forming in the corner of his eyes. At last Rebecca Rooks was in control. "Becks I'm so messed up. Nothing works anymore without you in my life. I thought if I moved away I would just get over you but," he paused and looked directly into my eyes, "it just won't happen. I'm sorry for the past. I just need you in my life again."

I sat back and folded my arms in front of me tightly. It would have been so much easier just to take him back into my life but as I looked at him closer he was no longer the man I loved, he was no longer my Danny Zuko. "Josh, the way you treated me in the past has made me realise that I'm worth more. I've moved on. I suggest you do the same."

He was gobsmacked and started to fidget about. You could tell by his body language that he was angry. "Becky stop being a drama queen, you know you still love me, so let's not waste any time getting back to normal. I can move back in today and we can put all this shit behind us."

He just wasn't getting it was he? He must have thought I was such a pushover. Looking at him in more detail I studied his lips. They used to be my favourite thing about him when we first met but now they were dry and cracked. Something was lying heavy on my mind and I needed to know the answer. "I know all about your other woman too. Do you think people don't talk because they do? It was just a matter of time before your secret fling was uncovered."

I was lying through my front teeth as I didn't have a clue who she was I was just bluffing him. My poker face just sat staring at him awaiting his answer. Josh was white and now he was sweating, small droplets of sweat were forming on his forehead. "I don't know what she's told you Becks but trust me it was all her. She did all the running; she was begging me for it if I was being truthful. Gagging for it she was."

I cracked my knuckles and pretended I knew who he was referring to. "No Josh it was all you. You was the one who wouldn't leave her alone."

Josh snapped and everyone started to look at us in the shop. "Gemma would say that wouldn't she. She wanted me to leave you from day one. So get your facts right."

Whoa... head spinning. I can't focus, heart beating in my chest. Did he just say my best friend's name? I had to remain calm and delve deeper. "Gemma wouldn't lie to me Josh, she told me everything." There was a silence and he banged his clenched fist onto the table.

"She was leaving Alex, she wanted us to start a life together. I bet she never told you that did she? Remember all the calls I got late in the night, well, who do you think that was? Come on... It's not rocket science. She's supposed to be your friend are you forgetting that?"

The Pudding Club

I was choking; I was so hot and felt like my head was going to burst. Standing to my feet I dragged the rat by the scruff of his neck. "And, you were supposed to be my fucking husband. Get out of my sight you prick. And, just to let you know, Gemma never whispered a word to me about your sordid affair, you've just told me." Josh ragged his hands through his hair in desperation, he was pleading with me as I left. "Fuck you," I shouted behind me in a loud voice. The other customers were looking at me in disbelief but I was upset, what did they expect?

Sitting in the car I reached for my cigarettes from out of my handbag. I needed nicotine and fast. This was too much to take in. Gemma was the one who had ruined my life. All those nights she'd sat with me telling me Josh was no good when she knew very well that she'd been banging his brains out. I had to try and think straight, there was no way this dirty cow was getting away with this. This was war and I was going to wipe that smile right off her cocky face. She was going to see what I was all about now. It was time to take the gloves off and crush that dirty bitch.

I don't know how I got home that day. My mind was all over the place. I was just in a trance and nothing seemed real. The more I thought about it all the more it made sense. Gemma was always at my house when Josh was there and she was always laughing and joking with him. What a fool I'd been not to see what was right under my nose. I bet she'd been laughing behind my back for years. Well, no more, revenge is sweet and now that I knew I was going to show her exactly what I was made of. She was due to meet me soon for training and I had to plan what I was going to do with her. There was no way I was telling her that I knew all about her sordid little secret. Where would the fun be in that? I knew what pushed

Gemma's buttons and I was going to do my best to make sure she knew exactly how much she'd hurt me. Gemma was no longer a pink lady. She was a black widow, a dark, dirty bitch who could never be trusted again.

Gemma walked into my front room all dressed for training. She looked good and there was no way you could take that away from her. The gastric band she'd had for years had worked wonders for her confidence, but now she was without it and prone to put weight on at the drop of a hat. Gemma could never stand any type of stress, she was like me. One bit of trauma in her life and she piled the pounds on like nobody's business. "Come on Rebecca, I don't want to be late, I've got some serious training to do tonight, look at my arse, does it look like it's got any bigger to you?" Usually I would have put her mind at rest, but not now. She was getting the truth whether she liked it or not. I kept a straight face as I answered her.

"I was going to mention it to you last week Gemma, it has got bigger. In fact your face is rounder than usual too. Have you been stressed or something like that?"

Strike one to me, she was devastated. Stood looking behind her at her backside she panicked. "No, I've not been stressed I don't think, but come to think of it Alex has been doing my head in lately, that could be the reason. Yeah, it's him stressing me out."

Head dipped as I tied my laces I spoke to her. "What ever happened to that guy you was going to leave Alex for? I mean, you must have felt something for him to leave your husband."

Gemma couldn't look me in the eyes; she rubbed her hands together and replied. "Let's not get into that Rebecca, that's so yesterday. Everyone has problems in their marriage don't they? Come on, look at you and

Josh."

I could have jumped up and strangled the two-faced bitch at that moment, but I kept calm. Standing up I sucked my stomach in and paced the front room. "I think I've lost some weight you know? A lady from work said it to me last week. I can't wait to get weighed; I bet I've lost over a stone. Ay, Catherine Bennett will be spitting feathers when I step on the scales won't she?" Gemma was quiet and you could see her hand patting her bottom behind her, she was just where I wanted her now and it was only a matter of time before I dug the knife in her, just like she'd done to me.

Strength camp started and Arnie commented on my progress. I was lifting heavier weights now and my body was starting to change shape. From the corner of my eye I could see Gemma working out with speed. She was paranoid now and desperate to look her best. Arnie made sure we were alone and placed his hand on my shoulder. "Are you alright tonight Rebecca, you look like you're on a mission or something. Has someone upset you or what?"

I just smirked at him and got ready to lift the weight set out in front of me. "Yeah Arnie, people who you think you can trust, just take the piss."

Arnie didn't reply and he just stood spotting me without another word. The other trainers were shouting outside and I lifted my head up to see what the commotion was. Gemma was on the floor and she was howling in pain. The dizzy cow had only gone and dropped the dumbbell on her foot. I know I should have been more concerned but I didn't give a shit if I was being honest. Arnie went outside and I could see him bent down talking to Gemma trying to calm her down, she was hysterical. Arnie came back inside and shook his head slowly. "She'll have to go to hospital. I bet her foot is broken, the barmy cow dropped twenty-four kilograms right on her foot. See what I mean about not concentrating, that's how accidents happen."

Maybe I should have gone with Gemma to the hospital but I just turned a blind eye and carried on with my training. She could rot in hell for all I cared. I'd asked Arnie for extra sessions too, I wanted this weight off me as soon as possible, I was sick of being fat, I wanted to feel like me again. I was going to the hairdressers tomorrow for a long overdue haircut. I'd let my hair go in the last few months and it was like rats tails if I was being honest. I was booked in for a colour and cut and after that a spray tan. Gary was also back on the scene. I called him today to apologise for my behaviour. Seeing Josh again had really shone a light onto my situation. Perhaps I needed this kick up the arse to get back on track with my life. Something was happening inside me and I didn't know what. I was starting to feel strong again and actually giving a toss about the way I looked. As from this moment my body was a temple and no forbidden foods were going to pass my lips again. I was on the ball now and my head was focused. The lard around my arse was going and my body shape was going to change if it was the last thing I did. I was sick of being round and fat. Today was the start of the new me. No, honest this is it, this time.

THIRTEEN

GEMMA LOOKED LIKE A SWOLLEN BALLOON. She must have gained at least two stone over the last few weeks. Her foot was still in plaster and she was no nearer having it off as the break was that bad. Me, however, I looked completely different. The weight was falling off me and I must have been fifteen stone now. My new hairstyle was great too, blonde and shoulder length just like I used to wear it back in the day. I've also been on the sunbed too so I look like I've just come back from holiday. I've been seeing Gary now quite a lot and his tea-bagging craze has now ended. I had to tell him straight. I was getting a rash around my mouth you know, a bright red irritable blemish on my skin, no, tea-bagging is a thing of the past. We're still experimenting in the bedroom though and he's come along leaps and bounds. Gary keeps talking about anal sex. I know he's hinting for us to try it, but that's a no-go area for me. Well, for now. My piles are sore anyway and I don't want them aggravated by any foreign objects up my back passage. It's funny how men think isn't it? Any crack or cranny they find they just want to shove their dicks inside it, no matter where it is or what it's used for. I'm sure if Gary could get his penis in my nostrils he would have a go at shagging them too, he's proper kinky.

Well, tonight I'm going to get weighed and see if my hard work has paid off. I'm driving tonight and Gemma is coming along for the ride. She doesn't get out much these days and she's always on the phone for me to visit her. Josh is still badgering me to get back with him. I like

The Pudding Club

playing with him now, he doesn't know if he's coming or going. I let him think he stands a chance then, pow... I knock the bastard straight back down to earth with a bang. It's funny how I've turned out really. I think I've become Josh and he's become me. I love the power I feel over him. I love the power I have over Gemma too. It's ironic that the two people who have hurt me the most in my life both need me now. It's getting near the time to tell Gemma that I know all about her fling with my husband. I can't hold it any longer. I want to pick my moment though, I want to humiliate her like she's humiliated me. I've confided in Gary about Gemma and he agrees with me that she was well out of order. He's such a nice man Gary, and I think I've found a diamond with him. Of course, he needs some training, but come on, don't most men. He's forever surprising me with little gift and gestures. I feel loved and cared for.

Gemma is like a lump of lead. Her weight gain is coming along nicely. She looks like she's storing nuts in the side of her mouth for winter. I'll mention that fact shortly too, she looks a bit too happy for my liking today. Sat in the car I put on my Grease CD. I actually sing now whilst I'm driving. I've surprised myself at the changes I'm making in my life. It's just small things but it all makes a difference doesn't it? Right, let me flick through the songs on this CD and find the one I'm looking for. Here it is, "There are worst things I could do." Oh, I love this song. I'm singing at full pelt and I know all the words. I look at Gemma who's in the passenger seat and she's not singing. That's not like her she loves this song.

"What's up Rizzo?" I ask with a chuckle in my voice.

Gemma turned to face me and growled. "Why are you calling me Rizzo, Rebecca? I've always been Frenchy not that slut Rizzo."

The Pudding Club

I don't know where it came from but this was the time to come clean and let the cat out of the bag. "Well, since you shagged my husband things have changed."

You could have cut the atmosphere with a knife, she was speechless and it took her a few minutes to answer me. "What the hell are you going on about; you're talking out of your arse if you ever think anything like that."

This girl had more front than Blackpool, bold as brass she was sat there denying everything. I pulled over and clicked my seatbelt from around me. Leaning over I could feel her hot breath on my face. Her chest was rising and she knew I meant business. "He's told me all about it Gemma. You dirty slut, you were my best friend. Get your fat arse out of my car and I never want to see you again."

Gemma was in a panic and she was still declaring her innocence. "Rebecca, stop being a dick-head. We're friends, I would never cross the line and touch your man. You know me better than that."

She was still adamant that it had never happened. It was time to up my game and put the fear of God into her. "Well, you can tell that to Alex then can't you, because once he knows the truth about his wife he'll kick you out on your sorry fat arse."

Gemma gritted her teeth tightly and she looked evil. I'd found her jugular and she was fighting back now. "You keep away from Alex. I swear to you If you say one word to him I'll..." She paused as I jumped into the conversation.

"You'll do Jack-shit because you've done your worst. How did you ever think you would get away with it? Did you think I would never find out? Get out of my car and get back in the gutter where you belong. You're a sly rat who doesn't deserve any friends."

Gemma opened the car door. She turned her head

back to me and screamed at the top of her voice. "You cheated with Peter, now we're equal."

There was no way I was having that, this was completely different. "We were kids back then. He wasn't your fucking husband; Peter was shagging anything with a pulse. I told you it was a mistake and you said you'd forgiven me. Is this what it's all about you sad cow?"

Gemma struggled to get out of the car. She wobbled a few times and had to steady herself on a nearby lamppost. I could see she was crying as she flopped down onto the floor. I probably should have got out of the car and seen if she was alright but at that moment my blood was boiling and I wanted to run the bitch over. Turning the engine on I pulled off from the kerb and joined the traffic. The music was loud and I carried on singing at the top of my voice. I knew Gemma wouldn't let this go and prepared myself for the battle ahead.

Catherine Bennett looked different tonight, she seems to have mellowed. I'm sure she just smiled at me. I don't trust her one little bit and if she thinks she's meddling with these scales tonight she's got another thing coming. The way I'm feeling right now I'll smash them right over her head. The other slimmers look well. You can see some of them have lost weight off their faces. They seem a lot happier and more confident. One lady who seems to have shed quite a lot of weight is dressed in Lycra leggings. What is it with some women, the minute they lose an ounce of weight they run straight out and buy some of these leggings? It's like the Holy Grail, I suppose, but you can't just wear them when you're still overweight can you? No, I'm not going near them until I'm at my goal weight. I don't want all my lumps and bumps showing. Catherine is heading my way, she's humming a tune and trying to sing. Looking cautiously around me she speaks.

The Pudding Club

"Where's Gemma tonight? Is she not coming along to get weighed?"

I don't know why, but I had to tell someone how I felt and it just blurted out of my mouth without any control. "No I think she'll be on her way back home. I mean, now I know she was sleeping with my husband, she'll have to make sure I don't turn up at her home and cause mayhem."

Catherine bit hard on her lip and stood nervously playing with her fingers. She grabbed me by the arm and took me away from the class. "So you know then? It's about time that slapper got caught. She's been at it for years you know. Even when I was seeing Josh she was still having sex with him. Josh told me himself so I know it's the truth."

This was getting worse by the minute. I was holding my hand over my heart and I felt as if I was going to pass out. Catherine held me by the arm and comforted me. "Josh came to see me you know. Two days ago he rang me and asked me to meet him. He said he still loved me and wanted for us to try again." The lying fucker, I knew it was too good to be true. I was speechless and felt like my windpipe was closing up. "He's been to see me too except he sent me a letter first. Declaring his undying love, he was saying he couldn't live without me."

Catherine chuckled and shook her head. "He's lower than a snake's belly that one is. I'll never trust him again after what he did to me, did you know we were engaged?" I did know they were going to get married but I shook my head in denial. "He nicked the money we had saved for our marriage and went on holiday to Ibiza with the boys. He spent every last penny of it and didn't bat an eyelid. When he came home, I told him straight that I never wanted to set eyes on him again. And, the next

The Pudding Club

thing I hear he's seeing you."

Why was I feeling like the other woman? When I met Josh he'd told me he didn't love Catherine and that's why he'd left her. What a lying toe-rag this bastard was. All the years I'd spent with him, and I didn't really know him. Why had I not seen this all before? I knew there was more than meets the eye with him. I sat down with Catherine and explained how I met Josh in Ibiza. She cried her eyes out, big thick salty tears streaming down her face. She was like me. Josh Thompson had made a fool of her. The anger stirred in my stomach and I wanted to destroy my ex-husband, but how? He was immune to pain and he could smell a rat a mile off.

Catherine dabbed the white tissue into the corner of her eyes and smiled at me. "I'm sorry for the way I treated you when we were younger. I was a bully and just saw you as an easy target. If it is any consolation to you I suppose I was jealous of you." What, was I hearing this right? Catherine Bennett was jealous of me. I took a deep breath and replied.

"It's water under the bridge now love. We all did things back then that we're not proud of." A loud noise stopped our conversation. Gemma had entered the room like a mad woman. She was livid and heading straight for me. I clenched my fists tightly at the side of my legs. One wrong word out of this scrubber and I was going to knock ten tons of shit out of her. The class was in silence and they huddled close together whispering. Gemma stood tall and placed her hands on her hips.

"You didn't think I would just walk away did you, when you're threatening to wreck my marriage, Rebecca? I want this sorting out now before it gets out of control."

I was clearing my throat to speak when Catherine piped in. "Listen you tart, just leave Rebecca alone. Don't you think you've done enough to her already? You're a sly evil bitch Gemma and I for one hope you get what's coming to you. You don't piss on your own doorstep."

Gemma growled and held the doorframe to steady herself. I should have just run at her and scratched her eyeballs out but I held back waiting on her reply. "Catherine, you just keep out of it, you interfering hussy. We can sort this out without any help from you. So fuck off and mind your own business."

Everyone was waiting on my next move, and they were not going to be disappointed. I could always look after myself and Gemma knew I would rip her head off if she pushed me too far. I walked slowly into her personal space and touched noses with her. "Get the fuck out of my life. I trusted you Gemma and according to Catherine this has been going on for years. You've seen how I've been over that bastard. I've cried to you and poured my heart out to you when all along you were getting your knickers off for him. We're done, me and you Gemma. As far as I'm concerned I never want to see your fat arse again."

Oh, she wasn't giving up that easily she was trying to talk her way out of it. The other slimmers in the group were hissing and I know they all wanted me to knock the cocky look right off her face. "He was the one who wanted me, Rebecca. I tried to fight him off but he kept ringing me and texting me. I was a fool too, you know. He ripped me off for over ten thousand pounds. He promised me everything and I believed him like a fool."

Red mist appeared in front of my eyes and I couldn't take it anymore. Dragging my coat off I rolled my sleeves up and sank my fingers into her hair. I gripped it with all my might and tossed her about the room like a rag doll. Gemma was on the floor now and I was sat on top of her.

The Pudding Club

The first blow was struck and blood surged from her lip. If Catherine and some of the others hadn't have pulled me off her, I would have been in prison on a murder charge. I was in the zone and I wanted to hurt this cheating bitch so she would never smile again. Gemma was helped from the floor and quickly taken outside. She never spoke a word as she left. The rage inside me was pumping and my head felt like it wanted to explode. I needed calories and quick.

Running into the toilet I searched deep in my cardigan pocket and pulled out the three sweets I'd stored there. Unwrapping them in a wild frenzy I pushed them into my mouth. Sweet, smooth, flavours. Rhubarb and custard sweets were so calming. Crunching, sucking, I could feel myself calming down. The voice from outside was low. It was Catherine. "She's gone love. One of the other girls has just put her into a taxi." Swallowing the evidence of my latest binge I slowly unlocked the toilet door. Catherine threw her arms around my neck trying to comfort me. This didn't feel right, I'd hated this woman for so long now and all of a sudden she was like my best friend. I pulled away and dusted myself down.

"Thanks Catherine, I just want to get weighed now and go home to lick my wounds."

Catherine seemed surprised and backed off with a concerned look on her face. "I'm here for you if you need me. Hold on, I'll get you my phone number." Catherine left me alone and I walked to the mirror hung on the wall. What a bloody mess I was, stressed wasn't the word. I was like a ticking bomb and ready to explode. I wanted to hurt Josh Thompson just like he'd hurt me. This needed thinking about. I had to be two steps in front of this bastard and one behind to ever outsmart him. I was going to show him who the fool really was. When I'd finished

The Pudding Club

with Josh he was going to be the laughing stock of the area. I knew what made him tick and if I mentioned any kind of money in the bank to him I would have him by the short and curlies. This had to be planned, no rushing in. Think, think, think.

On the way home it seemed like I wasn't there, my head was somewhere else and my mind wasn't on the driving. Stopping at the traffic lights I looked in the pet shop window. Budgies, lots of budgies, were dancing about inside the cage; a beautiful selection of coloured birds, blue, yellow and green. Would it have been an insult to Joey if I was to replace him so soon after his death? Was there a grieving time, some kind of law I had to follow? Before I knew it I was in the pet store and my fingers were poking inside the cage where the birds were. I felt warmth in my heart as I remembered Joey when he was younger; he was so full of life. I wanted them all, I love budgies.

The assistant came over to me and asked if I needed any help. Fucking hell, how long did she have? I needed desperate help and fast but that was just my personal life. I stared at her a bit longer than necessary and debated opening my heart up to her she had such a friendly face. No, I just wanted to buy a bird I was never going to burden her with my problems. "I want a blue one and a green one please." I said in a timid voice. That was it, the deal was done and my two new budgies were in a box on their way home with me. Olivia and John I named them after my two favourite people in the whole word. It's funny because I feel like I know Sandy inside out. She represents a nation of women. And, Danny, well, he's a typical man. He's out for as much pussy as he can get. I do love him though; all us women love a bad boy in our lives don't we? I'm no different I suppose. I wasn't sure

The Pudding Club

what sex the birds were but what did it matter that I'd named them Olivia and John, nobody would ever know. Well, unless my new feathered friends developed a six inch penis overnight, but apart from that you can't tell the difference between male and female. I can hear them in the box rustling about. I bet they're scared, how traumatic is this for them? One minute they are a singing away in a nice cage and the next thing, bang, locked away in a dark box not knowing what the future holds for them.

I've bought two birds for a reason. Joey always seemed so lonely and depressed without any company and I swore to myself I would never put another bird through the same kind of torture. Everyone needs a bit of company, including me. My two new birds will never hunger for company like I do. They will always have each other. I think the only love you get that's real is from your parents. They love you because you're just you. You don't have to pretend to be someone that you're not. My family is all I've got now. I've not seen my mother for a while though. I know I should call more often but it kills me to see her sat alone everyday without my dad sat by her side. I know it's years since he passed away but you never really get over a death of a parent do you? I often imagine what I would say to him if he ever appeared to me. Well, after shitting myself and hiding away I would find the courage to talk to him. I think I would just smell him first. I've missed his musky smell, stale cigarettes is what he smelt of, strong tobacco. I often think I can smell him in the room with me sometimes, especially when I'm upset. I think I would just cry and hold him in my arms. Every girl loves her father and I was his special princess. No man will ever love you like your dad does. My mother feels it too, so much sadness in her eyes. I can only imagine how she feels deep in her heart. How do you ever get over something like that? The man you've loved for years, gone forever. Oh, I'm getting tearful now, see what I mean. I only have to think about my father and I'm a blubbering mess. I wish Josh Thompson was dead, why does the Lord above always take the good ones? He should have taken that bastard and flung him straight into hell and watched him burn to cinders. I for one would love that, watching him burn a slow painful death.

Olivia and John are in the cage, cheerful they are and just what I need around this place to liven it up. They seem so full of energy and life and they've not kept still since I've put them in there. The green one is the singer, he must be the male. As I watch him closer he keeps sticking his little feathered arse out and fanning his feathers out at the side of him. The female is just looking at him, she's showing little interest. He's not giving up though, he's a tough cookie. He's at her side nibbling into her plumage.

Gary is taking me out tonight. I'm not in the mood but I need to try and make an effort. There's no point in sitting here staring at four bleeding walls is there? I'll go crackers if I'm left alone tonight. The phone has not stopped ringing. I bet it's her, Gemma. She'll be shitting herself in case I go to her home and tell her husband all about his seedy wife and her affair with my husband. I should ruin her life like she's ruined mine. I could come onto her husband and have hot steamy sex with him, I know he fancies me, it would be like taking candy from a baby. Alex has got a kink for big breasts and after a skin full of beer one night he told me exactly what he would like to do with my breasts if he got his hands on them. He's such a pervert. He said he wanted to give me a pearl necklace. At first I thought about it, come on girls, pearl necklaces are quite expensive and I loved jewellery, well, until he explained to me what it really was. The dirty

The Pudding Club

bastard wanted to ejaculate all over my neck; apparently a pearl necklace is the slang for this. I refused of course and called him a sick, twisted man, but he seemed to get off on it and tried sinking his head right between my breasts. That would be payback for Gemma wouldn't it? That would wipe the smile right from her cocky face. I need time to think about what I want to do with her. I'm not going to be predictable. I'm going to be sneaky and sly, just like she was with my bleeding husband. The phone is ringing again. I'm going to answer it this time it could be Gary trying to talk to me. He's tried my mobile phone all day but I just ignored him. I know I should have spoken to him, but he keeps me talking for hours and I never get anything done. I'll speak to him now anyway, he won't settle until I answer the phone.

I feel better already after talking to Gary. He does make me laugh you know, his sense of humour is so dry. I don't think he knows how funny he really is. Gary has lost some weight too. He's actually looking thin. I might let him slip me one tonight before he leaves. I have to get it while I can don't I? You just take sex for granted when it's on tap don't you? But, when it's gone, it's the only thing on your mind twenty-four hours a day. When I was going through a drought after Josh left me I took to watching porn DVDs. Not all the time, but once or twice a week. I just wanted to make sure I was doing it right. Nobody ever gives you a sex guide do they? So I called it research. I did learn a few tricks though, but I've never tried them out yet. Who knows, I might give it a go with Gary tonight. Men love porn don't they? Josh used to watch it on his own when I was in bed. He must have thought I was asleep but I wasn't. In fact, when I heard the music from the DVD I thought it was the ice-cream man outside doing a night shift, but once I was

The Pudding Club

fully awake I realised it was my husband jerking himself off downstairs. I never told him I knew about his guilty pleasure. I just turned a blind eye yet again and let him get on with it. Plus, I invested in a vibrator and I was pleasuring myself too.

When I first used the contraption it interfered with the TV signal. Gemma introduced me to the love toy. She took me to Anne Summers the sex store and urged me to buy the rabbit vibrator. At first it was just hid away inside my wardrobe but once I got to grips with it, it became my best friend. I could just orgasm at the click of a button, not just one either, multiple spine tickling ones. I nearly had a bleeding heart attack I can tell you. Josh never knew about my sex toys and I never told him, that was my secret. Looking back at my sex life with Josh I don't think he was that good between the sheets. He was just, well, all for himself. Our sex life usually consisted of me sucking him off and then when he was close to ejaculating he would slip it in me for the last few minutes. I did ask him if I could be the one who had the oral sex before sex and he just laughed, telling me that sex was all about pleasing him not me. What a wanker that guy was.

Oh, before I forget. I can actually see my lady garden now. Since losing some weight my stomach has shrunk and for the first time in ages I can see the top of my vagina. Only the pubic mound, but still, it's a start. I think I feel sexy after shedding some pounds. I'm livelier and I even laugh more. Helen has noticed it in work too and Sharon. She laughs over it saying I must be having plenty of sex to be smiling like that. I've not told them about Gary yet. I don't want to jinx it. Imagine me telling them all about my new back warmer and then he decides to leave me, I'd look a right dick-head wouldn't I? No, for now, he's my secret. Gary is on his way round to my house

The Pudding Club

as we speak, we're going to bingo tonight. I know that sounds boring to some of you but they have singers on tonight and you can get pissed on the cheap beer. I've never been lucky at bingo before, in fact, I've never won anything. It's the national tonight at the bingo hall and the kitty is predicted to be twenty- thousand pounds. I could do with that money if the truth was known. I just feel I've wasted my only chance of ever making it. Money doesn't grow on trees and I was foolish with the cash I had when I was younger. Well, the two birds have settled down now, they've been singing for hours. I liked it at first but after a while I covered them up with a tea towel. The little fuckers were doing my head in. I'm used to quiet, and if they think they can sing all night long when I'm watching my TV programmes they can think again. Joey always knew to be quiet when Coronation Street was on, if he made so much as a chirp he was covered up and left on his own until it was over. I hope these two budgies learn quickly, I'd hate to cover them up all the time.

I thought I would have cried more than I have already. I think I've dried up. My tear ducts are empty. I think you can only cry so much over a man then your brain reminds you that you should be moving on. I think it puts a block on the tears. I feel numb, I think. Well, let down, betrayed. How could she have done this to me? I wouldn't mind if it was just a drunken one-night stand but the bitch has been at it for years. I can never be friends with her again, never. Once the trust is gone between friends you may as well wave goodbye to them. Right, I better get ready for bingo, Gary will be here in a minute. I've not eaten yet, I've got no appetite.

Perhaps I'm becoming anorexic and don't know it. I look in the mirror and think I'm fat, so that's a sign isn't it? I've often thought about making myself vomit

The Pudding Club

after food but it just doesn't appeal to me. I did it once and I had a carrot stuck in the back of my throat for days. I coughed, and did everything to get rid of it but it wouldn't move. Eventually after a coughing fit I dislodged it. I will never stick my fingers down my throat again to be sick, it's not for me. My mobile phone is ringing, I bet it's Gary again, he's a right pest sometimes. He relays all his movements to me you know. "I'm at the shop Becks, I'm just at the traffic lights Becks," as if I need to know all that information. Gary is a bit insecure in our relationship. I think he thinks I'm going to leave him just like his own wife did. It's a shame really because when a relationship breaks down you're ruined for your next one. You don't love them unconditionally, you are always holding back aren't you? Rod Stewart got it right when he wrote the song 'First Cut is the Deepest' he must have been through heartbreak too. I answer my phone without checking the screen. Heart pounding inside my ribcage I realise it's Josh.

"What the hell are you phoning me for? If you carry on I'll phone the police and have you done for stalking, so do yourself a favour and fuck right off out of my life." I know I should have ended the call there but I needed him to know I knew all about his affair with Gemma and how long it had gone on. I waited until he'd finished speaking and popped a cigarette in the corner of my mouth. Lighting it and sucking hard on the tobacco I began to speak. "You and Gemma have been together for years. And, wank stain, I know all about the money you stole from Catherine too. What are you, some kind of weirdo? I'll tell you now Josh, if you come within an inch of me I'll stick a knife in you. I hate you."

The call ended and I was gasping for breath. This man just wound me up so much, he made my blood boil. I

The Pudding Club

wanted to hurt him and hurt him bad. Running up the stairs I ran into my bedroom and flung myself onto the bed. I wished I was invisible. I wished I was dead. Here it was, the emotion I'd stored, I knew it was too good to be true. I was crying like a baby, rocking to and fro with my knees up to my chest. My life was in ruins and I couldn't see any light at the end of the tunnel. Lifting my head up to the ceiling I spoke to my deceased father. "Dad, if you're listening, please help me. I don't know where to turn or what to do for the best. My head's in bits please help me." I stared at the ceiling for a few seconds hoping there might be some kind of reply but nothing, silence. A small white fluffy feather was floating in front of my face and I snatched it out of the air. People have always told me that if you see a feather floating near you it's a spirit from heaven. This was a message from my father for sure, he was listening and he hadn't given up on me. Blowing my breath into the white feather I felt a warm rush pass over my body. I carefully tucked the feather inside my bra. As long as it was with me I knew my father was by my side.

The letterbox is rapping, bloody hell who's knocking like I owe them money or something. Peeping from behind the curtain I see its Gary. I'm thinking twice about letting him in. I'm in no condition to have company. Oh, for crying out loud, he's seen me now. Heading down the stairs I try and wipe away my tears. I don't want him to see me like this, but I have no choice. Slowly I open the door and he can tell straight away I've been upset.

"Becks, what's the matter? Are you okay?"

I take a deep breath and shake my head slowly. I had to tell someone what was going on. I need support and someone to tell me everything was going to be fine. "It's Gemma, she's been having a affair with Josh for years,

The Pudding Club

not just once like I first thought, Catherine's told me all about it."

Gary guided me into the front room and held my hand tightly. Stroking my fingers slowly he spoke. "I'll bang the kettle on; a cup of tea is always a good cure for shock." I never answered him I just sat blubbering in the chair. Olivia and John just sat looking at me. I bet they wish they were back in the pet store away from all this misery. "There you go petal, a nice cup of tea for you. And look, some chocolate biscuits, you're favourites."

Food, yes that was just what I needed. It always made me feel better and stronger. Ripping the packet open with force, I sank a biscuit into my mouth it didn't even touch the sides. Gary tried to make conversation with me but my mind was on the biscuits in front of me. I was devouring them at speed. Why am I such a greedy bitch? I work my arse off all week trying to lose weight and one bit of trauma in my life and I'm like a pig in a fit filling my fat face. Gary doesn't mind me eating; he says he likes to see a woman eat. I bet he never expected to see a woman eat like I do. I'm like a Viking, a big fat overweight Viking.

I feel calmer now and my eyes have dried. It's amazing what a bit of comfort food does. Now, to face life again. Gary is smiling at me. He doesn't know how to cope with me I think. Men aren't that good at comforting crying women are they. Whenever I was upset in the past Josh used to snarl at me. "Sort it out, you emotional wreck". I could never understand why he treated me like that. I did ask him once and he told me as a child he was brought up to believe that tears were a sign of weakness. His parents were very military minded with him and I know he's not telling me everything about his childhood, something just doesn't fit. No cuddles, no kisses as a child what kind

The Pudding Club

of an upbringing is that? My father always showed us affection. Every time he came home from work he would always give us a kiss on the cheek. I'd give everything I owned at this moment for one of them kisses. Gary is rummaging in his pocket, he brings out two large pens.

"Check out our dabbers for bingo. You just stamp it on the number. I got you a pink one."

I smiled and looked at him. Did he want some kind of reaction from me? This was a pen not a bleeding diamond ring. See what I mean about me, that bastard Josh has turned me into such a selfish cow. I was never like this I always helped others and I loved the feeling I got from it too. I think life has drained me. All the love I had in my heart has been drained from me, like a steel sink being emptied from water going down the drain. I don't want to be unhappy anymore. I want to be one of those women who is always laughing and joking and taking life by the balls and not giving a dam. I take the pen from Gary and the corners of my mouth start to rise. I'm trying to smile but it's hard. The doctor gave me some antidepressants but they didn't do anything for me. In fact I was suicidal on them. They messed with my head and I didn't know if I was bleeding coming or going. Right, deep breaths, shoes on, I'm not letting this get the better of me. I'm going to bingo and I'm going to do my best to have a good night.

The bingo hall is packed out. It's like the blue rinse brigade in here. I feel like a spring chicken compared to some of these fossils. I think I'm the only one with my own teeth. Right, let's find somewhere to sit. The coffin dodgers are growling at me. They don't like new meat in the building. You can just tell some of these people have been coming here for years. They've got good luck symbols where they're sat and they are guarding them with dear life. I've brought my feather along, just for a

The Pudding Club

bit of luck too. Why not? Everyone else believes in good luck charms so I've brought mine along, just so I'm on an even keel with them. I can see two seats at the far side of the room.

"Gary, come on, let's get over there before the seats go."

Bloody hell, it's a struggle to move in this place. I can see an older woman eyeing up the seats too. I pick up speed and shoulder charge through some people stood near me. I'm nearly there. Victory, we have seats. I turn my head slowly and smirk at the pensioner. I know I shouldn't have but it's usually me who's the one who goes without. I've got three bingo cards in front of me and one national card. I've already decided that if I win the big one I'm having a gastric-band fitted. I know its extreme, but if it's good enough for Gemma Morley it's good enough for me. Tits, I'm having some nice boobs too. Round and firm perky ones. I've seen a few operations on the TV about breast reductions and they actually take your nipple off and sew it back on again in a new position. After watching it on the TV I went to bed and dreamt about it, it was a nightmare. I dreamt the doctor lost my nipple and sewed a button on instead. A big black button it was with six holes around the edges. I was scared of any kind of surgery after that and always said I would never go under the knife. Well, until now. Beauty is pain and I will do whatever it takes to have a half decent body. I don't want a bikini body, just a normal body that's not full of blubber and cellulite. The bingo caller starts the game and you can hear a pin drop. There is a slight noise behind me but that's the pensioner struggling to breathe. She's annoying me and I'm finding it difficult not to say something.

I'm alive inside as I wait for the number seven to be called. I whisper over to Gary. "I only need the number seven to win the line." He pats my hand and dips his head back into his bingo card. My heart is racing, the adrenalin is pumping. My palms are sweating and my mouth is dry. A loud voice from the other side of the room shouts out in a shrieking voice. "House," everyone's stretching their necks to see who the lucky winner is. I'm gutted, the old hag has won two hundred pounds for the line. The woman is about eighty-six. What on earth is she going to spend the money on, she could be dead tomorrow. She looks like one of them women who will go home and hide the money under her mattress. My mother used to do that too you know, it must be an old person thing. I mean, the only thing you'd find under my mattress is toffee wrappers and the odd piece of mouldy toast.

Gary goes to the bar and comes back with our drinks. I'm gagging and nearly neck all the vodka in one big gulp, my nerves are on edge. The night is going well so far and everyone's waiting for the big game to begin. Bingo is on a break for half an hour and the tribute act comes on to pass some time. Well, fuck a duck, it's a Grease tribute act. Now we're talking. My mood is lifted instantly and my hips are swinging. Let the party begin. "You're the One That I want," is being played. I'm singing in a loud voice like a strangled cat. People are looking at me and growling. What's to do with this lot, don't they know how to let their hair down? Gary is singing too, he actually loves the song and we make a great duo. The miserable old gets around me are looking at me with disgust. If I was singing a bit of Vera Lynn they wouldn't mind would they? It's just because they don't know the words to the song that's all. I smile at them and carry on singing there's no way they are stealing my thunder. I've drank nearly eight shots of vodka now and it's fair to say I'm pissed as a fart. I can still see straight though so that's a good thing. Once my eyesight goes I know not to drink anymore

The Pudding Club

alcohol. The band was brilliant and just what I needed to cheer me up.

All the old codgers are getting back to their seats now before the last game starts. It's funny to watch them on their Zimmer frames. The bingo caller is excited as he announces the amount in the kitty for the next full house. It was twenty thousand pounds. The crowd is excited and they are all waiting eagerly for the game to begin. My eyes are concentrating on my bingo card. I can hear the old woman speaking behind me. Every number she gets she feels the need to let the whole table know. She's doing my head in and if she's not quiet I'm going to ram her bingo card right up her old wrinkly arse. It's sad being old isn't it? Hair that's white as snow, no teeth, and legs that don't work anymore. I want shooting at the age of fifty-five, I've already decided that. What's the point of living when you're washed out and ready for the knackers yard? I know there are some fit healthy pensioners about, but most of them are miserable and angry. When I'm working in the doctor's surgery the blue rinse brigade are always moaning about one thing or the other. Mabel Wilson is one of the patients there and she moans to me every time she comes in. I know everything that a person could know about her piles and her bowel movements and any other ailments she might have. I'm sure she just makes up her sicknesses just so she can come into the surgery. Older people like company too, they never shut up talking. I wouldn't mind if it was interesting but it's about the price of bread or the bleeding weather. Mabel's favourite subject is death. She feels the need to tell me about everyone who's passed away recently. She talks to me as if I know them too. I'm sure she's goes to more funerals than the funeral directors do. Every time you see her she's dressed in black and she has a sympathy card in her bag. No, I never want to end up like Mabel. I'll be quite happy to pass away before I end up like her.

I've never really thought of my own death before. I wonder who would miss me? I don't even think many people would turn up for my funeral. It's sad that I never had any children. At least then they would have mourned my death. The only person I have is my mother, but she's on her last legs. And my brother too I suppose, but he's in another country now living the high life with his posh tart. Five years younger than him she is. I think she's a gold digger too. I mean, she only started to take an interest in him when he got his inheritance. He treats her like a princess too. Nothing is too much trouble for him. What she wants, she gets. I wish I had someone like that who loved me as deeply as he loves her. I'm jealous of people in love. I crave it so much but it just turns its back on me as if I don't exist. I wonder if anyone will ever love me again? I'm not a bad person really and I do have a heart of gold. It's just the trust issue now I think, how could I ever trust another man with my heart? My heart is cold and I have to face that fact, I will never feel love in it again. Look at me now, getting all emotional. It's the vodka that, one too many and I'm an emotional wreck. Right, pull yourself together Becks, the game's about to start.

Eyes down, everyone is concentrating, me included. Gary hasn't uttered a word since it started. Everyone's eager to net the fortune. I've only got three numbers left. I hope nobody shouts house before me because I need this money more than them. Gary is tapping his pen on his front teeth; he must be near to winning too. He always does this when he's nervous. Heart beating now one number left for a full house. Whispering behind me tells me I'm not alone in my quest to win the game. Number eight is my lucky number too, come on bingo caller dig deep for my ball. Two more numbers pass, neither of them are mine. I should just rip my bingo card up and throw it into the air. I've never had any luck, why should it change now? Sneaking my hand down the top of my blouse I tickle the edge of my lucky feather. The bingo caller shouts out the next number. "One fat lady number eight." Mouth dry, throat dry, I'm wriggling about. Standing to my feet I shout out from the pit of my stomach. "A bleeding full house. Come to mamma."

There's moaning from the other tables. A look of disapproval from the coffin-dodgers. My face is beetroot as my card is checked. Gary is by my side and he's checking the numbers too. Rebecca Rooks is a rich woman, it's official. I have only gone and won the bleeding national. The place is alive and the atmosphere is electric as I walk to the front of the stage to collect my winnings. Even a few of the oldies are clapping now they've got over the initial shock of somebody else winning. This is a dream come true for me, a second chance at life again. The bingo caller hands over the cheque and lights are flashing in my face from the press. Gary runs to my side and speaks. "I can't believe we won." I look at him and I'm not sure what he means, surely I've won and the money belongs to me. Gary grabs the microphone from the host and speaks to the crowd.

"We are so happy with our win. I'm going to buy a new car and treat myself to a good holiday," he chuckles. What the fuck was going on here? I was the one who won the game. I needed to make things clear to him before this got out of hand. "Gary, it's me who won, not you." He quickly turned his head to me and giggled. I think he thought I was joking.

"It's the rule of bingo Becks, you always share with your bingo partner."

The Pudding Club

I was embarrassed; nobody had ever mentioned this to me before. The two old dears sat near the stage giggled and spoke to us. "Me and Ethel have been coming to bingo for over twenty years and we always share no matter how much the money is. It gives you two chances of winning instead of one doesn't it?"

I felt a fool. I was being selfish. It was just that I thought I could do so many things with the money I'd won. I touched Gary's shoulder who by this time was quite nervous and smiled. "Of course we can share. I would rather have half of something than all of nothing."

You could see the relief in his face; he started to breathe normal again. "Bloody hell you had me going then love, I thought you were bailing on me."

I smiled and shook my head. "Would I do something like that? Come on you're talking to me now." Gary bought my story and believed I was sharing from the start. Even though I've still got ten thousand pound I still feel the whole amount should have been mine. I'm not greedy, don't think that for one minute, but once I've paid for my gastric band and my new breasts I'm barely going to have enough money left for anything else. The photos are still being taken and my face is aching now from smiling. Gary is all over me like a rash and you can tell he doesn't trust me. He keeps mentioning the money to check he's still on a share of it. I wouldn't do that to him anyway. He's never hurt a bone in my body, and I will share the prize money with him no matter what.

I'm pissed now and my eyes are blurred. Gary is still at my home and he's as drunk as me. Olivia and John are jumping about on their perch and they seem to be happy for me. Gary is sprawled all over the sofa. We tried to have some sex but his penis is like a coiled snake, there's no life in that baby tonight, let me tell you. I could have done

The Pudding Club

with a good old leg-over too. Sex just helps me to relax. Gary is falling asleep and I can't be bothered telling him to go home. He can sleep on the sofa, I'm off to bed.

Well, what a day today has been. It's been like a prostitute's knickers. One minute I've been up and the next I've been down. They say money can't buy happiness, but I think they've got that wrong. Money does talk and everybody craves it. Especially Josh Thompson, he's ruled by it. Now is my time to wipe that smile right from his face. Let the games begin. My eyes are closing slowly and I don't even need my usual chocolate bar to munch on tonight. I'm content and drift off to sleep with no problems.

FOURTEEN

EYES OPEN AND THE SUNLIGHT BEAMING through my bedroom window. It's a glorious day outside and I feel good. I no longer have to roll on my side to get out of bed and I can sit up now without a struggle. What a great day. My surgery is booked for tomorrow and I'm nervous, in fact I'm shaking like a shitting dog. I've thought about cancelling the appointment but I'd only regret it in the future. I'm like that; one minute I'm all up for it and then fear takes over me and I regret the choices I've made. I've been pulling at my breasts all day just to see what they would look like. That's what the surgeon did and I must admit they looked incredible. Round, firm and perky just like I'd imagined them to be. I've used Sellotape to keep them in place. I still have the fear that they would lose my nipple during surgery though so I've put two buttons in my pocket just in case. Beige coloured they are to match my skin tone. I always have a plan B when it comes to stuff like this.

Gemma has sent me a letter and she wants to meet me today. I was going to ignore her but I'm intrigued as what she has to say. After all, she's the one in the wrong not me and it would be nice to see her grovel and beg for forgiveness. Josh has heard about my windfall too, he must have, it's been all over the local newspapers. I've told him I want to speak to him soon too, not straight away he can wait until I'm ready. I have plans for him, big plans and I have to pretend its all rosy in the garden to get him where I want him. I've not heard a lot from Gary since I gave him his share of the winnings. I'm sure he's gone back grovelling to his wife. He never stopped loving her if I'm being true to myself, and who am I to tell him what to do with his life. He was only a back warmer anyway, a fuck buddy wasn't he? Oh well, life goes on doesn't it, and I'm not holding any grudges against him we both served a purpose for each other. And, I suppose he did introduce me to tea-bagging, so it's all good isn't it? It was just some fun.

I need to get everything prepared for my stay in the hospital. I've arranged with my neighbour to look after my house. Olivia and John don't need much looking after anyway but it will be nice for them to see a human walking about the place until I get back home. I know I shouldn't have but I've had a full English breakfast this morning, last chance saloon I call it. Once my gastric band is fitted I won't be eating food like this again, so it's kind of a goodbye meal. I wonder if I will survive the operation. It's just my luck to die under the knife. My mother thinks I'm going to a health spa for the weekend. She'd have kittens if she knew the truth. I can hear her now, "Oh, don't mess with your body, Rebecca. If God wanted you to have a perfect body he would have given it to you. You're dicing with death having surgery. I've seen on TV what can happen when it all goes wrong." My mother is so negative and she'd never agree with anything modern, she's so set in her ways and hates change. Even fashion, she's worn the same kind of dress for years, even her hairstyle, nothing ever changes. I can't wait to wear fashionable clothes, skinny jeans, low cut tops and even a bikini. I'm going to flaunt my body once my surgery is done. And, why not, I paid for it?

Right, I better get my arse into gear. I'm meeting Spencer at my mother's today before I go and see Gemma. Spencer has brought his new woman home to meet us all. I can see it now; he's a right pussy when it comes to women. My brother used to be so down to earth and you could have a laugh with him, but since he moved away he thinks he's above everyone, he's a toffee-nosed arse-hole who thinks the sun shines out of his arse. Well, he's not getting away with it today. I'm going to put him in his place and tell him how it is. For years I've listened to his verbal abuse and now I'm putting my foot down. Spencer hates the fact that he had a fat sister. He was embarrassed about me and whenever he brought his mates back to my mother's house he always made sure I was out of the way. He didn't hide the fact either, he blatantly told me to go up into my room until they were gone. I did venture downstairs once or twice when all his friends were there but as soon as they saw me they all joined in the name calling. Pie eater, porky, lard arse, were just a few of the names they had for me. I learned from an early age how to cope with this. I put a big smile on my face and ignored it. Once I was alone though I binged on food and anything that was bad for me. Twelve doughnuts I ate one day after Spencer's friends had put me down yet again. And, it didn't stop there, one packet of chocolate digestives and five bags of crisps, all washed down with a litre of coca-cola. I felt better after eating it and just brushed the comments off as if I didn't care.

Food is a soother for some people and I think it's the way my parents brought me up. You're not born fat are you? So, I've come to the conclusion it must be something that my parents did when I was growing up. I've asked my mother about this and she denies all knowledge of overfeeding me. But I know she's lying. I've heard her telling her friends she used to put extra rusk into my bottle so I would sleep longer, so there is some evidence. Every time I was upset as a kid my mother was

The Pudding Club

always passing me food. If I close my eyes now I can see her. "Here, Rebecca eat this cake and you will feel better. It's just a scratch on your knee; you're not going to die." She was right I did feel better after eating food but the relationship I had with it was not healthy. If I watched a sad film on TV and a few tears fell my mother used to pass the sweets over to me. "Stop crying and get a sweet, it will help take the tears away." I can't really blame my parents for my obese body can I? I have to be accountable for my own actions. It's not like I'm a kid anymore is it? And nobody has been forcing me to eat junk food for years, that's been all my own doing. I wonder if I will ever get over my addiction to food. People say you swap one addiction for another. God help me if that's the case I'll probably end up a sex addict. I like sex, well, in my day I did. I was never shy in the bedroom and even though I was fat I always made sure I had fun. Josh loved my large round body, he used to call me names but in a fun kind of way and I never seemed to mind. He said big birds were sexy and they turned him on. He definitely had a fetish for the fuller figured woman. I wonder what he will do when he sees me thin again with big tits and a skinny waistline? His face is going to be priceless. I know exactly what I'm going to wear when I first see him too. Yes, it's already in the pipeline.

My mother is sat blazing another cigarette, she smokes like a trooper. She's on at least thirty fags a day now. She's near the backdoor and the wind is circling inside the kitchen. "Bloody hell mother, close that door will you, it's freezing in here."

My mother looked at me and she is distressed. "No, just leave it open for a bit to get the smoke out. Our Spencer will be here in a minute and I don't want the house stinking of smoke. He's got Rita with him and I don't want him upset."

I walked to the backdoor and banged it firmly shut. "Listen, let's get one thing sorted before he comes. We are who we are and if he doesn't like it he can do one. We're not pretending to be people we're not. If you want to smoke, well smoke, it's your house not his."

My mother shook her head and blew a great big cloud of grey smoke through her mouth. "Don't you start Rebecca, it's been months since I've seen my son and I don't want you and your big mouth spoiling it for me. Spencer wants to impress this woman, so just be nice for a change."

Someone was knocking at the front door. The letterbox was rapping with speed. My mother was a nervous wreck and wafted the smoke from around her face. "Quick, spray some air freshener, that will be our Spencer and Rita." There was no way I was budging, I just picked up the newspaper from the table and started to read it. I can hear Spencer talking in the hallway. Bleeding hell, my mam is putting her posh voice on. She only does that when she thinks she talking to someone who's important, she never uses it for me. So, here he is - the prodigal son returning home. I can feel his stare and lift my head up from the newspaper. He's smiling for a change and he's not thrown an insult yet. Rita now joins him and I have to admit, she is a beauty. I've seen more fat on a chip but she is gorgeous.

"Rebecca you've lost weight," he says. I watch him carefully and wait for the abuse to start, but nothing. I'm on my guard but thank him. "So everyone, this is Rita," he announces. Did he want us to bow to her or curtsy? He was waiting on some kind of reaction from us, but I wasn't moving I just smiled at her. Mother is running around the front room now, she's like a blue-arsed fly. She

The Pudding Club

can't do enough for this woman. You can tell by her face she's stressed, her cheeks are blood red and she looks like she is going to burst.

"Rebecca, go and make Rita a cup of tea," she shouts over to me. I snarl at her and she could see I wasn't happy. I never brew up and I didn't see why I should have to start now.

"Oh, I don't drink tea Mary, but if you have any green tea that would be fantastic," she said in a sweet low voice.

Fucking green tea! Where did this woman think she was, in the bleeding Hilton? My mother had never heard of it and looked at me with a blank expression.

"We have PG tips, is that like green tea?"

I wanted to burst out laughing but held it well. I opened my mouth to speak and there it was too, my posh voice. "No, mother it's not. Rita, my mother doesn't even know what it is, she's drank the same kind of tea for years and she'd never dream of drinking anything else, even if it was buy one get one free."

Spencer stood playing with his fingers. This wasn't good and his aim to impress this woman just wasn't working. "I'll nip to the corner shop Rita don't worry. Anyway it will give you a bit of time to have a chat with my family whilst I'm gone. Ay Rebecca, don't you be telling her all my dirty secrets." He let out a false laugh and left the room. He was such a plonker and I wanted to reveal him for the dick-head he really was.

"Don't worry Spencer your secrets are safe with me," I shouted after him. There was a silence now and we all looked at each other and smiled. There was no way I was making any conversation I wasn't in the mood plus I had my own problems to think about. My mother was still talking in her posh voice. It was so funny to listen to. Rita had a soft voice and it was strange to listen to her

The Pudding Club

American accent.

"What are the men like in the USA?" I asked in an excited voice. Rita looked at me as if I was a nutter and flicked her chestnut coloured hair over her shoulder.

"The men are okay, but not a patch on English men. Spencer just swept me off my feet when I first met him and I've been smitten ever since." Just what I needed to hear. Another bleeding love story about the happy ending I always dreamt off. Why the hell do I put myself through this? Everyone seems to have a happy ending except me. I just think I'm destined to be alone for the rest of my life. Suddenly there was a text alert on my phone. Reaching into my handbag I read the message quickly as I listened to Rita talk about how much she loves my brother. It's a message from Gemma asking if we can meet earlier. I suppose I could if I wanted, plus it would give me an excuse to leave my mother and Rita and their boring conversation. It's only a matter of minutes anyway before my mam gets the family photo album out. That's all I need, Rita commenting on my obese body as a child.

"Mam, Rita, I'm sorry but I'm going to have to leave. Something has come up that can't wait."

Mother's face is on fire, she knows I'm just making excuses. "Can't it wait Rebecca? I mean, Rita has come a long way to meet us both so it would be nice for her to get to know you while she's here."

No eye contact whatsoever I stood up and grabbed my jacket. "I wish I could stay but my friend is in desperate need. I'll try and get back as soon as possible." Rita didn't seem to mind it was just my mother, you could see it in her eyes that she wanted to start shouting. A quick kiss on her cheek and I left the room.

"Nice meeting you Rita. I hope I get the chance to see you again before you leave. Got to rush, see you

The Pudding Club

later mam." I left the room before she could reply, I was smirking and loved the fact that I'd been saved from hours of boredom. Getting into the car I texted Gemma back and told her I was on my way. Music blaring I pulled out from the street and headed to meet the mistress of my ex-husband.

Gemma was sat waiting when I arrived. She's piled the pounds on and she was a shadow of her former self. Fat, round and spotty. I walked into the coffee shop and ordered my drink. I could feel Gemma's eyes on me and I knew she would be looking at my new slimmer backside. I clenched my bum-cheeks together and sucked my stomach in. Once I had my drink I walked slowly to where she sat. There were lots of other customers in the shop and I wasn't going to make a scene. I was keeping my cool and ready to listen what she had to say. Placing my cup down on the table I began.

"Right, make it quick I haven't got all day. I have a life to lead you know?"

Gemma swallowed hard and you could see tiny balls of sweat forming on her brow. "Rebecca, I've had a long time to think about this and it's killing me inside. We're best friends." I wasn't listening to this shit and stopped her dead in her tracks.

"Were best friends Gemma, get it right."

She knew by my face that this wasn't going to be easy. And, hats off to the girl she was doing her best to patch things up. "It was Josh who did all the running. I swear to you that it was him. I turned him away so many times and he just kept coming back begging me to see him."

I was listening to her every word, my stomach was churning and I felt sick inside. "You were my best friend Gemma, why didn't you tell me? You knew how much I loved him, why didn't you just give me a clue that the

The Pudding Club

man was a bastard because I would have done it, if it had been Alex coming onto me."

I thought about what I'd just said and realised that I should practice what I preached. Gemma's husband had come onto me in the past and I'd kept my mouth shut too. Was I as bad as her now? Looking her straight in the eye I unveiled truths about her own husband. Once I'd told her it was a whole different ball game, she was livid.

"So, you're telling me my Alex wanted sex with you?" I sat up straight and loved the blow I was about to deliver. "Yes"

Gemma shook her head and got on her high horse. "How can you preach to me when you've kept this secret from me too. I don't believe it Rebecca, you have double standards."

Now she was winding me up and I wanted to scratch her eyeballs out. "I kept my knickers on love not like you. I told Alex no, just like you should have told Josh no, but you never did you? You just went ahead and dropped your knickers for my husband. You're a slut, no other word can describe you." I could feel my temper rising and out of the corner of my eye a few of the customers were whispering to each other. I took a few deep breaths and spoke in a low calm voice. "We can never be friends again Gemma, that's just the way it is. I don't trust you anymore and I've lost all respect for you as a friend. Don't worry about me telling your husband your secret because I wouldn't do that to him. He's a good man and you don't deserve him. Perhaps," I sniggered, "I should sleep with Alex and we would be equal. How does that sound to you?"

Gemma was biting her tongue and you could see she was ready for snapping. I was pushing all her buttons in the hope that she would start shouting and make a fool of herself but she remained quiet. "Gemma, please don't ever try and contact me again. I want you out of my life for good. You and Josh, you both deserve each other if you ask me. I'm getting on with my life now, so you do the same. Nothing has changed since we last met and I'll be honest with you, I just feel like ripping your hair out every time I look at you, so it's for the best."

Gemma wiped the tears away that were rolling down her face. She was genuinely upset, but I had no forgiveness in my heart for this woman. Looking closely at her fat fingers I chuckled to myself. Gemma was piling the weight back on like nobody's business and for me that was justice. I knew she hated being fat and to lose all the timber she'd put on in the last few months wasn't going to happen overnight. That was enough for me, the score was settled. Standing up from my seat I picked my coat up. Gemma was looking at me with such sad eyes and I nearly told her that we could be friends again but something inside me made me stop.

"Can you rethink about us being friends Rebecca, We've been so close for years, what am I going to do without you in my life?" I turned my head slowly towards her and paused as I prepared my words.

"Eat Gemma, just eat. Because that's what I did when somebody in my life betrayed me. Eat and enjoy." I could hear her sobbing as I walked away from her. Not once did I turn back and look at her. My heart was so cold these days and I wasn't going to be a pushover any more. Rebecca Rooks was finally standing on her own two feet.

★

Sat in my white gown I prepared to go down for surgery. My heart was racing and I needed to calm down before I gave myself a coronary. I'd already been given the pre-med and slowly but surely I was calming down. I was feeling mellow as I lay back on the hospital bed and nothing seemed to matter to me anymore. I was in a place that was peaceful and nobody could hurt me. I can hear the voice at the side of me asking me to count to ten. "One, two, three," eyes shut.

I feel sore and heavy. Eyes opening slowly I start to panic. "Where are my nipples?" I scream at the top of my voice. "I've got two buttons here if you need them?"

The nurse comes to my side and strokes my hand slowly. "Rebecca, just calm down. You're back from surgery and everything went well."

My hands immediately touch my breast. These babies feel firm and perky just like I imagined. I'm still too dizzy to see them properly. My eyes won't keep open, they're so heavy. I need sleep.

Well look at the super sexy breasts sticking out in front of me. No spaniel's ears anymore, just perfect breasts. I'm overjoyed with the results. They are still sore and I have to wear a special bra for six weeks but I'm sure the pain will pass. My waistline seems smaller too. The gastric band is now in place and eating any large amounts of food is impossible, trust me I know. I tried eating a sandwich earlier and it just got stuck in my throat. I was gagging and thought my days were up but it dislodged itself after a few minutes. The doctor has given me a diet to follow and I'm on my third week of it. I do miss food if I'm being honest and it's a big void in my life. I've cried a few times too, I don't know why but I just broke down and sobbed my heart out. I'm going back in work today, it's been over a month since the girls have seen me and I think they will get a shock when they see me for the first time. I've told Sharon where I have been, but just her. The surgery where I work just think I'm suffering with

The Pudding Club

depression and allowed me some time off to sort myself out.

It will be nice to see the girls again. I've missed them all. Well, not Helen, but I suppose I may have missed her a bit. I've changed my hair colour too. I'm now ash blonde again. The colour change makes me feel sexy and alive just like it did when I was younger. I think I look like Olivia Newton-John, well, when I've lost another couple of stone anyway. It's my birthday soon and I'm planning a big party. The theme of it is Grease so I will get to wear them black Lycra pants I've always dreamt of wearing.

I've invited Josh too, yes, I know I need my head feeling but it's time to lay this problem to bed and I feel strong enough inside so I should be able to face it all. Josh has been ringing me constantly and I have spoken to him for hours throughout the night. I needed to. I just wanted to know why he treated me like he did. I think he's regretting losing me, he told me he'd never love anyone like he loved me and I think I believe him. I know he thinks I've still got some money left from my winnings and that might be the reason he's hanging onto me. He's going to come to earth with a bang when he knows I've spent the lot of it isn't he? I was cunning when I asked him to borrow me some money until my cheque had cleared and he keeps asking for it back. It was only five thousand pound, but it makes me smile to know I got some of my inheritance back. He'll go ballistic when he knows I've had him over, but ay, does this face look like it gives a fuck. An eye for an eye I always say. Josh thinks I've got the money to give him back and I've told him when he comes to my party he can have back what is owed... He got a loan to borrow me the money you know, that's how desperate he was to get back in my life. Revenge is sweet and I want nothing more than to break this man in half when I tell him the truth. How have I become this ruthless bitch? I was never like this before. I was always so laid-back and understanding. I don't like the person I'm becoming but I don't seem to have any control of her anymore. Olivia and John are bouncing about on the bottom of the cage. I think they are in love. They're always huddled together now and pecking at each other's feathers. I'm jealous and actually thought about getting rid of them both. I will see how I go though; it's pretty tight just carting them because they are in love.

Oh, guess what? Gary rang me last night too. Apparently he's been mixed up and needed to sort his life out before he could see me again. He's a lying fucker and he thinks I'm daft. I know exactly where he's been and what he's been doing. I'm going to wait until I'm face to face with him and tell him I know. See what I mean about the person I've become, I'm an out and out bitch.

The office is quiet as I walk inside. Helen sees me first and her jaw drops. "Oh my God Rebecca, you look bleeding fantastic, what the hell has happened to you?" I raised a smile and tried to keep a straight face.

Sharon was now in view and she winked at me. "I've just been looking after myself Helen. I think the break did me good. I feel like me again, so you won't be worried about me anymore."

"What diet have you been on because the weight has just dropped off you?" I should have told her the 'fucked up life' diet but I held my tongue and lied.

"It's the cabbage diet. I've tried it before ages ago and thought I would give it another go. It's really good and I don't feel hungry one little bit."

The girls in the office were jotting the name of the diet down and googling it on the internet. Little did they know that my gastric band was the only reason I was

The Pudding Club

shedding the pounds. My eating habits had changed so much in last few weeks. I was gutted I had the band fitted now because all the nice food I craved was just a distant memory. I couldn't swallow anything properly. I had to be careful when I was eating too because when the girls saw me gagging after trying to eat food they would put two and two together and realised I was lying about my new diet and that the band was the only reason I was shedding the blubber.

Dr Weston rang me and now I have to take some files down to his office. I can't wait to see his face when he casts his eyes on me for the first time. I'm hoping his penis bursts out of his trousers and he drags me onto his desk and makes mad passionate love to me. I've often fantasized about that you know? Call me a filthy mare, but it's true. He just excites me so much and I would love just once to have some fun with the man of my dreams. Dr Weston is single and so am I. So it wouldn't be any skin from his nose to slip me one would it? I would respect his privacy too, no one would ever know. The circle of trust would never be broken. As I walk down the corridor I roll my skirt up a few times above my waist, it's a lot shorter than it was but ay, I have to try and impress. Breasts pushed out in front of me, my cleavage is showing. Opening the door slowly I can see him sat at his desk. He doesn't even look at me.

"Just put the paperwork on my desk Rebecca," he said in his husky sexy voice. My heart was pounding inside my chest. I had to get him to look at me, I coughed loudly. Dr Weston turned his head and he was gobsmacked. "Erm, wow, is that really you Rebecca?"

I wanted to rip my knickers off and jump onto his lap. I had to calm myself down. "Yes doctor it sure is. It's about time I started to look after myself isn't it?" I could

The Pudding Club

see his hand disappear under his desk and I could see him tweaking the end of his penis. He was still looking at me, drooling.

"You look absolutely amazing. I can't believe how much you have changed. Even your hair colour has changed too?" He'd actually noticed me in the past so this was a breakthrough. I smirked at him and licked my lips slowly. Oh I was working it now and he knew I was hot.

"I got sick of being boring and they do say blondes have more fun don't they, so I'm just waiting to sample some of that too."

He chuckled loudly and tapped the end of his pen on his front teeth. "I know we are work colleagues Rebecca, but if you want I'd like to take you out for a few drinks. We can celebrate the new you."

My face was on fire, I was beetroot. I never expected this in a million years. I wanted it, God knows I wanted it, but now it had come down to the crunch I was crapping my knickers. He was looking at me waiting for an answer. Why the hell had my mouth dried up, I couldn't speak? Swallowing hard I tried to keep calm and relaxed. I didn't want to seem desperate. "That would be great; I'll call back in your office later and give you my phone number."

Brian smiled and nodded his head. I'm sure he was undressing me with his eyes. He had sex written all over his face. "That's great, I look forward to it," he replied. Well, fuck a duck this was amazing news. I left the room and tried to keep my composure. I wanted to run and shout out my news to everyone who was there, Rebecca Rooks had a hot date it was official.

I walked back into the main office and Sharon clocked the smirk on my face straight away. "What are you smiling at?"

I ran to her side and sat down next to her. Helen

was on the warpath and I had to be careful she didn't overhear our conversation. She could be a right pain in the arse sometimes, and if she got a whiff of this gossip she would have thrown a spanner in the works for sure. Helen was mad for Dr Weston and for months she'd been throwing herself at him with no effect, even though she was a married woman. "I'm going on a date with Brian," I sniggered.

Sharon covered her mouth with her hand and made sure no one was listening. "How on earth has this happened? Did you ask him out, or did he ask you?"

I sat proud in my seat and flicked the invisible dust from my black skirt. "He asked me, I swear to you, I was just stood there and his eyes were all over me. He was gagging for it Sharon." Both of us sat giggling like two teenagers.

Helen turned her head and growled at us. She was a right miserable swine and it was very rare that she would have a laugh in work's time. She wasn't always like this, no, before she was just an office worker like us but once she got her promotion she changed. She's so far up her own arse she can see her own tonsils. All the girls think she changed too but none of them will ever tell her to her face, except me. I told her once when we were all sat in a meeting how horrible she was and she nearly dropped down dead. After that she made my life a misery for ages so nobody ever challenged her again. I think she has personal problems at home. Do you know when you can just tell something is not right with a person? She's had the odd bruise on her arm too and a swollen lip but she always says she fell or she banged into something. I don't believe her story for one minute. I've heard the conversation she has on the phone with her partner and you can tell by the tone of her voice that she's shit scared

The Pudding Club

of him. I've met her husband a few times when he's come to pick Helen up from work, he's a right womaniser. His eyes were all over me and the other girls. In fact, rumour has it that he passed his number to Nancy, a woman who works in the office with us. Helen's husband is a big tall man, good looking too. He looks like he works out at the gym because his biceps were bulging underneath his tight grey t-shirt. I definitely think he's raised his hand to his wife in the past, not that she would ever admit it.

I suffered a bit of domestic violence too from Josh, mine was more mental than physical though. He did raise his hand to me on a few occasions but he only slapped me twice. Josh was much too clever to ever leave signs that he was a control freak; he messed with my mind so nobody could ever see the scars. He knew his game well. Love does make you blind though and for some reason you can't see the situation you're in until it's too late. My scars are deep in my mind and I'll never forgive Josh for the way he treated me. My hairs are stood on end now, just the thought of ever being with him again makes me feel sick inside. I used to crave him every day when he first left but slowly but surely he's left my mind for good. Teresa my therapist said I've made great progress with my sessions and she hopes after a few more talks we can say goodbye to each other. I think at one point she was seriously thinking about having me sectioned or put in a straight jacket. I do admit I was temporarily insane, but come on, wouldn't you be if you were in my shoes?

I tried to end my life once too. I've never told anyone not even my counsellor. Everything was planned and my 'goodbye cruel world' letter was written. When I went shopping that evening I put four packets of paracetamol in my shopping trolley. An overdose was the way I was planning to do myself in. I remember the cashier's face as

The Pudding Club

she picked the tablets up to scan them, she was alarmed and looked at me with a concerned face.

"I'm sorry love, you can only purchase two packets of tablets at any one time." I looked at her and tried to keep a straight face.

"Are you being serious or what?"

The lady confirmed the store's policy and she was smiling to herself as she whispered to me. "Some people just buy loads of painkillers from here and they top themselves with them. That's why there is a limit on what you can buy." I didn't know where to look. I was one of the people she was talking about. I chuckled and replied to her, there was no way I was admitting I was a non-coper.

"Oh, so I suppose I'll have to cancel my suicide now until I can get some more tablets. Damn blast, I've planned my death as well. It will have to go on hold."

The woman roared laughing and so did I. That was the end of my suicide attempt. I felt better after the little giggling session I had with the checkout girl. I bought six bars of chocolate instead. When I got home I ripped my goodbye letter up and binged on the chocolate and crisps instead. They nearly killed me too. I ate that much that I couldn't move a muscle after scranning them all. I thought I was having a coronary. Honest to God, on my life, pains were surging through my chest, there were pains in my arms too. I thought my number was up. I rang the emergency services and requested an ambulance in a stressed voice but as I was talking to them the pain eased and I told them it was no longer needed. The second I put the phone down I let out the biggest fart that anyone had ever heard. If Roy Castle and the Guinness Book of Records would have been there I would have had a world record under my belt. Gas can cause you so much

The Pudding Club

pain you know? Many a night I've been doubled up in pain – trapped wind the doctor calls it. It's embarrassing too because when this wind wants to come out there is no stopping it. I have to cough to disguise it but I'm sure on a few occasions people have heard me.

Helen is walking over to my table now, she's holding her hands behind her back and chewing on her bottom lip, she means business. "Ladies can I ask you to get on with your work and stop chatting. We have lots to do and we have a deadline to meet." I swear, I wanted to put this woman between the cheeks of my arse and squeeze the life out of her, she was doing my head in and this was only my first day back. I wasn't standing for it a minute longer.

"Helen, why don't you loosen up and relax, ay? Is there something on your mind because you seem stressed? Have you got problems at home or something?"

Helen was defensive and she swallowed hard. I'd hit a nerve I was sure of it. She twisted her body around and inhaled deeply. She was holding back the tears I could see them forming in the corner of her eyes. "Rebecca, my personal life would never affect my work here. Any problems I may or may not have I leave at the office door each morning. It's a shame we're all not like that isn't it?" she stressed as she shot a look at me. Helen was on her high horse now and she was pacing up and down the floor. She was on one. "I'm sick to death of you girls thinking you can walk all over me. I bend over backwards every day to keep things moving in this place and what thanks do I get?"

Sharon nudged me in the waist and whispered. "Who the fuck does she think she is, it's not her practice, she's just an employee just like us."

I agreed and nodded my head. I had the backup now. I thought it was only right that I voiced my opinion

The Pudding Club

on behalf of us all. "Helen, just take a few deep breaths. Nobody is saying you're not doing your job. We're just saying that you need to treat us with respect. You know I have already had issues with you about bullying and I think in my opinion you're doing it again. We're a team here and if you want to be part of it you need to start treating us with respect."

You could have heard a pin drop, Helen was hyperventilating and her chest was rising with speed, she snapped and ran at me. "Well you gobby fat fucker. Why is it always you who has something to say? I'll tell you what; the lot of you can fuck off. I'm sick of carrying you all. Let's see what happens when I report you all for not doing your jobs. Yeah, we'll see whose laughing then won't we?"

Sharon stood up and gritted her teeth tightly together, this was war. "Helen, do whatever you're going to do. We're sick of your threats, just do whatever you're going to do and get it over with. We girls all stick together and I'll promise you now that we will all put in a statement into management telling them how you treat us. So, Mrs fancy fucking pants, off you trot, do your worst."

A round of applause followed Sharon's speech and we all stood tall, we were sisters-in-arms. Helen shot a look at me and shook her head. She left the room in a hurry. Once she was gone all the staff got together and planned out our next move. If Helen was reporting us then we all needed to get our story straight. Sharon was the hero of the hour and she was congratulated by her fellow workers. A storm was brewing in the office and we all knew Helen would have something under her belt for us. She was never one to walk away from an argument.

At lunchtime the girls got their sandwiches out. Mine usually consisted of a massive butty with crisps and a selection of chocolate bars and crisps. Today was different, for the first time ever I was munching on rabbit food. Two carrots and a few leaves of lettuce. Sharon looked at my lunch box and chuckled. "You really are sticking to this diet aren't you?"

As I nibbled on the carrot I smiled at her. "Yep, it's now or never. And, if Brian wants a piece of this fine arse I better keep in trim hadn't I?"

Sharon roared laughing. "Oh, fucking Brian is it now and not Doctor Weston?"

I was blushing and got her to lower her voice. That was the last thing I needed an office drama. If Helen got a whiff of it she would have had my guts for garters. I knew she had a crush on Brian too and she would be wounded to know he'd picked me over her. All the girls are sat eating their lunch. Looking around at them eating their goodies I can feel my stomach craving the calories. I'm still addicted to food and somehow I don't think that will ever leave me. I think it's like being a smoker, I suppose once you stop you still crave the nicotine. That's like me isn't it? I still crave food.

Dr Weston walked into the room and Sharon nudges me. "Here's lover boy. I can't believe you two are getting it on. You're so bleeding lucky. I'd swap my hubby anytime for him, he's sex on legs. Look at him Becks he's gorgeous. Oh, I'd let him shake my bones, I can tell you." Sharon was actually turned on as she looked at Brian; she was licking her lips slowly and craving his masculine body.

Brian walked over to me now and passed me a small white piece of folded paper. He gave me a cheeky wink and left the office. Sharon watched him walk away and she was clocking his perky arse. "Becks, you're one lucky woman, he's mint. I swear, if you don't bang the life out of him I will." Sharon was so funny and her way with words were second to none. She was a happily married woman but it never stopped her having a laugh, she was only joking when she said she would sleep with Brian. Well, I think she was anyway. Opening the piece of paper slowly I realise its Brian's phone number. My heart flutters and I hold the piece of paper up towards it. He must really be into me to come and give me his number. I wasn't going to fuck this up, no way. This was a chance of happiness with a man who was respectable. I was going to be on my best behaviour and try and impress him. Gary can go and take a run and jump now anyway. I was considering seeing him again, just to keep the cobwebs off so to speak but now he's history, I've moved on. I want a real man with real potential.

I'm so glad I came back into work today. I was considering packing this job in, but now the tides have turned I'm glad I changed my mind. Helen's back in the office and she's hovering around me. I know she will call me over in a minute to chat to me. I can just tell she's waiting for the right minute to shout me over. Here we go, knew I was right. "Rebecca, can I just have a quick word with you," she asked.

Placing my last bit of lunch in my mouth I walk towards her with a cocky look on my face. I wasn't scared of her and she knew it. I placed my hands firmly on my hips. "Do you want to talk to me here, or in private?"

Sharon was at my side now and she piped into the conversation. "If this is a work issue I will come with her. She's entitled to have someone with her if this is a disciplinary meeting."

Helen brushed her comment off and answered her in a soft voice. "No Sharon, this is nothing to do with work, it's a personal matter. Thanks for your support though, but Rebecca doesn't need you."

The Pudding Club

I raised my eyebrows at Sharon and shrugged my shoulders. I was unsure of what this woman wanted me for now, if it was nothing to do with work, then what could it be?" Helen led me into a small side office. Once we got inside she walked over to the window and opened it slowly. "Can I get you a drink or something Rebecca?" I declined and sat down on the chair, there was no way I was taking a drink from her she could have poisoned it with Arsenic or something. Helen sat down facing me now and her lips were trembling. This wasn't good and I dipped my head low waiting for her to begin. "Rebecca, you're right. I do have family problems, and you're also right about me being snappy with you. I just can't do it anymore. My husband is making my life a misery. Every day I wake up and wish he was dead. Take a look at my arms." Helen rolled her sleeves up and revealed two large bruises, they looked purple and sore. "This is what he did to me last night, he's off his head. I'm scared of what he will do next if I stay with him any longer."

My heart went out to this woman and any anger I felt towards her left me. She was in need of help just like I had been when I was married and there was no way I could turn my back on her. "Helen, you need to leave him. He'll never change trust me, I know, I've been in the same place you are and I know how hard it is to move on." Helen was sobbing her heart out now and I had to drop the catch on the door so nobody could come inside. "Helen, why haven't you told anyone about this before? I knew something was going on with you. You should have said something to someone."

Helen dabbed the tissue into the corner of her eyes and snivelled. "And, what then? Nobody can stop him. He's told me if I whisper one word of this to anyone he will put me six foot under. He's not right in the head.

The Pudding Club

Honest, I'm scared of what he will do next. Since he's lost his job he just seems to have lost the plot."

This wasn't what I was expecting to hear, this woman was in big trouble and there was no way I could leave her when she needed help. She was a bitch yeah, but nobody deserved to be going through what she was. It was time to drop my armour and help her. "Helen, I'm so sorry for the way I've acted with you. If I would have known what you were going through I would have done something to help you. I've been where you are now and look what happened to me, I broke down I couldn't cope." Helen was listening as she cracked her knuckles on her lap. "Josh, my ex, led me a dog's life. He ripped me off with my inheritance money and wait for it," I took a deep breath and swallowed hard, "he was having an affair with my best mate for most of the time we were married." To even tell someone this was therapy in itself. I stood tall and looked at Helen. "My husband broke me in two with the way he treated me. Look how fat I got, I was ready for bursting. I ate to comfort myself. So don't ever think anyone copes with this kind of abuse."

Helen smiled at me. We were the same, yet different. I was going to take her under my wing and make sure she was alright. I don't care if she was a bitch in the past, it had all changed now and I was going to help her get through it. I sat back down and took hold of her hand in mine. "Together we can get you through this. You need to sit down and tell him you're not putting up with it anymore. If he wants to change he will, otherwise you will have to be prepared to leave him. You can always come and stay with me if things get that bad."

Helen sobbed and patted my shoulder. "Thank you so much. I feel better already. I just feel now that I've told someone about this that a weight has been lifted off my shoulders. You're right, I'm going home now to tell him it has to stop." Helen stood up and hugged me, she had the eye of the tiger and you could see she meant business. "Thanks so much Rebecca, I owe you my life. I hope we can be friends from now on?"

I smiled at Helen and nodded my head. "I will sort the girls out and as from now on, we can start afresh." Helen was crying as she left the room and somehow I knew she was going to be fine. She was a strong woman and she just lost it for a short time that's all, just like me I suppose. I was alone in the room now and I was proud of my actions. Who would have thought it that I, Rebecca Rooks, would one day be handing out advice about relationships. This was a day I would remember for the rest of my life. Something was changing inside of me and I felt strong for the first time in my life.

My D-Day was looming and Josh Thompson was going to fall flat on his face for the way he'd treated me. I missed my best friend Gemma but I could do without her for now. She'd betrayed me in the worst way possible and she has to learn that you can't treat people you care about like that. Anyway, chin up and move on. I'm going out tonight with Brian so that's something to smile about. Things are looking up for me and I finally feel like me again.

★

Everything is going to plan. Brian is picking me up at eight o'clock. I've been ready for hours and now I'm just sat here clock watching. I've groomed all of my body too. I've shaved my lady garden just in case, and all my monkey fluff has disappeared. You have to be prepared don't you? I'm not planning on having sex with Brian but if it should be offered to me I'm not going to refuse it. Come on, I've not had any slap and tickle for ages, I'd be mad to turn down a quick leg-over. Olivia and John are singing together on the perch, they are so in love. They have never really replaced Joey but I suppose they've helped with the pain in my heart. Josh has been on the phone all day too, he's becoming a right pain in the arse, he's so desperate. He keeps asking for his money back and I love hearing his desperate voice when I tell him he's getting everything he's owed soon and to stop worrying. He knows I'm being a bit shifty, but ay, all's fair in love and war isn't it?

I'm wearing a nice dress tonight; I've not even gone for my usual black colour either. I'm wearing red tonight for a change, red is sexy. I hope Brian likes it. I look rather good in it if I'm being honest with you. There are still a few ripples of fat around my stomach area but hopefully that will be gone soon. I've got my lucky knickers on too. I call them lucky but as of yet they have not brought me any luck. A car is honking its horn outside. Oh my God, it's Brian. I just lifted the net curtain up and waved at him. My heart is pumping, I feel nervous. I don't know what's happened to me, I've been fine all day. Right deep breaths, in out, in out. I feel sick, my stomach is churning inside. I think it's because I have had nothing to eat. I'm trying to save myself for the meal; I didn't want to be greedy. Gas, lots of it, is circling around in my stomach, this can't be happening to me. I need to break wind and fast. That's all I need on my first date isn't it. I can see it now, me sat there with my arse-cheeks clenched tightly together unable to move in case I explode. I need to do some quick stretches before I go outside to meet him. Griping pains, my bowels feel strangled, oh, oh, oh, goodness. I'm bent over the chair. My face is bright red, knuckles turning white. There she blows. Thank goodness

The Pudding Club

for that, I couldn't have moved until that gas was gone. I was like a ticking bomb. Olivia and John are staring at me in disgust. I snigger to myself and grab my handbag from the side. "See you later guys," I shouted over at them.

Brian is watching me as I walk out of the garden. I'm trying to walk as sexy as I can but I'm not used to high heels, I'm wobbling. Usually I wear comfortable shoes but I'm sick of my legs looking stumpy and fat. The heels make my legs look long and slender. I'll just have to cope with them. "You look stunning Rebecca, you scrub up well," Brian says. Nobody had ever said anything like that to me in years. Even on my wedding day nobody said I looked stunning, not even my family. I can see why they didn't back then because I looked like a pig in a fit. I was a big fat sumo squeezed into a bridal gown.

"Thanks Brian," I said in my sexy voice. As soon as the car started moving Brian began talking. It was weird speaking to him like this, usually we only spoke in a professional manner. Opening his window a bit he reached over and popped a cigarette from the packet. I was gobsmacked that he smoked. I thought doctors were all health conscious and all that. "I didn't know you smoked," I giggled.

"There's a lot you don't know about me Rebecca. I'm not as white as you might think. People always assume that doctors don't have a life and they stay up all night studying the latest diseases, but I'm not like that at all."

Correct, he'd hit the nail on the head; I did think he was a bookworm. I never really thought that he would abuse his body in any kind of way. I hoped he would abuse my body though, he's gorgeous. Looking at him closely I realised how handsome this guy really is. His eyes are so warming and when he smiles he has a cute dimple in his chin. "I hope you like steak Rebecca because I'm

The Pudding Club

taking us to a steak house".

I nearly shouted out, "Rip its horns out and wipe its arse and bang it on my plate, I'm starving" but I kept my big gob shut. I was being a lady tonight. The music on the CD set the scene it was calming and not that head-banging shite everybody was listening to these days. I wondered if he liked the same kind of music as I did and quizzed him.

"Do you like house-music and all that, or are you more for the quieter songs".

He tapped his fingers on the steering wheel as he continued driving and chuckled. "I have a guilty pleasure in music I kind of like the cheesy stuff, you can call me gay if you want but I'm more your Grease fan than all this hip-hop crap that's about."

Well, fuck a duck, this was amazing. This man was ticking all my boxes now. I had to know what his best track was, so I asked in an eager voice. "One of my favourite songs is "Summer Loving, what's yours?"

He smirked at me and lifted his head back laughing. "I just always wanted to be John Travolta in that film and strut my stuff. That black leather coat he wears is the dog's bollocks and I just sort of always fancied myself in one. I bet you think I'm a right geek now don't you?"

I nearly collapsed, this was so unreal. I'd never met a man who loved the film Grease like I did, this was fate. Now was the time for my confession. "I'm a big fan too. I'm always playing the soundtrack in my car, in fact, it's the only CD I play." We both sat giggling, the ice was broken and we relaxed with each other. His favourite track from the CD was "Beauty School Dropout," a bit gay for a man to like I suppose, but still, he was a big fan just like me. As we drove along the country lanes we passed a car in the lay-by. Head twisted I clocked the driver and his passenger. It was Josh and Gemma and her son Jacob. There was rage burning in my stomach and I nearly jumped out from the car as it was moving with speed. These two were definitely taking the piss out of me now. Why on earth were they both eager to be back in my life yet they were still seeing each other? Taking deep breaths my mind was doing overtime. Brian placed his hand on my lap.

"Are you okay Rebecca, you seem to have gone all quiet. I hope you haven't gone off me now, thinking I'm a geek for listening to cheesy music?"

I knew I had to pull myself together and touched his cheek softly. "No, have I 'eck Brian. It's a long story but just ignore me, I'm alright now."

Brian knew in the past the troubled life I'd had with my ex-husband and he tried to make me feel better. "This is a first for me too, you know. I split up from my wife four months ago and I know how hard it is to get back in the dating game. I'm not even sure how to treat a woman anymore."

This guy was lovely; his sense of humour was on top form. I still couldn't believe he was the man I'd worked with for all these years. "You're doing fine Brian. I've been out on a few dates with guys before now but none of them seemed to be what I was looking for." I was thinking aloud now and I forgot who I was talking to. "It's just a sex thing really. I mean apart from that I am fine living on my own. Nobody moaning at me, no one to cook for, it's bliss if I was being honest to myself."

I realised what I'd just said and covered my mouth with my hand. Brian was blushing and his shoulders were shaking as he sniggered. "Well, I'm not sure if I can give you the sex you're looking for but I will have a damn good try if you're up for it?"

The Pudding Club

Now it was my turn to blush, my palms were sweaty and I didn't know where to look. I apologised for my crude mouth and tried to backpedal. "Oh, you know what I mean Brian. I don't mean we need to have sex, but," I paused and swallowed hard. I was going to take what I wanted from now on and chances like this didn't come along every day and I carried on speaking. I was being upfront for a change. "It would be nice though wouldn't it?" Brian was stuttering and I'd taken him by surprise. Come on people, this guy wasn't a stranger I'd just picked up from a nightclub or something. I've known him for a long time and we were friends. I wasn't a slut was I? Laughter filled the car, but he never answered me. Pulling up in the car park I could see the restaurant in front of us. My stomach was rumbling and I knew if I didn't eat soon I would collapse. There was no way I could eat a steak though, I couldn't get that down my neck, no way. I'd have to have soup or something soft so I could digest it.

I watched Brian eat every scrap of his steak. I was dying to taste it. He relished every piece of it. I ordered some mushroom soup and a bread roll. It wasn't much but it was all I could stomach. Brian was a chatterbox, he never shut up talking. I know I can talk, but he was giving me a run for my money I couldn't get a word in edgeways. Brian was a lonely man. You could see it in his eyes a sort of sadness looming inside them, emptiness, and lonely eyes. He started to tell me all about his wife too and why they'd split up. It was just another sad love story and you could see he was still not over her. I asked myself the question. Did anyone really get over heartbreak? I think once you've been hurt, your heart never beats the same again does it? Hearts build a stone wall around them and you never let anyone get close again. My heart has got a banner around it saying 'Closed for Business Until

Further Notice'. I'm sure of it. I'll never give my heart away again, never.

After a few hours of eating and talking it's time to leave. Brian's not sure of his next move; he seems edgy. His mouth is moving but no words are coming out. I speak up and end his trauma. "Do you want to come back to mine for a coffee and a shag?"

I was joking of course but to watch him nearly keel over and die was so funny. I couldn't hold my laughter "I'm joking, I'm joking," I laughed.

Brian came to my side and I felt his warm breath on my face. "I'm not joking, let's go back to your house and I'll give you a good seeing to. We can play doctors and nurses if you want?" Now it was my turn to blush, I'd created a monster and he was like a dog on heat. I studied him further and my mind was made up. We were both consenting adults and what did it matter that we were going to have a bit of fun, nobody was getting hurt, it was just some adult fun.

Olivia and John were squawking as Brian ravished my body on the sofa. If they could have spoken, God knows what they would have said. They were definitely traumatised by seeing me being dragged about the front room by my new lover. Brian ripped my clothes off and he was on fire. Before I knew it he had my legs over my head and he was doing things to me, I'd only ever seen on TV. Oral sex was brilliant; he was between my legs for a very long time. I was surprised at what he did next too because I'd never experienced it before. I felt a warm flick on my bum hole at first, and then he was all over it with his warm wet tongue. I was going to stop him from doing it, but to tell you the truth it was nice, a bit ticklish, but nice. I hoped he didn't want me to return the favour though because there was no way I was doing it back to him. That wasn't my game. It's funny isn't it that you think you know all there is to know about sex then all of a sudden you learn something new. I won't be telling anyone about this though, no way, it's way too embarrassing. I wonder how many people have done this. Brian is kinky for sure, this must be some new European craze that's going about or something, because I've never heard about anyone doing it before, not even Gemma.

Sex was mind blowing. Brian was a brilliant lover. During sex I played my Grease CD and he serenaded me whilst we were making love. I never thought in a million years this guy would ever be as adventurous as he was, you just think doctors are boring, don't you? We're both lay naked next to each other now and from the corner of my eye I can see my red knickers hanging over the edge of the birdcage. Olivia and John are looking at me in disgust; they are still hopping about on the perch. Brian lights two cigarettes up and passes me one. We both enjoy a mellow moment and relax in each other's arms. It's nice to be cuddled after sex isn't it? Josh never cuddled me, he was so cold to me. He never really showed any emotion. When I think back to how we were with each other, it wasn't really nice. Even in public he would never hold my hand or anything, I should have known then that he didn't really love me like he said he did.

Why am I still thinking about him? And, why was he with Gemma? There are so many questions in my head and they torment me most nights before I go to sleep. I lie looking at my latest lover. Brian is husband material. I can just tell this guy would love his partner with all his heart. He's like me, a hopeless romantic. The silence is broken by Brian. "That was amazing Rebecca, you're a fantastic lover. You blew my mind." I was speechless for a few seconds and didn't know what to say back to

The Pudding Club

him. I've never really thought about how good I was in the bedroom before now and just thought I was about average. This was incredible news and my self-confidence was going through the roof.

"Do you really think so Brian, or are you just saying that?"

Brian grabbed my hand tightly and looked me straight in the eye. "I mean every word I say Rebecca. I wouldn't lie to you. I think you're a sexy woman. Any man that has the privilege of being loved by you is a lucky man."

Was he having me over or what? This was all too much for me to take in. I know I'd already dropped my knickers for him and he didn't need to say the things he was saying to me, so it must have been true.

"That's the nicest thing anyone has ever said to me you know?" I replied.

Brian smiled and his pearly white teeth were revealed. "I've always had the hots for you Rebecca but I've never had the chance to tell you before. I've dreamt of this moment you know?" I should have been over the moon with what he was saying to me but I felt a little bit sick. I like a man's man, someone to keep me on my toes, not someone who would jump through hoops for me. Was I normal? Why was I always looking for the bad boy? You know the sort, who treat you like dirt and make you cry all the time. There was something seriously wrong with me I wasn't normal. I felt a shiver rush through my body and goose-bumps appeared on my skin, I sat fidgeting. Brian could see something had changed and pulled me closer to his body. "I know what I'm saying seems a bit weird and I don't want you to think I'm some kind of sissy. I just needed to tell you how I felt."

I wanted food and lots of it, this was all too much for me to handle. I needed chocolate, crisps, chips, pies anything. In a panic I pulled away from him. "I'm just a bit mixed up at the moment Brian. I don't want to lead you on. I'm fucked up in the head if the truth was known. I just can't seem to give my heart to anyone anymore. You need someone who will love you like you deserve, not someone like me."

Brian pleaded with me, he was desperate and red in the face. "I'm sorry Rebecca. I just wear my heart on my sleeve. If you want, we can just be friends until you're ready. I don't want to scare you off or anything." He was right, he was scaring me off. I was shitting my knickers. I needed him to go home as soon as possible and passed him his clothes. I was tapped in the head I know, but he was doing my head in and I wanted him out of my sight. Brian could tell he'd messed up and slid his trousers back on and never spoke another word. Once he was ready I was eager for him to leave. My words were few and he could see the date was over.

"It's been amazing Rebecca. I hope we can do it again sometime?"

I licked my dry lips and nodded my head. "See you soon," I whispered in a low voice.

Watching him walk down the garden path I felt my heart in my chest racing. Here was one of the nicest men I'd met in a long time and I was letting him go. I didn't have it in me to shout after him. I was such a fool. Closing the front door I ran into the kitchen and opened the fridge. Food and lots of it staring at me. Grabbing a tub of ice-cream I sat down at the table and dug my spoon into it in a wild frenzy. I was devouring it with speed, wet, cold, creamy food sliding past my lips. My gastric band seems to know when I'm upset and allows me to eat during this time. I should have been back to the hospital to have my band checked because for me, my appetite is

The Pudding Club

returning and I seem to be eating more and more each day. I just don't have the time though, the hospital can wait for now. I'm going to make the most of this eating time too and I'm going to eat every scrap of ice-cream there is. Fifteen minutes later and the ice-cream had gone, empty containers all scattered about the table. Five tubs of it I've eaten. I don't feel guilty either. I just feel calm and comforted. I'm going to bed now. I'm a fat ice-cream munching slut and I'm ashamed of the way I've acted tonight. Brian must think I'm a right nutter. I just turned on him for no real reason. He could be right too. I'm not sure if I'm coming or going anymore - my head's all over the place. It's only one week to my birthday bash and I've got a lot of planning to do. Josh Thompson is getting what's coming to him, the life wrecking bastard. It's his fault I'm like this. His days are numbered.

FIFTEEN

EVERYTHING IS PLANNED for my birthday party and all the invites have been sent out. All the guys are coming from strength camp too; even Tarzan and Arnie are making an appearance. It will be good to see them all again, it's been a few months since I last saw them. Let's see their faces when they see my new slimmer body. I'm off to town soon just to pick up some last minutes bits. My birthday party theme is Grease so I'm expecting everyone to dress up in fun costumes. I'm wearing black Lycra pants and a black off the shoulder top, just like Olivia Newton-John wore in the film. I admit, I'm not as slim as her and perhaps my outfit won't look as good on me as hers did but I'm wearing it anyway. This is my party and I'll do what I want. My mother is even making the party, God knows what she will turn up in, she's a right miserable get and I doubt she will even make the effort. I'm surprised she's not made some excuse why she can't come, that's what she usually does, but ay, there's time yet. My brother Spencer may be coming too. He's split up from his partner Rita and he's been at my mam's for months. My mother said he's been in a bad way and he's piled the pounds on already. Two stone she said he's put on. Spencer will be devastated, he hates being fat and I can't see it lasting long. Part of me is laughing inside though. I know it's wrong, but come on, he's called me a blob for years and always put me down about my weight. It will be nice to see how he's coping now the timber is piling on him. Perhaps, I should give him some tips on losing weight, God knows, I should know them all.

The Pudding Club

It's a shame his relationship has ended but life does go on, doesn't it? Look at me, who would have thought I would ever breathe again after my marriage failed. Inner strength, that's what gets you by, trust me. I didn't know I had it, until lately. Everyone's strong enough to move on in time, even me.

Walking through the town centre I clock Alex, Gemma's husband coming towards me with his son Jacob. I try and keep my head low but he's seen me now. For fucks sake, he's going to ask me about why I have not been around to his house. "Hello sexy," he giggled. "I thought you'd passed away I've not seen you for that long. Where have you been hiding?"

I was struggling to speak, what could I say? Should I tell him the truth that his wife has been banging the brains out of my husband for years, or should I keep my lips sealed. "I've just been so busy Alex, how are you anyway?" I switched the subject and he was more than happy to talk about himself. Jacob, his son, was stood munching on an ice-cream and he smiled at me. The blood drained from my face and I nearly collapsed. Surely not, my head was messed up and I was imagining it. Alex took me by the arm and led me to a row of chairs nearby, I was unsteady on my feet.

"I'll get you a drink Rebecca, just take deep breaths and try to calm down. Jacob, just keep your eye on her while I get her a drink." The kid sat next to me staring at my pathetic panic attack. I looked at him closer and I knew what I felt in my heart was true. Jacob was Josh's son. The more I studied the kid, the more I could see his father. Alex was back at my side and he was pushing a cup of water into my mouth. "Get a swig of it Rebecca, just take your time, small sips should do it. Just try and regain your breath back." The plastic cup was shaking in

The Pudding Club

my hand and I wasn't coping. I reached over and grabbed the ice-cream from Jacob and rammed it deep into my mouth. The kid was moaning but Alex told him to sit still and stop being so spiteful. The food hit the back of my throat and slowly I started to breathe normal again. Alex was by my side and he was stroking my hand softly. "Gemma told me you were in a bad way, but I thought she was exaggerating, you know what she's like for telling stories."

Oh, I did know she was good at telling stories and this one was one she never had the balls to tell her own husband. Jacob was Josh's son. Why had I never seen this before? The kid was a spitting image of his father, even the dimples in his cheeks when he smiled, he was a mirror image of him. Why the hell had I not seen this before, was I that much up my own arse that I couldn't see the woods through the trees. I needed to tell someone and Alex was the only one there. I asked him for a quiet word alone.

"Jacob, here's some money, go to the shop over there and get another ice-cream for yourself, get me one too. I'll have strawberry, if they've got it." Jacob took the money from his father's hand and ran to the shop facing us. I was alone with Alex. I needed to get this off my chest and there was no way I was keeping his wife's seedy secret for a minute longer. Why should she be happy when she'd wrecked my life for good? I dried my tears and snivelled. Alex placed his arm around my neck and tried to comfort me. He was a friendly man and I knew what I was about to tell him would break his heart in two.

"Alex, Gemma has been having an affair with my husband Josh, that's why I haven't been around to your house. It's been going on for years. I've only just found out myself."

There was an eerie silence, Alex played about with

The Pudding Club

his fingers, nearly yanking them out of their sockets. Clenching his teeth together he snarled and banged his fist on the bench at the side of me. "I fucking knew it. I had a gut feeling something was going on between them two. He was always on the phone to her and turning up at the house. I thought they were just good friends. What a prick I am." The cat was out of the bag, Gemma's dirty secret was out in the open. Alex was surprisingly calm as he spoke. "I knew the scrubber was up to something, she must have been with him last night too because she told me she stayed at your house with you. I believed her too, she said you were suicidal and you couldn't be left alone." Well, the cheeky tart, how dare she use me as her excuse! Correct, yeah, I might have been feeling down in the past, but I would never take my own life, not now anyway. I had to tell him what was lying heavily on my mind. It was there on the tip of my tongue.

"I think Jacob is his son too."

There, I'd said it. I was waiting on his reaction. He dropped his head and held it in his hands, he was devastated. "What, my Jacob?" he sobbed. This was heartbreaking and I was the one doing the comforting now. "I think so, Alex; he's the spitting image of him. Josh is a bad man you know. He ripped me off for my inheritance money and I'm sure he's getting money from Gemma too."

Alex was bright red and he clenched his fist together in tight balls at the side of his legs. "Yes, that would explain the missing money from our bank account. I know Gemma likes to spend but there's thousands gone missing, she must have give it that scrounging cunt."

Jacob was back now and he looked at his father, who was upset. "Dad, what's up? Why are you crying?"

Alex shook off his emotions and held a stiff upper lip. "I'm fine, son. I've just got something in my eye that's all."

He held his open arms out and Jacob came to his father's side. He was hugging him tightly and you could see his knuckles turning white. "You're my boy aren't you, son. You always will be no matter what." Alex stood up and he was wobbling. "Rebecca, I need to go home. I will call and see you later tonight if that's alright. I have a few things I need to take care of first though."

I nodded my head slowly and watched him leave. Jacob waved to me and smiled before he left. I stayed where I was for at least another fifteen minutes. My legs were weak and my shopping was ruined. I just needed to go home and eat. The truth was finally out and Gemma would now have to explain to her husband all about her affair. I felt a little bit bad for what I had uncovered but why should I be the only one who gets hurt. It's about time Gemma got what was coming to her and I for one will be happy to see her fall flat on her face. Picking up my handbag I head back home. I was in no mood for shopping anymore and even though I should have been excited about my birthday bash my mood was low. I was going to call my therapist when I got home for an emergency meeting. This was a code red and I needed help as quick as could be. I was losing the plot.

Sat alone in my front room, I sobbed my heart out. I would have made a great mother to any child. And, if Josh would have told me about Jacob we could have worked something out. I would have forgiven him. Yeah, that's how desperate I was to keep him. Perhaps that's why he slept with another woman. How could I expect him to go through life never fathering a child? This was my fault. If I could have had children he would never have sought love from another woman. The doctors told me that my womb was tilted and any chances of me carrying a child full term was nil, but there were other options for us to

The Pudding Club

look at, we could have got through it. I want to smash this house up now! I want to destroy it from top to bottom! There is anger in my body and it's not leaving me. I'm scared of what I might do next, I'm losing control.

Sat next to the fridge several hours later, I have eaten everything that would fit into my mouth. There is one jar of pickles left, then I've eaten everything. I feel sick and bloated but still I'm eating anything in sight. I don't want to be thin anymore. I want to be fat and happy. I don't know why I even pretend to myself that being thin would change my life. It's me who needs to change, not my eating habits. My therapist is unable to see me today either, she has a busy day and can't even squeeze me in for a quick session. When I spoke to her and told her a bit about my situation she was shocked. I think she knows that I'll still be on her books for years to come. Just when I thought I was on the road to recovery, the shit hits the fan. Typical, why did I ever think I could be happy again. I am a washed up old fat cow who doesn't deserve anything in life accept to be fat. I was cancelling my party too, there is no way I wanted to celebrate another year of being me. I was a disgrace, a fat messed-up woman who would live the rest of her life a lonely old fool. Food was all I needed in my life and as from today I would never try to diet again. Fuck dieting and fuck life, I want to die.

Gemma is ringing my mobile phone constantly. I've ignored her for hours but now I'm ready to answer her call. She's screaming down the line and I gather that Alex had confronted her about her affair. I spoke in a confident manner and invited her around to my house to speak about it. Gemma is screaming and shouting so I've hung up and placed my phone back in my handbag, I don't have to listen to her shit anymore. I know Gemma will be around shortly and I've prepared myself for World War

Three. This is it, this woman was getting twisted up and I'm going to rip her to shreds, leave her half dead on the floor begging me to spare her. I should have knocked ten tons of shit out of her when I first found out about the affair. I don't know why I never did in the first place. I must have been mad in the head letting her think she could walk all over me. Running upstairs I change into something more comfortable. There was no way I was fighting her in my skirt and blouse. I was putting my trainers on and a pair of tracksuit bottoms. I could move about in them more freely. Heart pumping inside my chest I bent down and touched my toes, I needed to stretch, loosen up. A couple of jabs here and there and I was ready for whatever the bitch had to throw at me. The two budgies are singing downstairs, they must sense something is wrong. I better get down there fast and cover them up. There is no way I want them to see me brawling about the front room. I want to put Gemma through pain, the kind that she has put me through. I'm losing my head, I can feel my mind slipping away I'm not thinking straight. Slow, heartbreaking pain I want to give her, to see her suffer, yes, I want her to suffer. There's no way she's talking her way out of this one, her number's up and she's getting what's coming to her the dirty slag.

Knocking at the door, the letterbox is banging loudly. Deep breaths, blowing through my mouth I go to open the door in a wild frenzy. My jaw drops as I see them both for the first time. Josh and Gemma together. A couple. My eyes bounce from one to the other. I'm ready to strike and they know it. Josh swallows hard and speaks. "Can we come inside Becks? I don't want to air our dirty washing in public. Can we just come inside and be civil about this?" I left the door open and walked inside. I'm boiling hot and ready to explode. I've always had a problem with

The Pudding Club

my temper and I knew once I snapped there was no turning back. My mother always had me down as some sort of lunatic when I was annoyed and although I hate to admit it I think she was right. I watched my back as I stormed into the front room because I knew Gemma would strike the first blow given the chance, she was like a ninja; sly, cunning, and devious.

"This is all a big mess Rebecca. I don't know why you've told Alex about me and Gemma. He never needed to know. I mean, look at Gemma she's in a right state. You're such a selfish bitch."

Was he on this fucking planet or what? Did he not understand what had actually happened here? There was no way he was turning the tables on me, not this time. I blew my lid. "I don't give a flying fuck about Gemma's life. What about me ay? What about how I feel? She's a dirty scrubber who deserves everything that's coming to her."

Josh dropped his head low and walked over to where I was stood. He touched the top of my shoulder and patted it softly. His touch made my skin crawl. I pushed him away and growled at him. "You two think you are so smart. Why didn't you just tell me Jacob was your son?"

Josh bit hard on his bottom lip; he shot a look over to Gemma who was shaking. "It just happened Becks, we never meant to hurt you." There it was the truth. Why didn't he just deny it and defend himself. It would have been so much easier to handle if he lied to me.

Gemma collapsed onto the floor and rocked to and fro with her knees held up to her chest. She snivelled and began to speak. "You couldn't have children Rebecca and this was Josh's only chance of fathering a child. How could I deny him that?"

This was my worst nightmare coming true. "Oh, so

that's your excuse is it? Go on, rub salt in the wounds, we all know I can't have children. Who do you think you are, thinking you can have kids with my fucking husband? Are you right in the bastard head or what?"

I'd lost the plot now, a red mist covered my eyes and I ran at her full force, she was getting it. Dragging her up from the floor by her hair I sank my nails deep into her cheeks and delivered two strong blows to her head. She was screaming out at the top of her voice and Josh was wrestling me, telling me to leave her alone. This just made me worse and I was lashing out as if my life depended on it. I was in a zone and there was no coming back. I wanted to kill her stone dead. "Rebecca just give me back the money you owe me and I'm gone. I thought I still loved you but it's Gemma I love and my son. We're going to be a family; we've decided to move away and start afresh."

His words crucified me, deep pain suffocated my heart. My words seemed locked in my mouth and I couldn't breathe, I was hyperventilating. This man would stop at nothing to get what he wanted, he was a lying, cheating bastard. I ran at him and screamed at the top of my voice.

"There is no money! I've spent it all. Did you think I was just going to hand it over to you after you stole my inheritance? You're not getting fuck all from me, not a penny."

I sank to the floor and I could feel a warm liquid running down the side of my face. My vision was blurred and everything seemed to be moving in slow motion around me. I could hear shouting but the voices were muffled. Holding onto the corner of the sofa I reached for the brass candlestick holder and gripped it tightly in my hands Josh was bent over trying to help Gemma up from

The Pudding Club

the floor. I saw my chance and staggered towards him with hate in my eyes. Before I knew it I had been taken over by a force within me. I had no control of my actions. Hands held back over my head I smashed the candlestick over his head. I know I should have stopped after the first blow but the hurt this man had caused me throughout my life just made me carry on. Blood splurged all over the walls as I carried on hitting him. I loved that I was in control and the bastard I once called my husband was finally getting what he deserved.

Josh fell to the ground as the last fatal blow struck him on the side of his head. His body shook a few times and he just lay staring into space. Gemma slid down the wall and cowered with her hands above her head. I should of stopped I know, I know I should have. But it was too late; I attacked Gemma like a woman possessed. She was the root of this evil and she was paying for her betrayal too. Gemma screamed like a banshee as I gripped her by the neck. I threw the candlestick down on the floor and pinned her up against the wall. Squeezing her windpipe I could see the colour changing, she was turning blue. Her eyes were popping out of her head and I knew within seconds her final breath would be taken. Looking at her suffering was the revenge I had been waiting for. Her cheeks creased at the side and her legs twitched as I held her up by the throat. There were croaking sounds, her body shuddered for the last time as she dropped to the floor. Stood watching them both I felt a wave of hatred leave my body. It was over, they both lay lifeless on the floor. Heading straight into the kitchen I opened the fridge door and grabbed the last bit of butter in the tub. Hands scooped inside it I shoved it into my mouth. This was an eating frenzy that wasn't normal. Sat on the kitchen floor the reality of what had just happened hit home. Sneaking back into the front room I looked at the two bodies sprawled out across the floor. Tiptoeing back inside the room I kicked at Josh's body slowly. He never budged, he was dead. Gemma wasn't moving either, she was a snidey bitch and I had a feeling she might be faking it, she was like that. Sat down on the floor next to her I turned her over and slapped her face a few times. There was nothing, she never flinched. My head didn't feel right and I seemed to be in a world of my own. I started singing a track from my Grease CD.

Night-time fell and I was still sat watching the lovers on the floor. They were dead and I'd killed them both. I needed food and plenty of it. Grabbing my coat from the side of the chair I ran to the car. The local supermarket was still open and I knew if I hurried I could make it before closing time. Still humming the tune from the CD I walked up each aisle and gathered what I needed. My trolley was overloaded with sugary snacks. I made sure I had enough to last me for a few days. My mobile phone was ringing constantly and I just flicked the power button and turned the device off. I didn't want to speak to anyone ever again. I was going home to lock myself away from the world and hopefully die from overeating. A heart attack would be good, or even a stroke. I wasn't bothered just as long as it was quick. I didn't want to die slowly, no way, I was too scared.

The house seemed strange; the smell of death lingered in the air. My crime will be detected soon and I know I will go to prison for my actions. Prison might just be what I need. At least then I might have some friends, people like me who are different and don't fit in. Society has always rejected me and this is what happens when you're pushed over the edge. I feel sorry for my mother. The shame of it all will send her to an early grave. Perhaps

The Pudding Club

I should ring her and warn her about what has gone on. Maybe I should ring Teresa, she will know what to do. Perhaps she will realise now that I did need her help when I called for an appointment.

My head is so messed up, what the hell am I going to do now? Sat munching on a bag of crisps I notice Gemma is missing. In a panic I run about the house looking for her. Nothing, not a trace of her. I knew she was faking to be dead. I've seen her do this before when we were younger. She'd lie in the same position for over an hour and control her breathing so people thought she was dead. How could I have forgotten this trick? In a panic I drag Josh's body to the side of the room. It's a good job I've been in training otherwise I could never have shifted his heavy torso. What have I done?

"Josh why did you treat me the way you did? I loved you and look what you have made me do. We could have been so happy." Josh is lying on my lap and I stroke his blooded face. He's still my Josh and I'm glad he will never love again. The living room door flies open now and I can see policemen, lots of them. Slowly they approach me and speak in a calm voice. I'm not angry anymore and I lift Josh from my lap and stand up. "You'll get no trouble from me officers," I said. Within seconds I'm cuffed and stood up against the wall. After the police officer reads me my rights I'm escorted from the room. This was the last time I saw my Josh and tears streamed down my face. I struggled as the reality of it all hit home. "Please, let me say goodbye, please." My words fell on deaf ears and I was dragged from the front room. Olivia and John sat on their perch just watching me. As I got outside the neighbourhood was out in full force. I'd never seen so many of them out at once. You could see them whispering amongst themselves and pointing their fingers at me.

The Pudding Club

Gemma was sat with an officer in the car and as she watched me being flung into the back of the police van. She was screaming at the top of her voice. "I hope you rot in jail, you sick bitch. Me and Josh could have been happy together, it's all over now because of you Rebecca. You're a sick woman who needs help; you're a bleeding crackpot."

I never replied to her. I feel no remorse for what I've done and in a way I feel at peace now that the debt had been settled. The doors bang behind me and I sit alone on the platform at the back of the van. Tunes spinning around my head, lots of songs I hadn't heard for years reaching my lips. "Hopelessly devoted to you," being sung at full pelt. The shit has well and truly hit the fan this time. I knew I was a bit tapped in the head, but a murderer? I never thought I would go that far. What about my job? What about my life as I know it? Things will never be the same again. I'm set for of a life of imprisonment, no loving arms of a man ever again, no loving touches.

Total bliss.

SIXTEEN

It's my court day tomorrow and I can honestly say I'm crapping my knickers. The girls from The Pudding Club have written to me and they are sending their love telling me everything is going to be alright. Even Tarzan and Arnie have written a letter offering me their support. I never knew I had so many friends until now. Brian is coming to court today as a character witness for me. I don't think anyone will listen to him though. Gemma is giving her evidence to the court, and she'll want me banged up for years, the silly cow. I wish I could say my weight has dropped with all the stress but do you know what I've gained two stones in the last few months. The gastric band is no longer working and the weight is piling on me just like it always has.

I don't regret what happened, I just wish things might have turned out differently. I feel let down by the people I loved, betrayed and tossed aside like an old boot. My mother is at her wits end, she's told me so in every letter she's written to me, she's so ashamed. The press have been hounding her and they are offering her large amounts of money to tell her story. Everyone thinks I'm a nutter, the other inmates stay well clear of me and I'm still isolated from the main prison until I've been sentenced. I'm lonely, I'm aching for friendship, and any kind of a friend will do. Just somebody to talk to, someone who will listen to me. When I've watched films before on TV even the harden criminals have someone to speak to, why can't I?

I've had lots of visits from doctors too. We talk for hours but they are not friends, they are just trying to get inside my head and see if I'm a mental case or not. They think I'm daft when they fire their questions at me, I'm onto them though, I'm no fool. The medical team bring me food too, lots of treats, they know that's my weak spot. They sit watching me eat and know when to ask their questions. I take them on a wild goose chase sometimes, just to let them think they are getting somewhere, it entertains me for hours. Prison life is not as bad as I first thought. Not one lesbian has approached me yet though, that's strange isn't it? They will probably wait until I'm settled until they make their move on me. I'm open to any kind of loving now I suppose. I'll have to get it while I can won't I?

Freedom seems far away and I'll be a wrinkled old woman before I'm freed from jail, so yes, I may turn to women for some comfort. When in Rome do as the Romans do, that's what they say isn't it? I wish I had a pad mate, just someone to talk to throughout the day. The hours drag behind bars and I'm even talking to myself now. Yes, I sit and talk to myself for hours. I think I'm cracking up. Today my mother is coming to see me with my brother, Spencer. At least I can get out of my cell for a few hours. Mother just sits crying on the visit and she can't understand why I did what I did. I don't understand what I did myself really so how can I ever explain to her what I was feeling. I just lost the plot. I don't remember a thing. The doctors say this is normal sometimes but surely I should remember something. Sometimes at night I see Josh's face staring at me from the ceiling. I have to turn the light on I'm so scared. I can remember my husband though, but it's just the bad things he did to me.

The doctors have asked me time and time again what pushed me over the edge, but I can't answer them as I don't really know. My heart was broken and I think I just

The Pudding Club

couldn't take anymore, I tell them, but they always dig deeper trying to get a big confession from me. Janice the prison officer is here now anyway so it's time for my visit. I hope my mother has brought enough money this time for the canteen. The last time she came I only had three chocolate bars on the visit, I was starving.

No doubt Spencer will give me a lecture about how I have disgraced the family name. He's a right dick-head sometimes and I've told him if he carries on harassing me he'll be next on my hit list. He doesn't know if I'm serious or not when I talk like that, he just backs off. I like this control I have over him. I'm no longer the weaker sister. Spencer is like a balloon. His double chins touch the top of his chest. I know I shouldn't laugh but I just can't help myself. My mother still treats us like children and even when she goes to the canteen she always makes sure we get equal shares of the goodies. She a funny old soul and sometimes I can't help but laugh at her with the things she comes out with. On the last visit she actually asked me about my sex life inside the prison walls. On my life, I swear to you, she sat there with her arms folded tightly across her chest and just blurted it out. "I hope you're not going to be one of them lesbian things now you're locked up. You still have standards even if you're behind bars." She meant every word she said too; there was no beating around the bush with her, she just said it how it was. I smiled and answered her, I loved winding her up. "Mam, if I'm going to be in here for years what do you expect me to do. It's normal in here for two women to fall in love." My mother went white, the colour drained from her face and she looked disgusted. "That's shocking. I don't want to know anymore. If you become one of them please don't tell me. What I don't know won't hurt me will it?"

Spencer giggled at the side of her, he knew I was playing with her and joined in the banter. "Mam, if Rebecca finds women attractive then who are we to judge. Who knows, you could turn lesbian if you got locked up." I held the bottom of my stomach as she sat there spitting feathers. "There is no bleeding way I would touch another woman's private parts. It's not right, it's not natural. When God made us he didn't make two women he made Adam and Eve, if he wanted us to mix he would have done so." Here it was, the bible lecture we always got when she was lost for words. She was like that she always quoted from the bible when she knew she was wrong. Spencer giggled as she slapped him across his arm; she was on one.

Today the visiting centre was busy. I wasn't put with all the other inmates, I was secluded in another part of the room with the other nutters. Everyone looked at me when they came into the room and you could see them whispering to their friends. I was labelled a head the ball I'm sure of it. Just for fun sometimes I growled at the visitors and twisted my eyeballs at them. It's funny to watch their reaction, they nearly collapse. I'm marked as a dangerous criminal, I know, me dangerous. I don't know where they have got that from, I'm the most caring person anyone could meet. Well, I used to be before this. It's a good feeling inside though, knowing people fear me, I like to play the part of a psycho too when it suits me. It gets me the things I want. Even at dinner time when I'm getting my food in the canteen I only have to growl at the server and she bangs more food on my plate. I got two pieces of cake too just because I kept my plate out after she put the first piece on it. I'd seen this before in a film and I loved that for the first time in my life I was the leading lady. When I said jump, the people around me said

The Pudding Club

'how high?' I was the lady of the manor for sure, a force not to be messed with.

Mother looks drained today, somewhat different. I'm sure she's going to pop her clogs anytime soon. I've forgotten how old she is, she must be at least seventy-five now. I think she's just waiting to die if the truth was known. Her life is so miserable and lonely, what does she have to live for? There's no grandchildren to spoil, no husband to love and care for, nothing. I've never really thought about it before but our family is coming to an end. Nobody is going to carry our family name on. I don't suppose it's a bad thing really, come on, I wouldn't wish our genes on any child. Fat, lonely, and secluded, and that's only the half of it. I wonder if I'd be missed if I died. Olivia and John have probably forgotten about me already the little bleeders. My neighbour has taken them now and I know they are being looked after.

"Do you want a drink and some chocolate Rebecca?" my mother asks.

Spencer was already giving his order and I had to wait until he'd finished before I could tell her mine. He was a greedy bastard, three bars of chocolate he asked for plus two sandwiches. He always pissed on my parade and today was no different. Here I was ready to be sentenced and all he could think about was filling his fat face.

"I'll have the same," I muttered. Spencer sat looking at me then turned his head scanning the visiting centre.

"What's she in for over there? She looks like a right hard fucker." I looked over to the woman he was referring to and smirked. She's nowhere near as dangerous as me, she was a trustee and an arse-licker in the jail. I sat proud and spoke to him.

"She's in for council tax fraud, she's only in for a shit and a shave, three months she's doing that's all. All the harden criminals are sat over here with me."

Spencer clocked the other women sat a few tables away and started to rub his chubby arms. "You can see it in their eyes can't you? I mean, look at her there, I'd hate to meet her on a dark night, she looks menacing. What's she in for?"

The woman he was talking about was in the next pad to me and I didn't really know her crime so I made it up to keep him interested. "Oh, she's a crank. Six men she killed, her nickname is 'The Manchester Mauler', she just picked her victims up and done them in." Spencer's jaw dropped and you could see the colour drain out of his cheeks. I kept talking hoping to put the fear of God into him. "She said to me she would have killed more men if she hadn't have got caught. You're lucky Spencer because she only lived a few miles away from us. You could have been the next on her list." I tried to hold my laughter but I was struggling.

Spencer looked at me and tried to make light of the matter but I know he was shitting his pants. Mother was back now and placed the food on the table. We both grabbed our grub and sat munching on it straight away. My mother never bought herself any food, she just sits sipping on her cup of tea watching us eat. "How you feeling about tomorrow love, it's a big day for you isn't it? At least then you will know your fate won't you?"

I gulped hard and the hairs on the back of my neck stood on end. She was right though; the next day would determine my fate. "Whatever will be will be, won't it mam? I can't see me getting out of this place though. Come on, be realistic about this. I killed my ex-husband, they're not going to slap me on the wrist and send me home are they?"

Spencer chomped on his sandwich and spoke with

his mouth full. "No, you're right there Rebecca, they're going to sling the book at you. You should be looking at getting life for what you've done."

I think he was speaking aloud and forgot who he was talking too; he went bright red as my mother nudged him in the waist. "Bleeding hell Spencer, it's not what your sister needs to hear right now. We should stick together and support her. I know what she did was wrong but she's our blood and we know how mixed up she's been lately."

I looked at them both and shrugged my shoulders, they thought I was crackers too. "I am sat here you know, bloody hell, if I get life than I get life. I can't turn back the clock can I?"

Spencer leant over the table and made sure no one was listening, he cupped his hands around his mouth. "Did you mean to do him in or what, or was it just an accident?"

My mother was listening with anticipation too and I knew I would have to answer. "It just happened, he hit me first and he was going to start a new life with that slag Gemma, what did he expect? I was protecting myself. I know I went a bit too far but you know what I'm like when I lose my rag don't you?"

Spencer chuckled and nodded his head. "Yeah, we do know what you're like, you're a bleeding idiot. Mam, do you remember when she tried to strangle me when I ate her last toffee when we were kids; she was like a mental patient trying to get at me."

My mother was laughing as she sat back thinking about the days gone by. I'm sure a tear was forming in the corner of her eye but she held it back and held a stiff upper lip. "You're dad would go mad if he could see you now, Rebecca. He had so many hopes and dreams for you when you were growing up. He had dreams for both of you and just look at you both now, you're a bleeding mess. Slobs you are the pair of you."

Spencer banged his fists onto the table and looked her straight in the eye. "Ay, I've not killed anyone. It's her who's off her head not me."

I shook my head and waited for the usual family argument to start. "Well, look at the size of you both, you're both obese and even though I try and help you both cut down on your food you're both like gannets, greedy bastards in fact."

There she was again, straight to the point, she never held anything back. Spencer was wallowing in self pity as per usual and I just brushed her comment aside, I was used to it. "My solicitor said Gemma is a witness tomorrow at court, I don't think I can face seeing her after what I've done."

My mother was still on one and chirped into the conversation stopping me in my tracks. "Well, it's not like you just had an argument is it? You tried to kill her, she's still in a bad way and the doctors have said she will never be able to talk properly again, you've damaged her windpipe."

I closed my eyes and it was coming back to me now. I remember her face as I gripped her up against the wall. What had I become? I was an animal, I was out of control. Spencer finished his last bit of food and spoke about his own life. He was always a self-centred prick and he hated that he wasn't the centre of attention. "I'm thinking of signing up on a dating website for larger men. It's supposed to be good for people looking to start up with new partners."

I knew the website he was talking about and grinned to myself. I cracked daft and let him carry on talking about all the different people you could meet on it. Our family spent another hour talking about life in general. I wasn't missing much on the outside and my life behind bars seemed much more exciting. The officer walked over and told us to finish our visit. It was time for me to go back to my pad. I'd heard enough of them two bickering anyway, they were doing my head in. I've started reading books since I've been locked up and I can honestly say I'm enjoying the novels I'm reading. Words can mean so much when they are said in the right way, they can change the way you feel. One minute you're happy and the next you're sad. I just connect with all the characters I read about and feel their pain in every page I turn. A lot of people write about love and happy endings. I like these kinds of stories and sometimes I get lost in the world that isn't my own. I often think of the writer and feel each one of them has been through some kind of pain to be able to write about it. Perhaps I should take up writing? I've got nothing better to do with my time have I? What would I write about anyway? My books would be depressing and I'm sure the suicide rate would double after people had read about my sad life. I suppose I could change my life in a book though couldn't I? I could be the slim heroine who found her true love and lived happily ever after. That's something I might think about doing in the future. I'm going to have a lot of time on my hands so I may as well make the most of it. I could become a best-selling author. I could change my name and nobody would know it's me who's writing these classic books. I could reinvent myself as a whole new person – an interesting woman.

A wet kiss from my mother's lips is planted on my cheek, just a peck. There's no hugs exchanged between us or any heartbreaking words spoken. Spencer just nods his head as he leaves me and waves his hand over his shoulder. Bloody hell, his arse is massive, what the hell has happened to him? Love is a strange thing and it does weird things to people doesn't it? Spencer had it all; he had a great body, and a woman he loved with all his heart. To look at him now you wouldn't know that man he was once ever existed. He's a fat, lazy, calorie consuming mess. They're gone now and it's time to leave the visit. The walk back to my cell seems longer today. My feet have swollen and my toes are sore. They look like fat red sausages. The other prisoners are still wary of me and it's doing my head in now putting on this nutter act. I want to talk to people and make friends. The screw is walking at the side of me, she's butch and loves her job, you can just tell. Right, here goes let's see if I can break the ice.

"When do I get to mix with the other inmates, is there a special time when we all get out of our cells?"

The screw looks at me and holds her head back and chuckles. "Where the hell do you think you are, Butlin's? Association time is usually after six o'clock but I'm not sure you will be allowed to go onto the main landing with the other prisoners, you're a high risk prisoner."

I growled at her and she could tell she'd rattled my cage. "What do mean by a high risk prisoner?" I asked. The woman walked in front of me and shouted back over her shoulder. "They think you're potty, to put it bluntly. You killed a man and they think you could kill again." This was not what I wanted to hear. I was a gentle, caring woman who'd made a mistake. I tried to fight my corner but the bitch was having none of it. "It's just the rules, darling," she hissed in her sarcastic voice. I was back in my pad now and once the door was slammed shut I ran to the small window for air. I was gasping for breath and my head was light. With my nose poked through the bars I let out a scream from the bottom of my stomach, I was desperate and scared. My cry for help fell onto deaf ears,

The Pudding Club

no one came running or no one was listening. It was just the same as it had always been in my life, I was alone. Falling onto my bed I dragged the small grey blanket over my head. I wanted to be invisible and never see another human being again. The bed was too small for me and I could hear a snapping noise. Crash! The bed broke in two and I was lying with my legs still up in the air. I was struggling to move, my body was too big to get back up. I shouted at the top of my voice for help and it was only after a few minutes before my cell door opened and I could see a group of officers looking at me. Laughing, giggling, they stood looking at the big fat mess sprawled on the floor. I have to admit I was laughing too and to add insult to injury I broke wind, a large explosive fart like a gale-force wind.

This was a turning point for me in the jail and as the female officers tried to free me from the broken bed a friendship was formed. The banter was rib tickling and I can't remember the last time I had laughed so much. Bessie Bunter they called me. I didn't mind the nickname one little bit; it just meant I was now accepted onto the wing.

An inmate was stood at the door. Once she clocked me she pissed herself laughing too. She shouted behind her. "Girls, quick, get on this, come and check this fatty out." The doorway was soon filled with convicts and they were all screaming laughing as they watched the officers trying to free me from the broken bed. I loved the attention I was getting and I made it more difficult for the officers to move me. Finally, I was sat up straight. They sat me on a chair and started to remove the broken bed.

The inmate at the front of the doorway smiled and walked into the cell. "Are you alright big 'un. That was as funny as fuck. What happened to you?" I explained that I

The Pudding Club

just lay in the bed and it snapped in two and she was still chuckling. "My name's Pat, I'm two doors down from you, nice to meet you." There was no way I turning down any chance of friendship and I introduced myself to her straight away. The screws left us alone for a few minutes and Pat started to make conversation. "So, you're in for doing your old man in aren't ya?"

I nodded and I was surprised she knew about my conviction. "What are you in for?" I asked in a low voice trying not to frighten her off.

"Nothing much love, a bit like you really. I killed a woman who was shagging my man." This was amazing; it wasn't just me who was crazy. I was on a wing of other women who had also lost the plot. Pat rolled a cigarette and passed me one. This was surely the start of a great friendship. I took the thin cigarette from her and popped it into the side of my mouth. "How long are you in for then? Have you been sentenced yet?" she asked at last.

I rubbed at my arms as a chill passed over my body. "I'm up at court tomorrow, so I'll finally know my fate."

Pat sat thinking before she spoke. She was in her mid fifties and held that menacing look in her eyes. "You'll probably get a ten year stretch shoved up your arse, but obviously I don't know the details of your case, so I can't be sure. Tell you what, pop down to my cell later and tell me more about it."

I was overjoyed, a friend at last but then I remembered what the officer had said to me that I wasn't allowed to mix with the other prisoners. I told Pat my concerns in an anxious voice and she sat twiddling her thumbs thinking about it. "Right, leave it with me, I'll have a word with the screw and see what I can do for you. She's alright with me, so I'll word her up."

Pat winked at me on her way through the door. I

The Pudding Club

sat back in the chair and thought about Pat a little more. She was built like a man and had short cropped hair. Oh my God, she must have been a lesbian. This was it! I was being groomed, why else was she being nice to me. I'm not against gay relationships or anything but I don't think I'm ready to be someone's bitch just yet. How was I going to get out of this one? Food, I needed some food, at least then I could think straight.

Wobbling over to the table at the side of me I grabbed a handful of Jelly Babies and rammed them into my mouth. I was distraught. I just had a vision of myself with a skinhead and large tattoos all up my arms. I need to keep busy, I hate worrying about stuff that's not even happened. I think I might start that book I was thinking about writing, but where do I start. Perhaps I should wait until I'm sentenced then at least I can concentrate on it properly.

The officers soon brought a new bed into my pad and once it was positioned up against the back wall they left me alone. It's surprising how quickly you can adjust to prison life. I just seems to be plodding along as if it's normal everyday life. I'm not even bothered about dieting anymore. I am who I am and if people don't like it then they can take a hike. Why should I change to please others anyway? No, as from today, I'm eating what the hell I want. I'm dressing how I want too and if anyone's got anything to say about it then let them. I don't give a flying fuck anymore. I'm going to have a little sleep. I'm done in today, no energy whatsoever. Eyes closing and sleep.

SEVENTEEN

THE NIGHT WAS LONG and I've not slept a bleeding wink. Dark circles were visible around my eyes and my fingers felt numb. I've eaten all I can this morning before court and I'm feeling sick after I've stuffed my face. Tunes, lots of tunes, are floating around in my head and I can't help but sing my songs out loud. The officer asked me if I was feeling alright when she came into my cell this morning as she thought singing was not normal before I went to court to face a murder charge. I don't care what anyone thinks anymore, if I want to sing, then I'm going to sing. Pat's just been into my cell and wished me luck. She kissed me on the cheek before she left. I swear she's got my name down as her next lover but I'm going to have to put her straight, there is no way I'm leading her on. I hope she understands, I'm not saying I'm not complimented that she might fancy me, but I'm just saying I would like to keep my options open for now. I dreamt last night that she broke into my cell and took advantage of me wearing a ten inched strap on. She was ramming cream cakes in my mouth so I couldn't scream too. I woke up sweating and completely terrified.

The ride to court wasn't that bad. They should make the seats bigger though, my arse was hanging off it nearly all the way there. My mother is coming to court today with Spencer. I hope she doesn't make a show of me when the judge passes sentence. She's embarrassed me lots of times before with her big gob. Even when I was younger and we were at sports day she was always the one who shouted out in the loudest voice. She didn't care

The Pudding Club

what she said either. There I was running in a race with other six-year-olds and she was screaming at the top of her lungs at sports day. "Come on lard arse, run quicker!" The teacher had to have a word with her about her language but she told her straight too. I never attended another sports day after that. My mother told the school straight, that if she wanted to encourage her child then she should have been allowed to. They barred her from attending any more sports days.

Sat in the holding cell at court I can hear a woman crying. I think she's in the next cell to me. Sobbing her heart out she is, bless her cotton socks. Banging on the wall with clenched fists I try and get her attention. "Hiya love, my name's Rebecca, I'm in the next cell to you. Don't cry honey, everything will be okay." Well, I wish I would have kept my bleeding mouth shut. She was hurling abuse at me and banging on her cell door. I don't think she was right in the head; she seemed disturbed, not a full shilling. Oh well you live and learn don't you.

This cell stinks of stale arse, a horrible stench. I'm gagging now head in my hands. It reminds me of visiting the stables near the park where I used to live. There is so much noise outside, I hope things quieten down soon my head is banging. Well, it's all going to be over soon. I expect to be slammed for years; after all I did kill a man didn't I? I think my solicitor is saying I'm a bit of a psycho, he said that should cut me a bit of slack with the sentence I receive. I'm hoping I stay behind bars forever, there's nothing on the outside for me anymore. Everything I had has gone. I suppose I have my mother and brother but come on, life has got to hold more for me than that. I've heard a few stories about prison life and it seems full of excitement. I love meeting new people and hearing about their lives. It's like an adventure to me. I long to have unknown adventures. Hold on, the doors opening, keys rattling.

"Come on love, it's time for you to go into court," the male officer said.

Waddling out of the cell I straighten my black dress. It's just a plain dress, there's nothing much to it. I like to call it my tent dress, it hides all my flab and lumps and bumps. I've had it for years. My hair is tied back today, I've not brushed it though because I want to try and look mental to the judge. I've got flat sandals on too and my plump toes are squeezed together through the front of them. My arse is twitching as I enter the courtroom. I feel jittery. Lots of people sit facing me. I can see my mother and our kid too; he's smirking at me, the arse-hole. The courtroom is hot and clammy. I hope they turn the air conditioning on soon otherwise they will have a death on their hands. My solicitor comes to see me and speaks to me as I'm sat in the dock. His words were endearing but I think we both know that today isn't going to be good for me. I'm a realist me, I know what lies ahead.

The judge enters the room and everyone stands up until he's seated. He looks a right mean fucker too and doesn't look to be in a good mood. He's around fifty-five years of age and thin, very thin. The people in the courtroom sit down and my case begins. I'm not really listening to what anyone's saying, it's boring, and only what I've heard a thousand times before over and over again. I feel like jumping up from my seat and just telling him to get it over with. "I did it, I killed Josh Thompson so just do whatever you have to do and get it over with." I've always been impatient, I hate waiting. Even in takeaways, I hate waiting around for my food that's why I usually make a telephone order. My local takeaway knows me anyway and they always make sure my food is ready for when I get there. It's funny when I think back, the Chinese people in the chippy always thought I had a partner as I ordered that much food. I never told them and went along with the story of me having a partner at home. I used to lie to them and make stories up about what me and my loved one were doing over the weekend. Shocking aren't I?

Gemma is taking the stand now. I don't know how I feel about her anymore. I just feel numb. She's looking over at me and I can see the anger in her eyes. I growl at her and she knows I mean business. So what if I'm locked up, I know if I put my mind to it I could run at her and at least rag her about for a few seconds. Gemma starts to tell the courtroom about her ordeal. I don't feel as if it's me she's talking about. She's making me out to be a mad woman. The tears are falling from her eyes and I feel the need to start clapping my hands together but I refrain. A voice starts shouting from the back of the courtroom.

"She's a slapper, she got what she deserved, how did she think she could get away it anyway. Rebecca was her best friend and she's gone and done that to her, what a bleeding scrubber."

It was my mother's voice shouting. I could see her being escorted out of the courtroom. Gemma was passed a tissue to dry her eyes, she was a blubbering mess. Once she finished her statement she looked over at me and pointed her finger. "You're a crazy woman you are Rebecca Rooks. You've left my son without a father you selfish cow." I could feel blood boiling in my head and for a split second I couldn't breathe. I had to grip my knees to control my hands I wanted to lash out and kick the fucking living daylights out of her. Closing my eyes tightly I hummed a tune, I was calming down.

Over the next few days the evidence had been heard

The Pudding Club

and the judge was summing up. The court was adjourned until after lunch. I was taken back to my cell and was told it would be another hour or so before I was going back to the courtroom. My stomach was rumbling for food. I hoped they would be feeding me soon because if not I would be writing a letter of complaint to the justice system. I know my rights and I am entitled to some food. Fists banging on the door I shouted out in a loud voice. "Excuse me, what time are we having something to eat; only I'm wasting away in here."

I cupped my hand around my ear and waited for a reply, silence. This was a piss take. I kicked my foot against the door now hoping that this time someone would hear me. The door opened slowly and a woman handed me a sandwich and a drink of tea. Was that it? Was that all the food I was getting? Before I could get my words out the door was slammed in my face and I was alone. I suppose it was better than nothing, wasn't it? Sat on the wooden bench at the back of the cell I munched on the crusty butty. Cheese and onion it was but if I was being truthful there was more onion than cheese. I'm still hungry, that didn't even touch the sides. It wouldn't have fed a bleeding mouse. Looking around the room I can read some of the words people have engraved on the walls. Some of it is heartbreaking. One reads, "My darling Jane, I'm sorry, I will love you until my dying breath." Now that's lovely that isn't it? So much love in so few words. I wonder who wrote it? I bet it was a man who through no fault of his own was parted from his true love. I wonder if they will ever meet each other again or did they just part ways when he was arrested? The mind boggles doesn't it? I hope it was a happy ending. I wouldn't know what to write on the wall, I don't have anyone that I love anymore, only my family. I love food though, so that could work. Imagine if I wrote something about it on the wall, people would think I was a proper dick-head. I'm going to do it just for the sake of it. "My dear food, curry and kebab, not long until we meet again. Until then keep safe." I scrape the side of the stone from the bottom of my shoe deep into the wall hoping that my statement remains there forever. As I read over it I giggle to myself. It's official, I have lost the plot.

I'm stood in the courtroom. Everyone's been fed and watered and ready to continue. My mother has been let back inside the courtroom and she's on her best behaviour after a warning from the usher. She won't keep her mouth shut though, no way. I've seen this one hundred times before, she promises to keep her trap shut but once something rattles her cage she can't help but voice her opinion. I bet she doesn't make it until the end of the sentencing, you just watch her, mouth almighty when the sentence is served. Mark my words she'll let rip and start showing herself up. The judge is back in the courtroom. It's all gone quiet. Everyone is watching him take his seat and he sits down. My arse is flapping now, I thought I could just take this in my stride but I'm crumbling. Hot sweaty flushes are crippling my body. My mouth is dry and my windpipe is tightening. This is it, my fate is upon me. My mother looks over to me and shakes her head slowly, she must know the outcome.

My solicitor has asked me to give a quick speech before the judge passes sentence, he said it might help but I'm not holding my breath. Standing to my feet I begin, there's not a sound in the courtroom and everyone's eyes are on me. Twisting my hands on the dock I clear my throat and try to talk. My legs are weak and I don't think I'm going to be able to stand for long. Right here goes, let's see if I can win this old bastard over. "I never thought this is where I would end up your honour. I'm disgusted I let myself get in this situation and I know my time in prison will help me reflect on the crime I have committed." I had to breathe, I was feeling light-headed and knew I didn't have long left before I fell flat on my arse. "My husband tormented me physically and mentally. I never meant to kill him. he was attacking me it was self-defence. I'll have to live with his death for the rest of my life and that in itself is a sentence." I broke down in tears now and I knew my words were over. There were tears in the public gallery, my mother was snivelling and she was being comforted by Spencer.

The judge read through his notes one last time and asked me to stand to my feet. My legs buckled and the guard at the side of me helped me up by holding my arms. "I've listened to all the evidence and I feel you were a victim in some respect but what you did was a cold, callous murder. A man has lost his life because of it. I have no other choice other than to sentence you to fifteen years in prison."

My mother was on her feet now and she was screaming at the top of her voice. "No, she can't do that long. It was that bastard who made her do it. I'm glad she done him in, it saved me a job."

"Take her down," the judge said completely ignoring my mother's pleading voice. A quick look over my shoulder and I could see Gemma smirking, she'd got what she wanted I was going to jail for years.

The ride back to the prison seemed to take forever. The sweat box seemed smaller than usual and I was finding it difficult to get comfortable. As we drove past familiar land marks I felt my heart break. It was going to be a very long time before I would see Manchester again. Twiddling my thumbs I looked out of the window.

The Pudding Club

"Goodbye Manchester," I whispered. I knew some tears would come but I didn't expect them so soon. I thought it would have been later on when I was lay in my cell alone. My shoulders were shaking and tears streamed down my face. I was a mess and shaking. Perhaps I was having a mental breakdown or something. They all think I'm crazy anyway, so they could be right. Banging my head on the side of the window I hoped my life would end. Style prison was where I was heading. At least Pat would be there for me when I got back, she knew how to sort me out and always made me think straight.

The door to the sweat box was opened. My eyes screwed tightly together as the light hit them. A female screw was stood looking me with a stern look on her face. "Come on love, I've not got all bleeding day," she said. I looked at her and snarled.

"Just hold your horses will you, there's no rush. I'm a big girl so it might take a bit of time." The woman chuckled and played with the bunch of keys in her hands.

"You can say that again, you're enormous." I clenched my teeth together and slid my arse from the seat. If I could have got to her I would have landed my fist right on the end of her nose, the cheeky cow. Here I was I've just got fifteen years shoved up my arse and she was thinking she could talk to me like that, no, she was getting told. Once I was out of the van I confronted her.

"Ay, vinegar tits. I might be fat sweetheart but I will put you in the cheeks of my arse and squeeze the life out of you if you carry on speaking to me like a dick-head. Just because I'm a prisoner it doesn't give you the right to think you can insult me does it?"

The screw screwed her face up and she made sure her work mates couldn't hear her. "Listen, big mouth, you can do things the easy way or the hard way, it's up to you?"

The Pudding Club

I wanted to strangle her, my fingers were tightening as she walked in front of me, the rage from inside me was bubbling and if she carried on she was going to see what I was all about. I know this wasn't a good way to start my life in prison but she was making my blood boil.

Pat sees me coming back onto the wing. She's shouting to the other inmates that I'm back. "So, what's the crack, how long did you get?" Pat was at my side now and when I told her I was serving a sentence of fifteen years she gasped her breath. "Fuck me, I thought you would have got a ten or something like that, but ay, it is what it is isn't it. Plus, I'm here with you so it's not all bad is it?" She was right, as long as Pat was here with me I knew I could get through some of the years set out in front of me. The other inmates come to see me now and they were shocked at my jail sentence. I felt loved, cared for even. These women who I hardly knew made me feel part of something. Walking into my cell I looked about the small room. This was home for me now. The next fifteen years were going to be spent in rooms like this. Perhaps they would let me paint the walls, you know to liven it up. At the moment the walls in the cell are painted grey and they look so depressing. I can make this place feel like home, I know I can. Lying on my bed I stare about the room, silence, not a sound. I feel strange, it feels like this is not me anymore, strange, strange feeling.

Night time falls and I'm lying in my cell watching TV. That's one good thing about this jail; at least I can still watch all my programmes. I'm starting to come around to the fact now that I'm a prisoner. I think I was just a little shocked before and disorientated. Pat's put me back on track and I feel normal again. She gave me some weed to smoke too, just a few blasts I took, but it did the job. Pat is main girl on the wing and there's nothing she can't get

The Pudding Club

inside the prison walls. Some of the girls get drugs from her and other luxuries; she'll be useful to me in the future. I'm glad I'm on the right side of her though as I would hate her to be an enemy, she's off her rocker. I've started to write my book too. I've just done a few pages up to now though. I'm taking my time I don't want to rush it. I've not even got a title yet but I'm sure in time something will come to me. It's about love and how it can change you. They say you should always write about something you know and I know more than anyone about the four-letter word that can cripple you for life. I've not decided my story line yet, or who my main characters are. I don't know if they will be good or bad people but I'm sure we will grow to love them or hate them. I thought about writing my own story, but the more I think about it the more I hate that I never stood up for myself in my life. Never mind, a lesson has been learned and I'll never fall in love again. Who knows I might write about my own life.

Looking out through my window I can see the stars shining brightly. I've named one of the stars Josh. It sort of helps me come to terms with what I've done knowing that he's still watching over me. I don't think he hates me. He's probably up there now smiling down at me wishing he was still alive. The gentle night air tickles my face as I stick my fat cheeks through the bars on the window. It feels like Josh is stroking my face just like he used to do when we were together, the hairs on the back of my neck are stood up, I shiver. I think he still loves me in his own way. My eyes are tired now and I've got some hard times ahead of me. My weight is something that I've given up on completely. I am who I am, and fuck it, that's what I say. If I'm fat then I'm fat. And let's face it, I've got fifteen years in this shit hole to lose weight if I decide to, haven't

The Pudding Club

I? Pat's getting me a job in this place too; it would be heaven if I get to work in the kitchens. At least then I can fill my face whilst I'm cooking can't I? I hope she pulls it off and gets me the job, the sooner the better for me. I can't wait to fill my face. Right, nightwear on, it's time for me to get some shut eye. Have you noticed how I'm using a lot of slang words now, it makes me laugh too. Me, Rebecca Rooks a hardened criminal using all this street talk. Eyes closing, day one of my sentence is nearly over. Let's see what prison life is all about then. Let's see what tomorrow brings inside this shit hole.

EIGHTEEN

It's been five years since I went behind bars and I'm still the same person I think. My weight is nearly thirty stone but I feel happy inside. I'm involved with the drama group inside the jail now and tonight is the night of the show I've helped put together. You'll piss laughing when I tell you what it is. Are you ready for it? It's a Grease production and I'm playing Olivia Newton-John and Pat is playing the part of John Travolta. It's a dream come true for me you know? I'll never be able to wear them black Lycra leggings I always dreamt of wearing but who cares, I can still play the part well. I know all my lines and Pat said I've missed my way in life and that I should have been an actress. When my sentence is up I might even go down that road and try my hand at a bit of acting, who knows I might be successful. Pat is my best friend and my lover. I've not told my family I'm a lesbian yet and I feel it's something I'm going to keep to myself for now. It's nice having somebody to love me even if they are the same sex as me. My mother would never understand it so I'd be wasting my breath trying to explain it to her. My mother has not been well either. Spencer said if she sees the month through we'll be lucky. I'm prepared for her death and know when the times comes I'll be ready to face my loss. Pat is here for me anyway, she knows how to make me feel better. It's usually with cakes and chocolate but I don't mind, it gets me through any traumas.

The show is about to start now and I'm dressed in my costume. Tears fill my eyes as I walk out on the stage to sing my first song "Summer Loving". The crowd of inmates love me and within seconds they're on their feet dancing along to the tune. This is heaven and I never want this feeling to end. I'm alive and for the first time in my life I'm confident.

My novel is nearly finished too. I know it's taken a lot of time to write but I wanted it to be right before I let anyone read it. Pat's sending it to some literary agents for me and hopefully I should hear back from them soon. I decided to call the book, "The Pudding Club" and maybe one day you will read my story about how I ended up in jail. I've got a few more books inside me I think, so hopefully I will carry on writing, but until then, I'll say goodbye. Keep smiling guys. Life's what you make it. Life doesn't give. You have to take what you want. Right, back on the stage to sing my favourite song, "Hopelessly Devoted to you,"

I love being me. Rebecca Rooks is finally happy.

THE END

Other Books by Karen Woods

Broken Youth
Black Tears
Northern Girls Love Gravy
Bagheads
Teabags & Tears
The Visitors
Sleepless in Manchester
Covering Up
Riding Solo

To order any of these titles visit:
www.empire-uk.com

'*Verliefd* is een nagelbijter van jewelste. De Bruyn weet met eenvoudige middelen de dreiging op te roepen waar dit genre het van moet hebben. En het laatste hoofdstuk is zeldzaam navrant.' – Het Parool

'*Verliefd* is een toonbeeld van niet-aflatende dreiging.'
– Vrij Nederland Detective & Thrillergids

'Patrick De Bruyn is de absolute grootmeester van de Vlaamse suspense. *Verliefd* is een zinderend vat vol suspense, op een Hitchcockiaanse manier vorm gegeven.'
– Crimezone.nl

'In een puur zakelijke stijl brengt De Bruyn topsuspense.'
– Knack

De pers over **Passie**:

'*Passie* voert de lezer in sneltreinvaart langs verscheidene stations van verbijstering en is de beste koop van eigen bodem die u deze zomer kan doen.' – Humo

'Sombere, spannende en ingenieus gecomponeerde tragedie van de Vlaamse *master of suspense* die ons moeiteloos het verkeerde pad opstuurt.' – Weekend Knack

'Het is indrukwekkend hoe in dit sombere drama iedereen manipuleert en gemanipuleerd wordt. Opvallend sterk blijf je als lezer permanent bij het verhaal betrokken terwijl je heel goed beseft dat ook jij gemanipuleerd wordt.' – De Morgen

'Zoals in zijn vorige boeken, houdt De Bruyn ons vooral een spiegel voor. Het is geen leuke wereld die De Bruyn schetst, maar een heel realistische.' – Gazet van Antwerpen

'*Passie* is een fascinerend verhaal over hoe één moment op de foute plek je leven totaal kan veranderen.' – Libelle

'De Bruyn is zonder meer de primus inter pares van de Vlaamse thrillerschrijvers.' – Humo

De pers over Indringer:

'De eerste honderd bladzijden zijn zowat de spannendste en snelste uit de hele misdaadliteratuur.' – De Morgen

'Het loopt uit op een zonder meer tragische finale die De Bruyn superieur in scène zet.' – Knack